The Silent Woman

The Silent Woman

Peter Tonkin

Severn House Large Print
London & New York

This first large print edition published in Great Britain 2007 by
SEVERN HOUSE LARGE PRINT BOOKS LTD of
9-15 High Street, Sutton, Surrey, SM1 1DF.
First world regular print edition published 2003 by
Severn House Publishers, London and New York.
This first large print edition published in the USA 2007 by
SEVERN HOUSE PUBLISHERS INC., of
595 Madison Avenue, New York, NY 10022.

British Library Cataloguing in Publication Data

Tonkin, Peter
    The silent woman. - Large print ed.
    1. Musgrave, Tom (Fictitious character) - Fiction 2. Feast
    of Fools - England - Cornwall - Fiction 3. Great Britain -
    History - Elizabeth, 1558-1603 - Fiction 4. Detective and
    mystery stories 5. Large type books
    I. Title
    823.9'14 [F]

ISBN-13: 978-0-7278-7596-9

Printed and bound in Great Britain by
MPG Books Ltd, Bodmin, Cornwall.

CHAPTER 1

The Man from Hell

London, Spring 1595

'*Hold!*' Tom Musgrave threw up his left hand as he snapped the order, and turned the rapier in his right hand safely off-line. Even as he acted so decisively, Tom saw that his opponent was committed to a lunge. Therefore he stepped aside as he spoke and turned, as though he were the most graceful of dancers as well as the Master of Defence.

Kate Shelton's blade passed harmlessly along the outer curve of his ribs while his armed right hand whispered around her waist and held her, breathless and unusually supine in the crook of his arm, as though they were truly about to dance. Or to kiss. Either was likely enough, for the beautiful, breathless woman was a rising star of the younger generation at Queen Elizabeth's court, and Tom's mistress. Down swooped his lean face until his lips just brushed her own. '*Listen!*' he hissed.

The echo of their swordplay still lingered on the hot air of his long practice chamber like the pealing of discordant bells, but his quick, sharp ears had heard another, more desperate, ringing beyond it. Where they fenced here for amusement, someone out in the street close below was fighting for his life.

They started up together like lovers discovered, turning towards the door that would take them out and down, but Kate froze, stricken. Their exercise since the noon bells had been hard and hot – as warm as the unseasonable weather, which behaved as though June were arriving three months early. Kate had come attired for Court before they had fallen to sporting with his foils, but their play-fighting had been as energetic as all their other pursuits. It had soon become obvious that fashionable clothing for court ladies was never designed to allow the brisk *passado* or the tempestuous *posta longa*. Consequently, Tom had served as maid as well as master and slipped off the tightest of Kate's clothing before returning to their bout. Now her ruff lay discarded on a chair with her sleeves beside it, their points loosed and their slashed silk soughed like snake-skins. Her thoughtlessly unpinned bodice had slid to the floor nearby and the dress-front that had been laced so demurely beneath it gaped now. And so, Kate realized wryly, did the damp shift below, which failed entirely to protect her modesty. From forehead to farthingale, she might as well have been standing naked to the world, like a whore at Bridewell stripped for the whipping. As Tom ran down, therefore, Kate clutched the staid, silken wings of her dress together and hurried to the window instead.

Tom ran out into the stuffy, sweltering street already drawn, supple and afire from his bout with Kate. He saw in a twinkling what the situation was and hurled himself forward. Black Friars was quite wide at this point, up at the Lud Gate end, where Master Aske's haberdashery stood hard against the City Wall and Tom's school towered above it. The ancient cobbled roadway was broad enough to accommodate a crowd of some half-dozen onlookers, a gang of four rough-looking footpads and a desperate young gallant standing alone against them.

No. Not alone. As Tom hurled himself to the lad's defence, so a second champion appeared. The two men Tom was set to join could hardly have presented a starker contrast, noted the Master of Logic, racing in Tom's keen mind; and in truth, his own tall frame could not have been in more immediate contrast to the pair of them either. For he was clad in elegant black doublet, unlaced to reveal snowy linen at his breast, black galligaskin trousers, wide at the hip and narrow at the knee – the very pinnacle of fashion – and thigh-high Spanish-leather boots.

The lad looked scarcely old enough to boast a beard, a callow country youth, well dressed

9

but ill armed – expensively and eye-catchingly dressed, indeed, in a uniform of livery, which Tom found old-fashioned, out of place, yet faintly familiar: corn-yellow silk, almost cloth of gold, figured with some device and buttoned in moulded silver. Across the breast of the figured-silk doublet was strapped a leather message-wallet, also crested and silver-buckled. Well enough dressed, then, if all too dangerously – seeming to be a very signal crying to all the world, *'I carry rich and important things – rob me!'*

And, in the face of his dangerous costume, the lad was ill-armed both in terms of weaponry and ability. The fashion of an older time was matched by a short-sword almost of antique years – and none too well maintained. Not that this made much difference, considering how ineffectually it was being wielded by the terrified youth as the four assailants crowded round him with their clubs and daggers briskly at work.

The second man, on the other hand, was massive – squat and square, ill-dressed in common clothes though these clean and well-mended if a-strain at every seam. He seemed a man of the streets, a local journeyman, like any other in the gawping crowd – utterly unremarkable, except, in the first instance, for what he carried and what he was doing with it. Almost lost in his massive labourer's fist, there gleamed a very jewel of the swordsmith's art: a stark Toledo blade in an ornate Toledo basket hilt. The priceless weapon was being employed, however, as a cross between a whip and a club. A lesser blade would have snapped at such artless ill-usage, but this one survived a little longer – long enough to drive the footpads back.

Back they stepped into the hissing arc of the Master of Defence's orbit. Loath to kill even a footpad without warning and run him through the back – for professional and legal reasons at the very least – Tom called out, 'Ho! Kit Callot!'

All four pads turned on his call and froze – as much at his familiarity with thieves' cant, Tom guessed, as with the all-too-immediate threat of his deadly Solingen blade – the match of the labourer's Toledo, but fashioned five hundred leagues and more to the north, in Germany.

Seeing how they were all but evenly matched in numbers now, and outmatched, indeed, in weaponry, the footpads simply took to their heels. Into the crowd they vanished like smoke; and the crowd, too, vanished, as the City Watch arrived to find Tom and the stranger alone in fashionable Black Friars, kneeling beside the fainting servant as he lay gasping in the gutter.

The big journeyman held the boy gently and Tom knew from the way he did it that he had been a soldier and seen companions die – in Flanders, like as not, or on the Scottish Borders. Tom knew them both through his own upbringing and adventuring, and recognized the stranger's gestures because of them.

He held the battered boy with an all too practised hand; and, looking at the hands themselves, Tom in an instant placed his big companion as a bricklayer. Or, looking more closely at his square, lightly-bearded face, an apprentice bricklayer.

'How is he?' asked Tom.

'Fainting like a girl,' came the answer in a rich, surprisingly cultured voice, much at odds with the body and the hands. 'Battered and bruised as Hector pulled behind Achilles' chariot around the walls of Troy, but I cannot see a wound.'

Tom rose and prepared to talk things through with Captain Curberry's men, the Watch. Here was assault, and perhaps worse than that, though only time would tell; and as the month was March and Her Majesty at White Hall, they all lay under Sir William Danvers' jurisdiction, therefore. For Sir William was the Queen's Crowner, the most powerful lawman in the land.

Sir William's crowner's quest could well come out from beneath the Verge as this deed had been done within thirteen miles of Her Majesty. All suspicious acts performed so near to the Queen's sacred person were subject to such close scrutiny, particularly if death came as their end result. The Queen kept her own coroner to look into the most important of them: Sir William Danby – who had been called, for instance, to the murder of Kit Marlowe, playwright and spy, at Deptford scarce two years since, while the Queen herself had lingered at Greenwich.

When Queen Bess was at Westminster Palace or White Hall, however, a judicial distance had to be maintained between what happened in the sewers and stews of London and what was likely to threaten the Realm itself. The Queen would not be threatened by the murder of a bawd or two or the death of a gallant in a duel – or, indeed, by the fatal robbery of a servant lad up from the country. Sir William Danby would never be unleashed for matters of such slight moment as these. In the meantime, north of the river at least, in the City it was Captain Curberry's Watch that held the square.

Their leader, Sergeant Virgil Grimes, knew Tom; and Tom knew him as a notoriously slow, deliberate man. Slowly and deliberately, therefore – though as swiftly as Tom could manage – they began to discuss the situation.

The slow conversation had only just begun between them, however, when a cry from on high called Tom's attention. Kate was hanging out of the end window of the practice room, as careless of her modesty as of his reputation after all. 'Tom,' she called. 'I see their leader; he lingers in a doorway just beyond the gate down into Water Lane.'

Tom turned on his heel and left the bricklayer to deal with the Watch sergeant. Down the street he pounded, eyes busy, mind racing. Racing, but hardly to any purpose: there seemed no pattern to this random robbery, nothing for the Master of Logic to

13

chew upon. Yet Kate had seen – understood – more than he. She had recognized, as he had not, that the gang of roughs had had a leader – and recognized which of them it was as well as where he went, lost to Tom's eyes amongst the vanishing crowd. So if Kate, aloft, had seen more, perhaps there was more still for Tom himself to see down here on the mean street – to see and to understand.

Tom hurtled under the arch that led out of the old Black Friars Priory and into Water Street, skidding to a halt at the first recessed doorway; and there indeed stood the biggest, most brutal of the four men he had called Kit Callot – thieves' cant for any footpad, robber or low-life. But the footpad did not stand alone: he stood with his back against the doorway looking out at Tom over the shoulder of a slighter man dressed indistinguishably in a travelling cloak and a slouch-brimmed hat. As the footpad's eyes widened in shocked recognition, so the stranger turned. Over his face he wore a cloth, guarding nose and mouth against city stench and easy recognition alike. Between the top of the cloth and the low-hung brim of the hat there gleamed a pair of cold and narrow eyes. They flashed in the shadows, almost as brightly as the barrel of the pistol that came up from under the cloak in the grip of a gauntleted hand. Had he been closer, Tom might have risked a lunge. As it was, he hurled himself sideways, rolled in the gutter, to the near-ruination of his velvet jerkin, and hurled himself down the slope towards the river. After ten steps he slowed, for there had been no shot. After five more he turned. The doorway seemed empty, but he could not see its shadowed depths from here.

Cautiously, Tom returned, heart thundering and chest heaving, eyes everywhere, until he could see right into the doorway again. In the shady recess stood no stranger, cloaked and armed – stood no footpad. Stood nothing but an ancient, black-wood door – which, when he pounded upon it, remained immovably locked and barred against him.

'Did you see them leave? Did you mark whither they went?' Tom asked Kate a few moments later.

She shook her head in reply, looking down as she modestly re-secured the strings of her dress-top. Her preoccupation was understandable, for hard on Tom's heels came the apprentice bricklayer bearing the battered boy and hard on his came the Watch. Nodding fatalistically, Tom turned and directed his new companion into the airy brightness of his own bedchamber, where the fainting boy was deposited gently upon his neatly made bed. The action seemed to stir something in the yellow-clothed messenger, for the dark-ringed eyes flickered in the ivory-cheeked face.

'Who are ye, lad? Where do you hail from?' asked the apprentice, his rich voice as gentle as all his gestures and actions so far had been.

15

In answer, the boy reached up. His arms clasped round the thick bull-neck. The pale lips pressed to the ear beneath the curling, oily hair, and a word or two was whispered, soft as the lightest zephyr of breeze. Then the boy fell back upon the bed and the square apprentice straightened, frowning.

'What did he say?' asked Tom, his open face also folding into a frown as he crossed to the pair of them, seeing with his experienced, soldier's eye the passing print of Death's own footstep here.

The stranger stepped back, his broad young face pale with shock. 'He said Hell,' he answered, dark eyes wide and burning, searching Tom's face as though some explanation might lie there. 'There's no mistake. I'm certain. He said he came from Hell.'

CHAPTER 2

The Dead Letter

'If Hell's where he came from, then Hell's where he's bound for,' observed Grimes mournfully, showing more wit than Tom, for one, had credited him with. The Watch sergeant stood between the bricklayer and the bed, looking down into the boy's staring eyes. Tom crossed to the opposite side and sat beside the still body, leaning forward, eyes busy and fingers itching – but restrained. All too regular, and recent, experience had taught Tom the simple rules of his calling as Master of Logic: eyes first and most; fingers second and least. Logic always but carefully, leaning on the proofs of his sharpest sense. Deep into the dead eyes he looked, therefore, wondering, *What could have killed you, boy?* For, as the bricklayer had said, there was no wound obvious, no deadly contusion on head or neck, no bleeding apparent from body, eyes or ears; but the wide, fixed eyes looked dead, and Tom's nose and cheek, brought perforce close to the sagging gape of the silent mouth, detected neither movement nor odour of breath.

The boy was dead, then, in spite of the lack of immediate, obvious cause; but the face was waxen – a thing of linen and ivory. The lips – so often blue in the corpses beneath Tom's sharp notice – were as bloodless as all the rest. As he looked at the frozen death mask, Tom was put in mind of the heads he had found spiked upon London Bridge last year, lopped off murdered women and placed as a warning to the world. But there he had known where the blood that should have coloured the pallid skin was gone.

Back, then, further still in time, to Julius Morton, murdered on the stage of the Rose Theatre in his friend Will Shakespeare's famous play of *Romeo and Juliet*, all the rage last summer. Morton, too, had been as white as this – and, initially, as bloodless, for he had been run through the chest from back to front with the finest of foreign steel...

Tom looked up at the apprentice, suspicion rearing like a monstrous hound within his mind. 'Your Toledo sword,' he said. 'Where is it?'

'God's my life, I left it in the gutter when I carried the boy aloft,' came the answer, and the big man whirled away through the door.

'Sergeant! Follow him,' rasped Tom. And for once Grimes was not slow to obey.

No sooner was he gone than Tom turned back to his task. Thoughtlessly, like a parent bereft of a hopeful son, he swept a tangle of straw-coloured fringe aside and closed the staring eyes. Then he restrained his eager fingers once again and looked away from the livid face, letting his acute gaze travel down the length of the slight, still frame. A ruff at the throat, the same colour as the flesh; the cloth beneath as yellow as daffodils, as heavy as brocade, with a woven pattern of cats and mice; buttons moulded in a strange shape to figure ... what? Nutmegs? The black pouch was buckled tight and held between white fingers that might have clenched had not their strength run out too soon. That gave Tom pause, for he suddenly saw that the boy's dead hands had not fallen loosely from the apprentice's neck: they had fallen here to clutch the message pouch with the very last of his failing strength. The pouch was the last thing he had thought of, therefore – the pouch, or the message it contained. *Several messages, perhaps,* thought Tom. For he noticed that the black leather was full and fat. Both pouch and messages would bear careful examination in consequence, when the eyes were finished and the fingers could begin their work at last.

Below the old-fashioned doublet were old-fashioned breeches of plain daffodil cloth; stockings – of white wool; new shoes, country-cobbled but soiled by London's streets. And that was all.

Mindful of Morton, Tom stooped forward and allowed his fingers some licence. As he had done with the murdered actor, he rolled the boy on to his side and checked the bright brocade of his doublet between his shoulders – but there was no mark on the cloth. Logic dictated, therefore, that there would be no wound on the flesh beneath – and yet ... Tom's ears were acute enough to hear a gentle slopping, as though he had tilted a barrel half full of ale, when he rolled the body back.

'Is he dead then?' asked Kate quietly, emerging from the practice room at last, with everything in place except for the points that bound her sleeves to her shoulders – which Tom would tie for her, when time and opportunity allowed.

Tom nodded in reply. Distracted a little by her potent presence, he fell to unfastening the laces of the boy's doublet and, beneath that, those of his shirt. Only that distraction, he

19

later thought, could explain why he did this first, without removing the message pouch that lay loosely clasped and tightly strapped across both; but so it chanced – and that made a great deal of difference in the end.

The skin of the dead boy's throat was as pale as that of his face, and so indeed was that of his breast as Tom uncovered it. Even the bruises born of the footpads' clubs were pallid, ghostly. The flesh of his torso was soft, cool and as hairless as a maid's, and yet, where it gathered into a valley between the firm hills of muscle, the white cup of the flesh contained the first hint of the truth. For there at last, oozing sluggishly along the valley, was a red finger of blood. Abruptly, it seemed, the lawn of the open shirt was bright and soaking with it. Tom's hands jerked up and Kate gasped.

'What's amiss?' demanded the rich, echoing voice as the apprentice returned with his Toledo sword.

'A dead man bleeding,' said Tom.

'That's none so strange. In Flanders I saw—'

'Blood from a bloodless boy,' persisted Tom, his voice made almost dreamy by the depth of his concentration. As he spoke, at last he reached for the message-pouch under the dead hands. He unbuckled it with growing urgency and lifted it easily free, though the white fingers retained their grip upon it briefly. All the witnesses gasped, caught between shock and sickness, for the leather pouch itself seemed to be bleeding. Certainly it left a thick, hot trail across the bedding and the floor besides until Tom put it into the empty ewer he kept near his bed for washing when he had bought water from the tradesmen down Water Lane.

Gently, Tom returned to the still body, whose chest was now awash, the daffodil brocade darkened to the colour of Seville oranges. He parted the slack arms, and folded back the edges of cloth. There, just above the dead boy's heart, where the message-pouch had been so tightly buckled, gaped the tiny mouth of a stab-wound. 'The killing stroke,' said Tom, his voice grown rusty on the sudden. 'Through the wallet, through the message and through his very heart, so I would judge. A lean, long blade, as sharp as sin and almost as strong as death. The match to your steel of Toledo, master bricklayer.' The suspicion he felt gave an edge to his voice and a suddenly confrontational power to his words – a combination that begat an instant response in kind.

'I am no bricklayer, you coxcomb! I am a scholar bound for Cambridge!' The resonant voice cracked with boyish outrage, the square face flushed brick-red with indignation. The round eyes rolled wrathfully beneath low, frowning brows.

'That's true at least. You are no bricklayer, for you'd need to be several years older than you are to be out of your apprenticeship and a master of the trade. Apprentice bricklayer,

21

by your dress and build and hands. Still, you speak like a Cambridge man – or an actor, come to that. You've been a soldier – not too long since, I'd guess – and you've knowledge enough of the classics for a scholar; but unless you've come to sell the sword you won in battle there in Flanders, you'll not be a gentleman scholar. A *poor scholar*, perhaps, like my friend Robert Poley.'

'You insult me beyond bearing! How dare you...'

'I tell the truth and less of it than I could tell, were I not engaged in more important matters – and obliged to you for your quick thinking and bravery in the matter so far. Stop huffing, boy. Tell us your name and your business. And stop waving that good sword around my ears or I shall kill you where you stand.'

'He will,' said Kate equably, when the bricklayer's rolling eye alighted on her. 'And you called him a coxcomb, so not even the Sergeant of the Watch would stir to save you.'

'Not even Captain Curberry himself,' confirmed Grimes, grimly amused. 'Whose close acquaintance you'll be likely to make unless you keep that temper of yours in check. If you survive this afternoon, of course.'

'Make up your mind,' said Tom, his voice suddenly icy as he stood to face his opponent over the corpse-laden bed. 'My bed's already ruined and big enough to bear a bricklayer's apprentice as well as this dead messenger.

Now would be the best of times for me. I'll be getting a cleaner in any case. And the Search-er. And a Crowner at the least, I'd judge.'

Their angry guest hesitated – hesitated, then capitulated. 'My name is Ben Jonson,' he began. 'My father was a cleric, and I'm as well born as any here.'

'Except for the lady, perhaps,' insinuated Tom, his voice still icy.

'Ah,' said Ben. 'Except for the lady, per-haps, as you say. I was sent hither from The Theatre hard by Finsbury Fields by a fellow called Shagsberd or some such, the scribbler of a trifling thing of fairies and confusion in love not a patch on Plautus from whom it was stolen in the first place, then mangled out of recognition...'

'So you went to see *A Midsummer Night's Dream*,' prompted Tom, 'and managed to talk with Will Shakespeare, who sent you here to me. To sell the sword – or to be instructed in its use, I'd say...'

He sat again and fell to further contempla-tion of the murdered messenger as young Ben Jonson explained his fortunes, his misfor-tunes and his mission this afternoon.

Every now and then Tom would look up and steer the voluble young man's narrative back on to its course with a tiny touch of his genius like Drake's own hand on the tiller of the *Golden Hind*.

'Your father died before you were born and left your mother destitute, you say. So she came to London – to Islington. Perhaps...'

'Ha! The brick-kilns of Islington. You persist with that—'

'It is in your arms and shoulders, Ben; and especially in your hands. You worked with bricks this very day before you strolled into Finsbury Fields with your Toledo sword and wandered – not by chance – through the door of The Theatre for the play. Your stepfather is a master bricklayer and you will do anything but follow the path he has mapped out for you. That much at least is clear.'

'My first escape was into scholarship. Camden himself...' Ben Jonson began to embroider on the earliest manifestations of his childish genius and how they had enabled his mother to bring him to the great scholar and headmaster's personal notice.

'You were at Westminster School? No wonder you know your classics and have an eye to go to Cambridge,' prompted Tom after a while.

'But when the junior scholarship ran out, no more could be found to carry me thither and so...' Ben's misfortunes began to be enumerated – the natural testing of great genius in the Classical, Stoical manner.

'The brick-kilns – until you escaped again...' Tom's eyes met Kate's, crinkling in a smile of almost paternal understanding of the young man's self-absorption.

'To Flanders. I joined the army. A gentleman volunteer. I learned much of soldiering. I killed my man. In single combat, hand to hand...' An epic description of the bout –

worthy indeed of Achilles pursuing the flee-
ing Hector and closing to his death.

'A Spaniard, and a rich one, whom you
stripped of armour and of sword, all of which
you have sold except for that,' concluded
Tom. 'And so we are come full circle. You
believe you have enough to start at least at
Cambridge. One way or another the sword
will secure you. Either your purse, if you will
sell it; or your safety, and again your purse, if
you will learn to use it well enough.'

'Even in Islington, the fame of this froth at
The Theatre is bruited abroad. Like the trash
about Romeo – no true tragedy at all to my
mind; it is the swordplay that dazzles. In
among the leaden tropes of Titania and the
sad mock-humour of Bottom and the rest,
the swordplay is all that is fit to stand. And
then I heard that it was you who taught the
wooden actors how to fence...'

'It cost you a penny to watch it, Ben. It'll
cost you a mint more than that to learn it. It
will cost you more to become a master of
defence here than it will to become a master
of the arts at Cambridge, boy. Did Will
Shakespeare not warn you of that?'

'Hardly! What, to discuss money with a
stranger, the merest acquaintance?'

Tom forbore to mention the far more
intimate details Ben had just shared with two
more mere acquaintances and the City
Watch. 'The nub, Ben. The pith. The moment. Are you come to market or are you
come for mastery?'

'I have come,' said Ben Jonson, pompously enough for Cicero addressing the Senate of Ancient Rome in the days before Mark Antony had him killed, 'to offer you my service in return for tutelage.'

Winded with simple surprise, Tom paused. Providentially he avoided Kate's eye now, for hysterics would have made an enemy of a potential friend and ally. 'Indeed?' he ventured at last. 'My apprentice in what art, mystery or mastery?'

'Well...' Now it was Ben's turn to hesitate. 'I had assumed in the Art and Science of Defence. I come well prepared...'

'He has his own sword,' observed Grimes, still surprising Tom with his dry but potent wit.

'And it's the equal of your own,' added Kate, a little gustily.

But Tom, confronted by a recently murdered corpse, chose to take the matter a little more seriously than they. 'I have seen what you can do with the sword you have brought,' he said gently, 'and I know what I can teach you if I choose to accept your offer of servitude. But I have other skills that are called upon at moments such as this. Come over here, therefore, and let us see if your wits are as sharp as your Toledo blade and as ready to study in Lord Burghley's university at Cambridge as you suppose them to be.'

As Tom spoke – and Ben obeyed – he turned away from the bed with its ghastly occupant and crossed to the ewer on which he had placed the messenger's wallet. Because of the strength and weight of the straps attached to it, the wallet itself had been sitting high above the bowl. Out through the hole that had been clutched to the dying heart had trickled the last of the life's blood pumped so strangely into it. The wallet was flat again, containing only one or so messages. As Ben – and the rest, for that matter – crowded nearer, Tom opened the silver buckle and lifted the black flap wide.

In went his fingers – steadily enough, all things considered – and out came the message like a mess of crushed blackcurrants between them. At first it seemed no more than a sodden little parcel, stabbed through the middle and soaking in blood.

'A dead letter, in God's truth,' whispered Ben, simply awe-struck.

'A letter indeed,' agreed Tom. 'A letter that, I believe, has cost the life of the boy who bore it. A letter of such import that cold, calculated murder has been done to stop it reaching its destination. A letter, therefore, of deadly pitch and moment, bearing within it life and death at the very least. But a letter from whom? And to whom? A letter saying *what?*'

CHAPTER 3

The Silent Cry

As Tom carried the dripping bundle across the room, his eyes and tongue were busy. 'Ben! Take the ewer off the table so that I may put this down. It is parchment, but so damaged it is like to disintegrate before much longer.' Tom laid the message on the little table and carried the whole thing over to the window where the light was brightest. He worked swiftly, for it was obvious to him that the blood was soaking into the parchment rapidly. A missive, from whomever to whomever, would be folded and refolded into the package he was studying. If he was swift – and only if he was swift – he might be able to open the sopping parchment and see what had been written upon it before the messenger's blood obscured it all.

The little tabletop was of ancient oak, close-grained and nearly impenetrable. Even as Tom automatically noticed this fact, so the next step became obvious to him. He lifted the sopping letter once more.

'Kate, I will lift the package one last time.

Put some cloth beneath it, if you please – something that will soak away the blood. The cloth beside the fire...'

Kate spread the thick cloth Tom used as a towel on the table and he put the letter gently down upon it. Immediately he began to unfold it, spreading out the parchment and trying to keep uppermost the side that had been written upon.

Leaf by leaf he lifted the parchment back, flattening each fold and spreading out the whole like a crushed poppy. No sooner had he done this than he saw that there was a narrow column through the middle of the whole that remained untouched at the last. Here, and here alone, the writing remained clear. On all other sides the neat, firm hand ran away into the darkening thickness impenetrably, becoming utterly indecipherable on the instant. The last section of clarity seemed to have survived because of the way in which the parchment had been folded and, as Tom spread the letter out, so it formed a little ridge. 'Ben, your sword,' Tom called and Ben brought it with commendable promptness. Tom slid the fine Toledo blade up beneath the pale ridge, supporting it as the thick blood ran away.

Tom stooped over the pale column with its endangered, spidery marks, his eyes busy.

'I have a tablet here,' said Ben at his shoulder. 'Tell me what you see and I will set it down, so if the original is lost...'

Tom could see the following, and this is

what he told to Ben, who wrote it down as he had promised:

grave
o-one e
erwatc
nger. A
ife, whi
ood in
nd men
ound he
een care
e. I ha
variou
ansfer t
w Year
ies pas
my deat
n I may
ed offic
that yo
opeful
nd take
of Elfin
Help me
argare
ess Cot

' "Help me",' said Tom again, the first words spoken after he had dictated to Ben what he could make out along the rapidly darkening ridge of parchment. Ben's thought had been a good one. For no sooner had Tom repeated the only words in all the message that stood clear and unequivocal, than the fiery essences within the youthful liquor, cooling though they were, sped on up according to their nature and the little ridge was consumed with all the rest.

' "Help me",' he repeated, his voice little more than a whisper as his mind sped away into the most abstruse of contemplation. He picked up the half-melted seal and looked at it in the strong afternoon light. ' "Help me"...'

'Help who?' asked Grimes.

'And how?' demanded Ben. 'As you said, Master, we do not know who sent this cry for help. Or where they sent it from. We do not know for whom it was destined. Or where he is. And we have not the least idea what help is needed or must be offered.'

'I am not your master yet, Ben. And even were I so, it is not my mastery of logic that you seek to learn. But it is logic that can aid us now, and it is here where I can prove my true mastery. For I do know the answers to all the questions that you have just posed.'

'Ha!' laughed Ben derisively, clearly believing Tom's boast to be empty, and his reputation overstated after all.

'Sergeant Grimes,' said Kate immediately, 'perhaps you had best withdraw. I would hate to see you take down the Master of Logic for witchcraft. For witchcraft' – she swung on Ben, with a martial glint to her eye and a challenging edge to her voice – 'witchcraft will it seem to those denser spirits close at hand who have never seen the Master of Logic at work.'

→ 'A thousand thanks, my love,' said Tom, amused. 'And you, Ben, keep your wits honed to see if you can follow where my logic leads, though it is not the logic of Aristotle, nor his *Organon*, so it may seem a trifle new-fangled to you and relatively worthless – like the plays of Will Shakespeare, for instance, when compared with those of Plautus, Aristophanes and Sophocles. But he fills The Theatre day after day; and I get the job done.'

'Well,' blustered Ben, 'now that you mention it...'

But the Master of Logic was in full flow now and Cicero himself could hardly have wedged in a word. 'I knew before the boy died where he had come from, for there is only one livery in England comprising cats and mice, with silver nutmegs cast as buttons.

'Who is he, therefore? He is a liveried servant come from Lord Outremer, or someone within His Lordship's household; and that is the more likely, for My Lord is yet but a boy.

'Whence has he come? From the country, by the manufacture of his footwear, and by horse, judging from the mud spattered on his fine white leggings. From Elfinstone, Lord Outremer's castle in Kent, therefore – and that swiftly, because he has had neither inclination nor leisure to change out of his livery clothing. And he did not ride alone, for see, the right side of his clothing is more stained with mire than the left. Another rode

32

beside him to guide and protect him, mayhap, almost to the last.'

'But whither was he bound?'

Tom stood up at that and looked around them. 'Ben, where else in Black Friars might you have been visiting when you came to call this afternoon?'

'The haberdashery below,' answered Ben readily enough, adapting to the Socratic method familiar from his schooling at Westminster of teaching through question and answer.

'A happy thought,' admitted Tom. 'Except, you see, that the boy carries nothing but his message-wallet. He is fully dressed in the uniform of his lord and master and wants no fripperies or fancies – which he cannot buy in any case. Not Aske's the Haberdasher's then. Where else?'

'What other shops stand nearby?'

'None of any note, unless he was bound down Water Lane to buy a pitcher of water. With no money...'

'And no pitcher, come to that,' observed Kate dryly.

'Mayhap he was passing through,' suggested Grimes, entering into the spirit of the thing. 'He could get a wherry down at the water steps.'

'And where would a wherry take a penniless lad? Especially one dressed in such finery?'

'I know where the wherryman would be likely to tell him to go,' said Ben.

'Precisely,' said Tom.

'But who's to say the ruffians that attacked him did not take his purse? He might have been well supplied with angels and all of them gone to Alsatia or Damnation Alley, or Islington...' Grimes stopped as Ben caught his eye. There were worse places than the brickworks in Islington, nevertheless.

'No,' said Tom decisively. 'His clothing is of ancient design. I see no pockets in it. There would be a purse fastened to his belt were he carrying one, and the loops and thongs that held it would still be obvious, even had the purse itself been cut away.'

'But then,' said Kate, 'on the other hand, who would let a boy out in London bearing nothing but a message, carrying not a penny piece for safety's sake?'

'Someone close by who has told him where to come and expects him soon to return. The man that rode up with him from Elfinstone.'

'Why, then,' said Ben, 'we can test your mastery in your logical art. If I have inferred correctly from what you have been saying, you suppose that the boy, like myself, must have been bound hither. Sent from who-knows-where? – this *Elfinstone*, you aver – but sent to see you. If that is true, then the man that sent him must come hammering on your door as soon as he realizes the boy has not returned as planned.'

'Good! Wrong, I believe, but good. Well reasoned.'

'If I have reasoned so well,' huffed Ben, 'how is it that I am wrong?'

'Because you have not included in your reasoning one small but vital element – which, to be fair, we have not discussed at length. It is this: the gang of footpads who attacked the boy was led by a man – the man with the foreign dagger, as like as not. A slim, strong, sharp-bladed weapon, of no English manufacture that I have seen. That man immediately reported to another man down in Water Lane. The footpads were *employed*, therefore, and this was no random attack on an unwary yokel lost in the dangerous city. These footpads sought him out and attacked him because they had been employed to stop the message getting to me. And if they could not stop the message they were employed to stop the messenger – as they have done, and so their leader reported, to their employer, the cloaked and masked stranger with the unusual pistol whom I saw.'

'Well...' allowed Ben, still not despairing of his own thesis.

'It would only be worth stopping the young messenger at such a price if the other man was also stopped – distracted, perhaps, if the boy were to be slowed, but stopped, as the boy has been stopped in such a final manner. Therefore, the next man to come knocking at my door is not likely to be looking for the dead boy, or even for myself.'

'Who, then?'

'Why, for the Sergeant of the Watch, here, to report another murder done.'

So saying, Tom turned to the letter once

again. Then, seeing that the last of the writing was lost beneath the tide of heart's blood, he fell back on Ben's transcription.

'As my would-be apprentice has observed, the letter is likely for me,' he began, once more the Master of Logic addressing his apprentice tutorial. 'The first word, then, may be expanded from "grave" to "Musgrave". And, as I am sure the seal will confirm when we have the leisure to test it all, the last words are the name of the only person in the household of the young Lord Outremer who might call on me for help – to wit, the Lady Margaret, Countess Cotehel, from whom the messenger said he came...'

'*Hell* – he said he came from Hell...' Ben was beginning to understand the power that the Master of Logic could wield when he chose to do so.

'It is the Lady Margaret who requests my help; and there is no great wonder in that...'

'Tom rescued her from a terrible fate,' supplied Kate, her voice carefully neutral. 'He saved her from rapine when she was scarce more than a girl. He came to rescue her from a mad room in the great house of Wormwood in Jewry where she had been locked because she could no longer speak, after giving birth to the child born of the rape. He saved her when she was ravished away to be hunted to some terrible fate by men who killed all her family except for her son and hoped to steal their inheritance. Finally, he saved that inheritance and revenged her wrongs and left her mistress of one of the richest estates in the land.'

'And she is *elderly* and *ugly*, is she, this heiress from a tale of fairies worthy of Master Shagsberd himself?' probed Ben.

'Neither,' snapped Kate.

'Scarred by her experiences so that only a blind man would look on her?'

'Not a mark on her that I have seen.' Kate's eye fell on Tom, and it was burning.

'Nor I,' he admitted, and Kate and he both knew that Tom had seen all of the Lady Margaret that there was to see.

'A drivelling Bedlamite, perhaps, maddened beyond recovery by the horrors that have come so close to her?'

'Save that she remains forever silent,' admitted Kate, 'she is perfect. Perfect in mind and body and fortune.'

'You have some greatness of spirit,' Ben assured her, sounding mildly surprised, 'though you are coloured like the veriest shrew and seem to be compounded of all the shrewish humours.'

'*What...*'

'I speak but of nature, lady. I do not seek to insult you; indeed, I sought to make a compliment, for greatness of spirit is rare in your sex. But you have, you must admit, the reddest of hair and the greenest of eyes – signals both of shrewishness at the very least, and witchcraft, indeed, in some learned authorities...'

'Let us agree, then,' said Tom swiftly, 'that

37

this is indeed a cry for help from a silent woman.'

Even this intervention would hardly have saved Ben's plump cheeks from Kate's sharp claws. But then someone started beating on the door downstairs and calling for the Watch.

CHAPTER 4

Dark Waters

'You found him?' asked Tom, looking down at the lad who guarded the wherry at the Black Friars steps.

The lad nodded.

Tom looked down into the thick, brown water where the second body bobbed, face-down, half-awash, with scum and detritus piling up on the upriver part of him, as though he had actually been the mudbank he so nearly resembled.

Tom crouched, reaching out to clasp the mooring post that made a little bay with the side of the steps into which the body had washed and where it floated now, amongst the other rubbish discarded into the Thames. From the thrust of the steps here it was pos-sible to see upriver past the out-wash of the Fleet Ditch and the footings of Bridewell.

The colour and odour of the water at his feet told Tom of the tide falling away downstream beyond London Bridge, and of the current here picking up speed and sucking stuff out of the open sewer of the Fleet Ditch that could have lain bottled there for hours; and that was where the body had come from, for the whole north bank was walled upstream, past Arundel House, Somerset House and the Savoy. Water Lane, Strand Lane and Ivy Bridge Lane were the only openings other than the wherry steps, except for the Fleet Ditch, between the Savoy and London Bridge itself.

Only the Fleet lay upstream of here, and it was plain to Tom that the corpse had come downstream, following the north bank to this place. A glance over his shoulder downriver towards the Bridge proved that, for the water was falling swiftly down there, seemingly being bodily sucked into the great water-wheels in its bankside arches. If the body had moved for an instant downstream from the little isthmus of these steps, it must have been swept away into the pounding maelstrom down there.

It must have come from upstream then, decided Tom with settled certainty. It must have come recently, for it had gathered so little detritus as yet; and the boy, silent now, seemed to have been quick enough in reporting his discovery.

The Fleet Ditch was the likeliest place for this second corpse to have entered the

Thames, therefore, and Tom knew it from all-too-close acquaintance; and he knew that it would be easy enough to check his theory. He looked up past the frowning face of young Ben Jonson and caught Sergeant Grimes's eye. 'You can pull him out now, Sergeant,' he said quietly.

One whiff of the deceased as he came up out of the thick, dark water was enough to confirm the matter of the Fleet Ditch for Tom, for the little river was nothing more than an open sewer these days. Any exposure to the filth that flowed in it left an odour that was as unmistakable as it was disgusting.

A good deal more than that was swiftly settled too: the man's age – he was of middle years, with greying hair and a neat beard silvering at the jowls; his standing – he was a chamberlain or some such, for he wore a solid suit of well-made clothes and a golden ring cast with his master's signet, of cats and mice; his origin – the dark cloth was brocaded with a pattern of cats and mice, his buttons were silver nutmegs.

'Much better suited to this dark cloth than the daffodil-yellow up in your lodgings, master,' said Ben, his voice uncharacteristically awed.

'He has attained his respectable darkness by service and seniority,' observed Tom, reaching down to pull back a flap of imposing over-robe to reveal the dead man's chest. He, too, wore a message-pouch. Ben reached down towards it but Tom prevented him. 'It will be empty, Ben. It likely carried the twin of the message in my room; and the man that employed the murderers holds it now, of course.'

'The same man?'

'And the same murderers,' said Tom. 'The same knife, at least, for look how precisely the throat has been slit. I have seen barber surgeons less neat with their finest razors.'

'They took his purse,' observed Ben. 'Look. It is exactly as you said it would be: the loops are left dangling from his belt. But if they took his purse, and, indeed, his message, why leave his ring?'

'Time and priorities, perhaps. The message would be first – particularly if their employer wanted to read it – for, as with our boy, there would have been a deal of blood. Then the purse in a twinkling – extra payment for a job well done, as like as not. And then the ring ... but you see how advancing age had thickened his knuckles. What went on easily some time ago will not come off so swiftly now. Men in too much of a hurry to linger over the lopping of a finger – even though they had sharp tools to hand; and, perhaps, men who knew that it would be risky to try and sell a ring bearing Lord Outremer's arms when two of His Lordship's servants lie dead and a hue and cry may be called.'

'So, you will call a hue and cry, will you, young Tom?' came a familiar voice, dryly mocking, but affectionate for all that.

Tom looked up, and there in the middle of

the crowd beneath the archway stood an old friend – the very friend of all others that Tom most wanted, but least expected, to see. 'Hello, old Law,' he answered, rising. 'What are you doing over the water and out of your bailiwick?'

Talbot Law, Bailiff to the Bishop of Westminster and principal law officer on the Bishop's lands south of the river, stood aside to reveal Captain Curberry, his local equivalent. 'Since the matter of the heads on London Bridge which fell into both our bailiwicks, literally as well as figuratively, you will recall,' said Talbot, 'Captain Curberry and I meet regularly. But I return your enquiry with my own. If you are here, where is the trusty Ugo Stell that bears you company at all times?'

'He has moved down to Bleeke House,' answered Tom. 'Still pursuing the fair and fortunate Mistress Van Der Leyden. I do not see him from one week's end to the next. But it is good news that you came north of the river on occasions...'

'As today, for instance,' said Curberry, interrupting the two old friends. 'What's amiss here?'

'Well...' began Tom.

'Two men murdered,' interrupted Ben officiously.

'Sergeant?' Curberry swept the interloper aside and turned to his own professional. Grimes folded his face into a slow and thoughtful frown. 'We-e-ell...' he began.

Tom caught Talbot Law's eye. An infinitesimal gesture of the head and the two companions of the Nijmagen campaigns, who had fought across Flanders five years before Ben arrived, and fought other, darker battles since, moved silently, side by side. Down into the wherry they stepped, unnoticed by everyone except Ben. His entry into the little vessel, hard upon their heels and a great deal less subtle than theirs, came near to upsetting the little wherry, and would have called their departure to Curberry's notice had he not been wrestling with the Gordian Knot of Sergeant Grimes's slow report.

At Tom's terse order, the boy began to guide the wherry up against the current and into the mouth of the Fleet. The little river was narrow, its waters shallow and thick. Soon Ben and the boy were pushing the little overladen vessel up the foetid stream by using the oars as poles. Tom crouched in the bow, apparently oblivious to the rancid stench, his eyes busy.

'You suppose him to have been cast in here?' asked Talbot at his shoulder, looking up at the low wall to their right that backed a series of gardens overlooked from their left by the towering garrets of Bridewell.

'Yes,' said Tom briefly. Then he began to expand upon his reasoning a little, glad to have his old friend securely at his side again. 'He is unlikely to have been killed in a public place. The footpads that killed the boy outside my school were driven to it by despera-

43

tion. No swift slice on a busy street and heave over the side of the Fleet Bridge, therefore. No. A swift quietus here, in one of the houses or gardens on our right is much more likely. But slit throats make swift messes, so on the bank and the wall above it, in the garden and mayhap even in the house where it was done there will be ... Ah!' He pointed. Something gleamed like rubies even in the shadow cast by Bridewell.

Talbot's hand clapped down on his shoulder. 'Witchcraft,' opined the Bishop's Bailiff almost silently.

Then, at Tom's command, Ben and the wherry boy guided their cockleshell vessel over to the bright red slick that slithered vividly down from wall-top to mud-slide to water's edge.

The wherry carried a mooring rope and a grappling hook as well as oars and boat hook, so it was only the work of a moment to secure a passage up over the stinking mud and the low but solid wall above it. Then, with Tom in the lead, the three went hand over hand up beside the trail of blood. Tom topped the wall and looked around a derelict and overgrown plot. Once, he guessed, this had been the herb garden for the cooks and physicians of the Black Friars in whose dissolved Dominican priory he now lived and worked. Many of the buildings from the top of Water Lane up to Lud Gate itself had been part of the religious complex for which the whole area was now named. Many of the buildings were finding new tenancies – as with the building he shared with Aske the Haberdasher. Others, like this one it seemed, were falling into ruin through neglect. Like the garden, the building was unkempt, overgrown, apparently derelict.

With these thoughts in mind, Tom leaped easily over the wall and landed in a fragrant area full of springing rosemary and sage. A bay tree stood a few yards down on his left, and his nose alerted him to the fact that he had landed on a patch of early-flowering garlic; but none of the sensuous beauty around him could tempt him from the path he was following. All through the garden, on stem and blossom, on leaves and the ground beneath them were splattered gouts of blood.

Tom began to follow this trail at once, dimly aware of Talbot and Ben in turn following him. What struck him as he moved through the little wasteland was the speed at which the body must have been carried – dragged here and there, as attested by broken branches and lines through grass and mud made by dragging boot-heels, but carried for the most part, by two men – one on each arm to begin with, then, later, less handily, one at each end, the one with the legs almost literally rushed off his feet.

Tom thought again of the ring, which a moment or two more work with that razor-edged dagger would have secured. It all bespoke a monstrous haste, he thought again. As he neared the back of the house, therefore, he paused and looked up to try to work out what the murderers might have seen to hurry them along. And he saw at once: the east-facing windows of Bridewell. Even now, figures came and went, some pausing to look out and to wave – prostitutes for the most part, locked away for plying their trade but using the windows to keep their hand in against their release. Thinking of Kate, whom he had first met in Bridewell, half-stripped and ready to be whipped in – disguised as a bawd while she sought to contact a prisoner in the deep dungeons there – Tom smiled and waved back, much to the disgust of Talbot and an unsuspectedly prudish Ben.

Then he turned, thinking further, *If the murder was done in a derelict house, then why not leave the body there?*

No sooner had the thought come than Talbot at his shoulder gave it words: 'Why risk dumping the corpse? It could lie in this place undiscovered till Doomsday by the looks of things.'

'Only time will tell,' said Tom quietly. 'Time and a little practice of the Black Arts.'

Behind him, Tom heard Ben suck in his breath with shock at this apparent blasphemy. 'Fear not, young Ben,' he said, in much the same tone as Talbot Law used when addressing him; 'I speak in thieves' cant – of lock-picking, not Devil-worship.' So saying, he slid out one of his long Solingen daggers and slid it into the lock in the ancient door against which they were crowding. The lock was of

46

the same vintage as the door itself and that had likely been fashioned when a Plantagenet was king. It yielded now as rapidly and completely as most of the women overlooking their break-in from the windows of Bridewell would have done.

The door led into a low room, wide and brick-floored – a kitchen, judging by the brick-built hearth against the side wall. In the middle of the room stood a plain table with a scattering of utensils, overturned for the most part, and some seats in like condition scattered on the floor – the whole bespeaking a quiet, friendly meal between several friends disturbed by sudden and violent action. Violent, for certain, because the tabletop and floor to the door were covered with dark, dry stains. The room stank of an iron sweetness all too familiar to Tom from the incidents of the heads upon London Bridge.

Defying the apparently logical assumptions of his two companions, however, Tom did not cross to the bloody table, in spite of the fact that this was clearly the end of his recent quest. Instead he led them through into a tall, silent hallway where a set of stairs mounted to silent, shaded upper rooms. Across the dusty hall he crept, with his two friends following, exchanging confused, enquiring glances, until he came up against the inside of the big front door. This was secured by a lock of equal age – and equal weakness to the Black Arts – as the one on the back door. In an instant he had opened it and swung the door back an inch or two, peeping out into the street. Then he closed it, locked it again and swung round to face the others. 'We must be swift,' he said. 'We will search the kitchen for more details and clues as soon as we may, but I think we must also look through the whole of the house.'

As he crossed to the stair he whispered to Ben, 'It is the house, Ben – the very house on Water Lane in whose doorway the leader of the footpads met the stranger in the cloak and mask as the boy lay dying in your arms. Remember: I saw them as I came past. And Kate, who watched the footpad run in, saw neither one of them come out.'

To Talbot he said, 'Take care, old Law, for these are dark waters – deep and dark.' Then he fell silent as the three of them climbed the stairs. As soon as they stepped off the top stair, Tom's eyes were on the floor. The house was as good as derelict, the flooring thick with dirt and dust; but there were signs of occupancy – to wit, footmarks. Tom followed the trail of these into a privy whose simple downward opening sat above a midden in the garden; then to a bedchamber, which seemed tidier than the rest so far – certainly the ancient four-poster was neatly made with clean linen – and still the footsteps led out and on, their number – or the frequency of their passage – dwindling, speaking of occasional, private, perhaps even secret, visits.

This last set of footprints brought them to a short, recurved staircase winding up into the eaves. At the head of this stood a gallery, almost a passage, some eight feet long, and at its end, a door. On their left an inner wall stood eight feet tall, built up to the high-point of the roof. To their right it sloped down a little, clearly towards the guttering. The door reflected this shape, for it was not quite square, but sloping a little down towards their right hands. Again, this one was locked. On the slightly shorter side, a padlock gleamed in the gathering shadows, and it was modern, well maintained: solidly fixed.

Tom looked at it and shrugged. 'This one is far beyond my mastery,' he said. 'Nick o'Darkmans and Kit Callot both would be hard put to pick through this.'

He and Talbot turned away, defeated, but Ben stopped them. 'Wait,' he said, flinging the word over his shoulder as he looked closely at the door itself, then crouched a little on the lower side. 'I know neither of the worthies that you name and doubt that I would like to know them; but if your masters of the Black Arts could not get you through this door, I know an apprentice bricklayer who can. For see, the wall built inward from the roof-pitch here is merely lath and plaster. The frame seems to be settled here and bricked in, but these bricks are near as old as Julius Caesar and are more sand than substance. And the wood, I swear to you, might well have been part of the Ark. If I were to put my shoulder here' – he suited the word to the action, obscuring the whole newly locked side

49

of the ancient construct – 'and if I were to push with all my might and main just here...' A groaning ensued, and a creaking splinter, and the whole door grated slowly open, taking the lock and the jamb to which it was secured right into the secret room with it. Because the hinge was secured to the taller, inner wall, and the door also opened inwards, away ahead of them into the room itself, the jamb settled back and the whole thing opened freely.

The three friends walked into a long room with a sloping roof, lit from their left by the rays of the afternoon sun. The place had the air of a chapel and, considering the provenance of the building, it might well have been one, once. In the room there were three things: a chair, of plain wood, its seat padded with leather and polished with constant use, before which stood a table, backed against an inner wall; and on the table stood a picture. The picture was a portrait of a woman, head and shoulders, extended almost to the waist, set against an indeterminate background of clouds and sea. It was not the work of a great master, but there was something about it of Holbein's liveliness and accuracy. Certainly Tom had no trouble in recognizing its subject – the golden ringlets bound up into that old-fashioned filigreed headdress; the even, golden brows beneath that clear, snowy forehead; those forthright eyes that stared straight into his, as still and deep as the most fathomless of pools; that decided nose, a partner for that strong, faintly dimpled chin; and, between, those sculpted, strawberry, ever-silent lips.

It was Lady Margaret Outram, Countess Cotehel, whose messages calling for his help and whose messengers who had brought them lay lost and dead within a couple of hundred yards.

No sooner had this fact burst into Tom's consciousness than so did two others, each one more urgent and disturbing than the last. The portrait had obviously been taken some time since – or for private purposes – for Lady Margaret was dressed in a high ruff plunging to a low point, revealing her breast, in a manner reserved only for maiden ladies, to a deeply shadowed valley; and that valley, of a sudden, put Tom disquietingly in mind of Kate lying in the crook of his arms at the beginning of all this a scant couple of hours ago. For Kate's stays had been unloosed, her shift a-gape and more than her cleavage on show. Tom crossed to the portrait, frowning, wondering why such an image should have come to his mind just then.

And he saw that, from throat-pit to breast-bone, the portrait had been cut – cut with a razor-edged knife, as though whoever wielded it had dreamed of cutting away the Lady's clothing. Perhaps even more.

No, certainly more, for, as he looked more closely at the thing, Tom realized that there were two more cuts across the canvas: one across the mouth, separating the lips exactly at their join, so that for a moment she seemed to breathe; but that was clearly impossible, for the other slit cut right across the throat, beheading her entirely.

Then the sinister slits in the portrait stirred again and Tom realized that the still air in the strange, unholy chapel had been stirred.

That a door downstairs had been opened.

CHAPTER 5

Greek Fire

Tom led them down the stairs, walking silently with his back against whichever wall was nearest, his sword leading in whichever hand was foremost. He was, at once, certain that someone had just entered the house, careful of losing the element of surprise, keen to overhear any unguarded talk and most potently in remembrance of the evil-looking pistol that the cloaked stranger had carried in the very doorway below. Talbot followed silently at his heels, walking more square-on, armed with sword in his right hand and dagger in his left, content to follow where Tom led and confident in his leader. Ben brought up the rear with his Toledo blade safely in its scabbard, Lady Margaret's ravished picture beneath his arm and his square face folded in a mutinous scowl – for he wished to be a warrior, not a beast of burden.

As they crept along the long, dusty hallway, it became possible to hear quiet voices weaving impenetrably upwards out of indeterminate sounds – scraping, bumping, a kind of muted thundering. Tom strained to make out the words, to guess how many men were below at the least – but all to no avail. At the end of the corridor he paused, straining to see down the stairwell. The sun, which had illuminated the room up in the eaves, was setting behind the bulk of Bridewell now and it was suddenly surprisingly dark down there. From what he could see, the hallway seemed empty. The bustle and whispered conversation had moved through into the kitchen area where a sudden, slopping liquid element was added to the strange sounds that came creeping through the shadows to his ears.

As careful as a hunting cat, Tom put his right foot on the top step and shifted his weight down on to it. The stair remained blessedly mute. Swiftly and silently he crept downwards, placing his tip-toes where the stairs promised to be strongest. Talbot followed in his footsteps like Eurydice following Orpheus out of hell. On the half-landing where the stairs turned, Tom paused and crouched, looking through into the kitchen area. It seemed brighter there, and shadows came and went monstrously through the half-open door. A shaft of light suddenly shot across the hall and settled, as bright as sunset, upon the inside of the main door. Tom saw that it was locked and bolted; but, on the sudden, this information took second place to other, much more vital. Ben stepped on to the stairs above him and they groaned like a bull at the baiting. The moment that he did so, however, what Tom could see and hear was swept aside by what he could smell. Under the kitchen door, under the shaft of sunset brightness, was pouring a thick liquid shadow that would have put him in mind most forcefully of blood had it not been for the overwhelming stench of it. It seared his nostrils – indeed, the whole back of his nose and throat. It was a terrifying odour – one that reared horrifically out of his young manhood at school with Maestro Capo Fero in Siena. It was a smell with the most terrible associations – from the one time he had seen someone being burned at the stake. The stench was that of naphtha. The thick black liquid was the legendary, unquenchable Greek Fire invented, so legend said, by Archimedes himself.

Revelation exploded in his head even as something much more dangerous and tangible exploded in the kitchen with a *whoomph!* that blew the kitchen door off its hinges and sent a wall of fire rolling across the black mess on the hall floor. Even as Tom sprang back and the two above him turned again, he saw a tall sea of flame come rolling across the hallway to batter like blinding surf against the back of the bolted front door.

Mounting the stair hard on Talbot's heels, then, he thought of Ben's words – how old, dusty and dry this ruin was. The element so actively ablaze beneath them would feed upon the fabric of this place like a starving man upon a pie. Even as he leaped up into the corridor, he heard the deep, rumbling thunder that is the voice of great conflagrations.

'I last heard a sound like that when we fired Nijmagen,' bellowed Talbot, echoing his very thought.

Ben led them into the first bright bedroom and Tom saw at once that the brightness would cost them dear in this situation. The window – their only way out – looked west over the herb garden, and that was well ablaze. The desperate temptation of a two-fathom leap was, of necessity, removed – unless they wished to roast. The second room Ben led them into was little better, the crazy flooring of the house adding another six feet before they came to a tiny window looking nearly twenty feet down on to the cobbles of Black Friars itself. Tom had escaped from a predicament like this one in times past by jumping out through one window and in through the window opposite, which usually stood a scant yard distant; but Black Friars was six feet wide at this point and the windows of the house opposite looked further away even than that. The next room they found was the privy and they paused here for a desperate moment, considering how best to rip up the plank with its one central hole and squeeze through to drop into the softness of the midden heap below. Unlike the door above, however, this wood was well secured in strong brick.

'A later addition, like as not,' bellowed Ben knowledgeably.

This time when they came back out into the corridor they were greeted by the sight of the stairhead gushing flames upward at a terrifying rate. A great cloud of spark-bright smoke came rolling along the ceiling towards them. Tom turned to Ben, coughing, choking and shouting, 'Is there any other part of this structure we can break through as you broke through the doorway upstairs? Think, Ben. It is the master bricklayer we must look to now, or we all get a taste of hell itself together.'

Ben paused, thinking, but only for a moment. Then he nodded and they were off. Up that curving little staircase and into the long room under the eaves he led them. Hard on his heels they followed, across the smoking floor to the solid chair and empty table that had recently held the picture that remained, still, firmly under his arm – until he turned and passed it back to Tom. Tom sheathed his sword and took it. The smoke in the room was growing dangerously thick disturbingly rapidly, pouring in strange lines and columns through the ill-fitting floorboards; and the boards down at the stairwell end were beginning to spit and smoulder themselves.

Ben pulled the table into position and

slammed the chair into place beside it so that he could use the one as a step up on to the other. Then, standing four-square on the table, he wedged himself at a half-crouch under the sloping beams in the ceiling above and, even as Tom's quick mind saw exactly what he was up to, he heaved with all of his square-bodied, bricklayer's strength.

So the three of them went through the roof. Ben went first, scattering old tiles and ancient timbers hither and yon. With the good eye of an apprentice to his trade, he had brought them through within easy reach of the central ridge. Thus he was able to kick himself out to the waist, use Talbot's shoulders as the Bishop's Bailiff leaped on to the table in turn, and squirm out. Then, holding the central ridge with one hand, he pulled Talbot past him as Talbot in turn kicked off from Tom's shoulders. Finally, the pair of them reached down for Tom, who needed more help because the room at his feet was well ablaze, because there was no one presenting shoulders for him to stand upon, and because he refused to leave Lady Margaret's portrait to the flames. Then, with Ben still in the lead, they ran north along the sagging roofs of two more houses until they were able to slide down a gentle pitch and clamber on to the top of the old gate by the opening into Water Lane. From here it was a simple matter for them to run down its internal steps and out into the street.

Tom's plan now was to put Lady Margaret

safely in his rooms, then to join the throng who were already fighting the blaze under the direction of the Watch. His exit from a burning house, through the roof itself, had by no means gone unnoticed, however; and if Talbot was well known in Southwark and Ben in Islington, everyone in Black Friars knew Tom, so no sooner was he safely out into the street than he found himself face to face with Captain Curberry.

Tom was used to terse, quick-fire debriefings under battlefield – and near-battlefield – conditions. He had given one such to the Earl of Leicester beneath the walls of Nijmagen – one that had founded his fortune, as well as those of Talbot Law, Ugo Stell and Will Shakespeare, who had been there with him. He had given one – and more than one – to Henry Carey, Lord Hunsdon and Lord Chamberlain, the Queen's cousin, half-brother and most trusted advisor, whose Man he was together with all of Will Shakespeare's acting troupe the Lord Chamberlain's Men. He had given one to Lord Robert Cecil, Master of the Queen's Secret Service, in a shadowed room in Elfinstone Castle. He had given one to the Earl of Essex, Master of the Queen's Horse and sometimes of her heart, as they had run across London Bridge pursuing a madman with an axe. He had given one to his uncle and namesake the Lord of the Waste at Bewcastle on the Scottish Borders as they had taken a war-band into the black heart of Liddesdale pursuing more madness, murderers and a monstrous, ghostly hound; and he gave one to Captain Curberry now as Ben once again became responsible for the portrait and the Bishop's Bailiff added observations of his own.

'I will have to refer this to Sir William Danby,' decided Captain Curberry in the end. His concern about the political impact of the situation outweighed other, more immediate, practical aspects. Not even Tom could turn him from his moment of hesitant deliberation while the Watch down Water Lane behind them oversaw the pouring of bucket after bucket of water into the blazing house. 'This is more than a simple matter of murder now. And if, as you say, there may be some threat against the House of Outremer, the Queen's Coroner himself will want to be involved.'

'And I had best refer it onward and upward also,' said Tom, exchanging a look with Talbot Law. 'For anything taken to the Crowner's ears had better also be taken to Lord Hunsdon, at the very least, and probably Lord Robert Cecil.'

However, a combination of events arising from the arsonists' use of Greek Fire and Captain Curberry's failure to take Tom's word that this was an important element to the problem confronting them took the matter to more general notice in any case. The water pouring into the front of the house swept through into the garden and thence it settled into the Fleet Ditch; but because

Greek Fire was composed of lighter, fiery elements, it rode upon the water's back and, instead of being quenched, it simply poured out of the garden and into the river. So that the Fleet river exploded into flames. The noxious gases given off by the rotting foulness in the dark water blazed for a glorious moment that threatened Bridewell Palace itself, then flames flowed out on to the Thames. Wherries, ships and shallops headed south. The dangerous floating conflagration spread along the river wall, past the Black Friars steps and threatened Puddle Warf, Paul's Warf and even Bayard's Castle before it petered out, broken up and smothered, not by the hand of man but by the roughness of the waters beneath the rapidly falling tide.

By this time too the fire was under control. The two houses beside the Gate were ruined beyond recovery, but the top of Water Lane and the rest of Black Friars was safe. Wearily, Tom dragged himself homeward with Talbot by his side. Ben had come and gone about various commissions and Tom expected to find him guarding Kate in his rooms above Aske's the Haberdasher. But Kate was gone. Not even her reputation was likely to remain unblotted were she found to be sitting half-dressed in the middle of a matter such as this one. She had rooms she shared with her sister Audrey and Audrey's affianced husband-to-be Sir Thomas Walsingham, nephew and heir to the Spy-Master, at Nonesuch House on London Bridge. Tom would find her there, when this matter was less dangerous to a hopeful lady-in-waiting to the Queen.

Ben, on the other hand, was by no means waiting alone. He was pacing up and down in front of the long mirror in Tom's practice room, making fearsome passes with his Toledo blade under the icily amused gaze of a tall, powerful-looking man whose assured, courtly bearing was at odds with his ragged clothes, dirty flesh and linen, and unkempt beard. Lady Margaret's portrait stood on the floor beneath the mirror as though she could enjoy the sight of Ben's wild rage and the stranger's dangerous amusement.

'Welcome home, Tom,' said the tall man dryly. 'Your ... ah ... *bricklayer*, here, said I should expect you at any moment. And then he went to some practice, which I see is sorely needed.

'As Master Law was no doubt about to tell you when the chance arose, I have been working in the Clink Prison under his personal jurisdiction this last week, apparently befriending some stupid men with traitorous plots toward who are resting there at present at Her Majesty's pleasure.'

Tom and Talbot exchanged a speaking look; and Tom indeed would have been glad of the information, had Talbot been swifter to give it to him. For this man was Robert Poley, the secret agent who worked in the dark world between the courtly lights of Lord Robert Cecil and Sir Thomas Walsingham. Lord Hunsdon himself, as Chancellor and Leader

of the Queen's Council, occasionally employed Poley about his most sinister and dangerous business. This was the man who had
posed as the lover of Thomas Babbington and
caused the death of Mary Queen of Scots by
exposing their treasonous plots. This was the
man who had murdered Christopher Marlowe in Eleanor Bull's house in Deptford.
This was the man who ruled many of the
streets where Tom had to walk with the power
of life and death. This was the man who, all
too often, was sent to give him his orders; and
if he was working with traitors in the Clink,
that could only mean he had reason to fear
some plot – instituted by Catholic Spain,
perhaps, and put forward by Jesuits and
secretly Catholic intellectuals in the great
houses nearby. Suddenly it did not seem so
irrelevant that the room from which he had
rescued the portrait so recently had looked a
little like a secret chapel.

'But,' continued Poley, his voice as light and
dry as sand whispering over silk, 'the moment
I looked out of the Clink, between the Rose
Theatre and the Bear Pit, earlier this afternoon – looked out in all innocence to see that
the Thames was ablaze from Bridewell to
Bayard's Castle, and half of Black Friars put
to the torch behind – something told me I
would soon be talking to you.'

CHAPTER 6

The Heart

They went to the tavern named The Heart on Carter Lane overlooking the old Prior's Garden, which still stood behind Black Friars. Here they secured a private chamber, a solid meal from the ordinary below, a gallon of ale and four leather tankards sealed with pitch. Then – over a stew of winter mutton, early carrots, leeks and greens spiced with rosemary and mint, served on great thick trenchers of dark bread – they came to the heart of the matter so far.

'It was a clever notion to write the message down before the blood consumed the last of it,' allowed Poley, looking down his long nose at Ben.

'Unexpected in a bricklayer, perhaps,' needled Ben, still disgruntled by Poley's treatment of him so far. Nevertheless, he laid his carefully written note in the middle of the table so that all of them, peering down their noses, over their tankards or through the steam of the mutton stew, could see:

grave
o-one e
erwatc
nger. A
ife, whi
ood in
nd men
ound he
een care
e. I ha
variou
ansfer t
w Year
ies pas
my deat
n I may
ed offic
that yo
opeful
nd take
of Elfin
Help me
argare
ess Cot

'Any thought at all is unexpected in a brick-layer,' answered Poley, sneering and narrow-eyed. 'And I observe you can even write. This is a revelation! And they say the education system is going to rack and ruin, Apprentice *Jobson*, is it?'

'It is *Jonson*, as I suspect you know quite well, Master Poley,' said Tom, leaning forward and gently taking command. 'And Ben's good thought has given us one of only two facts hard enough to grasp left after the blaze in Water Lane.'

'Apart from the corpses, of course,' observed Poley, incapable of letting another man take the final word.

'Apart from the corpses, of course,' allowed Tom, long-used to the game. 'But let us begin with the message, such as it is, before we return to what little is left of the messengers.'

'We had begun to consider this,' Ben advised both Poley and Talbot Law.

'We had,' confirmed Tom. 'But the weight of subsequent events is added to what seemed relatively trifling at the early part of the investigation.'

'Meaning?' demanded Talbot, the only auditor whose sole motive was to support the Master of Logic and further the investigation, while the others tried to score points as though they duelled with the wooden blunts that stood in the corner of the fencing room in Tom's school, seemingly unaware that this was a matter for sharps, if ever there was one.

'The message is apparently a call for help. It seems to have been sent to me, and may have come from Lady Margaret Outram, Countess Cotehel, to whom in the past, as Kate observed, I have rendered some trifling service. Beyond that we can establish little from the words themselves.

'The letter begins with my name. That seems clear. Then the next is "o-one e...". This must mean that in all her household at

Elfinstone Castle she has "no-one else" whom she can trust...'

'Except for the two she sent with her messages,' observed Poley.

'And if they were the last two she could trust, then her danger is compounded, is it not?' added Ben, not to be outdone in this matter of reasoning.

'Indeed,' allowed Tom. 'In more ways than one, perhaps. Especially if she sent two because she could not trust one alone to do her bidding and no more than her bidding. Now you see how events subsequent to the original arrival of the letter have added their weight and emphasized the danger. For "danger" is the next word but one, is it not? Or "anger", though they be terribly closely allied. And the word just before it must be "overwatched". The danger seems most puissant, moreover for it seems to threaten her "life", does it not?'

'Possibly,' added Ben, getting to grips with the puzzle now and confronted with the next few fragments of words, 'there is no "good in" the people beside her. No good women "and men" who stand "around her" at all. Even though she has "been careful", nevertheless she has – see where it says "I have" here – "various" suspicions. I confess I cannot see the relevance of "transfer" or "New Year" or indeed of "sundries past", but I think she clearly speaks of "my death". And if that is so, the fact that little else can be gleaned before she begs "Help me" and signs with her name and title seems to make little difference at all.'

'True enough,' allowed Tom quietly. 'And well expounded...'

'For an apprentice bricklayer...'

'For an apprentice in the Art and Science of Logic,' countered Tom before Ben became too distracted by this. 'I thank you, Master Poley.'

'Hum. But even so, master and apprentice both, there is precious little meat upon the lean bone of supposition,' Poley countered, his tone on the very edge of a sneer.

'True. And therefore would it seem a trifling matter, after all, had this been discovered in the filth of the Black Friars kennel, obscured by mud instead of blood. I return to my words addressed to Ben earlier, of the added weight of subsequent events. If that were the case, were this mud instead of blood, then all this exercise of logic would truly be a waste of time and effort. For there is not a word or part of a word in the whole missive that could not be interpreted some other, more innocent way.

'But we do have two dead servants come from Elfinstone wearing Lord Outremer's livery, the first of whom bore the blood-boltered missive itself, the second of whom might have been left in secret for the Greek Fire to consume with the house where he died – but who was publicly broadcast instead, at some risk, and therefore with some point. And we have the picture of Her Ladyship mutilated in that most sinister manner,

67

in the garret of the murder house, destined to burn with the house, for it is a dangerous piece of evidence. And we have the stranger, cloaked and masked, who caused all these things – who doubtless cut the portrait, and who, as like as not if my logic holds, is known to Lady Margaret, and covets Lady Margaret; who has overwatched her in the past, and closely enough to have aroused some suspicion within her breast; who has taken decisive action now; who wishes to cut her off from her friends, indeed from any hope of help, so that he may...'

'*So that he may what?*' demanded Poley, when Tom hesitated. 'So that he may do what?' he repeated, when Tom was slow to respond.

'Did you note the portrait we rescued from the burning house?' answered Tom, at last.

'Aye. Though your bricklayer danced around it like a bear while he swung his good sword like an ape with a club.'

'Did you note how it was cut?' Tom's words overwhelmed the outraged croaking of Ben Jonson, goaded too far at last.

'Of course. From throat to bodice. Across the face and across the throat. I had thought Apprentice ... *Hobson*, is it? ... had done it in his wild cavorting.'

'Jonson,' corrected Tom thoughtlessly. 'No. Our man did that. And it is *that* – whatever it might actually mean to him – that he is preparing to do to the Lady.'

'But,' said Poley, testing as ever, 'why now?

– if he has been content to watch and wait, to do so since the New Year, perhaps, as the letter says. What is there that has goaded him into action now?'

'Something we cannot fathom from this distance, surely,' said Talbot. 'Something we could only descry if we went to Elfinstone itself.'

'The New Year,' mused Tom. 'Why mention that at all? Unless...' He lapsed into thoughtful silence again. Then, Socratic as ever, he asked, 'Old Law, you celebrated the New Year with the rest of London, did you not?'

'I did. On the first day of January last...'

'But your wife, the good Lady Bess, at the Nag's Head Inn down in the depths of Winchester – when will she and her country friends celebrate New Year?'

'Ha! They will ever hold to the Old New Year! They will hold their festival at the end of this month and celebrate the coming of the year country-fashion, with feasting and foolishness. And, God's my life, that's less than a week hence! I had clean forgotten...'

'Thus, were the household at Elfinstone to be bound by ancient tradition, say, the reference to New Year might well be less innocent than Master Poley supposes – a moment in the safe past that the Lady first became aware that more eyes than usual were overwatching her. It becomes a date in the dangerous future – in the future but all too close at hand – when something fearful might be expected to occur, the promise of which might well have proved the good to set everything in motion: her call for help, his silencing of that call; his realization of how much she fears; his need to act before the fears lead to further danger to himself and his plans...'

'All at Old New Year ... Why then?' wondered Ben.

'At the very least,' said Tom grimly, 'the festivities must offer opportunities to the agile mind.'

As the thoughtful little party broke up each to return home for the night, Tom took Poley aside. 'I must go down there,' he said. 'I must go to Elfinstone.'

'All the way to Elfinstone? Does she not own properties much closer at hand where you might start instead?'

'Two houses here in London, but as you must know yourself, she never opens them; and after what she suffered within their walls, that is little surprise. She hates the town and resists all calls to come to Court. She fears to lose control of her life again, to lose her son once more...'

'To fall within the dangerous orbit of her ravisher, the boy's natural father,' purred Poley.

'On whom you and your masters keep the closest of eyes. Have you not got eyes riveted to the Lady Margaret as well? Or at least to her son, the young Lord Outremer?' As Tom spoke, so the speed of his words slowed, for his mind became distracted by a realization: that he had been tricked – hoodwinked, perhaps.

'We had,' allowed Poley grudgingly.

'Ah. So the body in the Fleet was not simply a message for the Lady Margaret. And there must have been two missing messages, both gone from the chamberlain's purse.' He took Poley's silence as a kind of admission and proceeded, still speaking slowly.

'Then you must take responsibility for the bodies and see what further you can find about them. I must to Elfinstone with all haste to replace your eyes and give the silent lady, at the least, a voice.'

'I think you must,' agreed Poley.

'Can you get me the passes and permissions? Or shall I to Lord Hunsdon? I've no wish to risk a whipping at every parish line I cross between here and Rochester.'

'Is this a matter for Lord Hunsdon? He is Lord Chamberlain and even though you are his man you should trouble him only with matters fit for the Council's notice. Or the Star Chamber's.'

'And you see nothing for either of them in this matter, Master Robert?'

Tom only used Poley's given name when he wished to focus Poley's considerable intellect on something of crucial importance. Poley knew it. 'I have overlooked something?' But there was just too much surprise in his dark, rich tones.

'I doubt it, but allow me to expound. There is still one aspect undiscussed – a crucial aspect, I would say. For who was it that

71

ravished Lady Margaret all those years ago? Who is the father that dare not own his child? Who, because of that, can never lay his hands upon the fortune that his bastard son stands heir to, though he is desperate for money and would go to any lengths...'

'The Earl of Essex,' admitted Poley, naming his master's greatest enemy at Court – his own greatest enemy, therefore; and Tom's, come to that. 'Lord Robert Devereux, the Earl of Essex.' His tone was that of a satisfied man and Tom saw at last exactly how Poley had been playing with him: distracting him by teasing Ben Jonson while subtly guiding the Master of Logic into the very position in which he found himself now; ensuring that he must take action – at a speed and with a purpose that suited Poley and his ever-murky ends.

'The Earl of Essex – who, you and your masters fear, would have the apparently disinterested goodness to step in and look after the child should any harm befall his sadly damaged mother?'

'Exactly,' admitted Poley.

'Who may well have, therefore, a very lively interest in seeing that some harm certainly does befall her? For he will by that one single stroke find himself master of one of the vastest fortunes in the country, two of the largest houses in London and two of the most important castles in the kingdom – Cotehel, if my memory serves, famously strengthened and armed by Henry himself over the matter of the French wars fifty years since, and further armed by Her Majesty since the Armada.'

Poley was silent for an instant. Then he said, 'Oddly enough, I have some passes here to hand. The very things you need, I think – though of course it would be madness to set forth tonight, even were you able to get past the Watch and over the river to your Bailiff's jurisdiction.'

'Marry, well thought on. I shall need a pass for Talbot; and, as we are bound for one of the greatest and most historic stone edifices in the South of Merry England...'

'One for the bricklayer. Of course. I had not foreseen the bricklayer. But that will take until the morning.'

'Until the morning, then. We have little choice in any case. But early.'

CHAPTER 7

Elfinstone

'It belies its name,' observed Ben cheerfully, swaggering in Tom's footsteps some few minutes after dawn next day.

'What does?' Tom was wrapped in thought – with much to think about, not least the implications of finding that his self-appointed apprentice had not gone home to Islington last night after all, but had crept into Tom's doorway in Black Friars and slept there, lucky to avoid the Watch's notice and that of the cloaked killer, who might well still be lingering nearby.

'Hog Lane,' said Ben simply.

Indeed it did belie its name, thought Tom. He had never really considered it before, but the thoroughfare upon which Poley partook of bed and board with Master and Mistress Yeomans belied its name in truth; and, when a man considered it, it belied its function as well. *Hog Lane* – it sounded innocent enough, like the veriest foetid kennel designed to join a pig-farm to a butchers' shambles. Instead it was the nearest and fairest of roadways just outside the City, north of the Hound's Ditch, which lay like a moat along the northern wall – and one of the busiest. It opened on the right hand out of Bishopsgate Street, north of Bishops' Gate, just north of Bedlam, the Hospital for Madmen. *And for Madwomen*, thought Tom grimly, remembering who had written the letter that had started all this.

The main path of the lane, which they followed now, meandered through the fair meadows that rolled away past the big, busy artillery yard behind St Mary's Spital towards the Butts in Spital's Field itself. This was one of the open areas where every hale city-dweller must come to practise archery – and such martial arts as would keep the warlike Spanish at bay – by law, on Sundays. Here,

74

where Hog Lane ran roughly parallel to London Wall, the solid, spacious houses stood, innocently enough, amid garden plots a-glitter with dew and fragrant with spring flowers – and separated the vital artillery yard from the great gun foundry that supplied it. *What a convenient place,* thought Tom, *for a spy and spy-master to be lodged.*

Even as the thought stirred, like a worm in an apple, so he and his apprentice in the Mastery of Logic perforce stood back while two huge wagons laboured past, packed with barrels of powder and pulling a great gun apiece. Ben would have stepped into the road again immediately in their wake, but Tom held him back, allowing the silent troop of well-armed guards to canter by before they proceeded.

'You brought a gallon of ale and a loaf the last time you called this early,' said Poley. He was full-dressed and pale-faced. The darkness beneath his eyes bespoke a sleepless night, and the pout with which Mistress Yeomans put milk and bread on the table between them confirmed that his wakefulness had not been spent with her.

'Have you the passes?' asked Tom urgently. 'I see you have been busy enough in the night.'

'I have them. And more. But...'

'What is it?'

'Matters that need not concern you.'

Tom nodded, but his eyes were narrow. He

75

had never trusted Robert Poley – not since their first meeting. Poley was as much master of equivocation – duplicity – as Tom was a master of logic – detection. Plain, blunt Robert Poley was a Cambridge man, graduate of Lord Burghley's university and seedbed of Walsingham's Secret Service. Poley had deceived the traitor Thomas Babbington, making the poor fool believe he could release the Queen of Scots and put her on the throne. Poley had deceived him, betrayed him and seen him tortured to confession and then drawn and quartered with all the rest of his sad confederates; and Poley had been at Fotheringay to see Mary Queen of Scots beheaded. Poley had deceived Kit Marlowe – Cambridge graduate, playwright, mentor to Will Shakespeare and spy – into believing he was safe at Mistress Eleanor Bull's big house in Deptford nearly two years since – deceived him, and held him still while Ingram Frizer ran a twelvepenny dagger through his right eye and into his too-clever brain.

No. Trust was never the strongest amongst the strange buttresses that held the relationship between Tom Musgrave and Robert Poley sound. Yet there was an obscure sort of affection – a respect for an equal if darker intellect, of the Glasgow graduate for the Cambridge man, of the Master of Defence for the Master of Duplicity, of the Master of Logic for the Master of Lies; the grudging love of Abel, perhaps, for his big brother Cain.

'What is it?' asked Tom, again, gently.

'Matters that need not concern you,' said Poley – again. In the silence that followed, another pair of powder-laden carts went creaking by on the lane outside and another troop of guards cantered after them, their tack a-jingle like duelling foils.

'Very well,' said Tom, abruptly. 'Then let us have our passes. And more.'

The *passes* were for three men about the Council's business, their bona fides attested by the Lord Chamberlain, Lord Hunsdon, himself; the *more* came from the same source: directives to the stable hands at the inn immediately opposite the opening to Hog Lane on Bishopsgate Street to release three of the first-quality black geldings normally reserved for messengers speeding up the Great North Road, into the charge of Her Majesty's most faithful and trusted servant, Thomas Musgrave – this in spite of the fact that he would take them not north, but south.

'This is the most powerful steed I have ever ridden,' called Ben, uneasily.

Tom, one set of reins easily in one hand and another loosely in the other, glanced back over the riderless horse he was leading, at his increasingly nervous apprentice. Ben had become a bricklayer again, suddenly. He was all elbows and knees – and none of them tightly in to where they were meant to be. 'You have five minutes to settle yourself,' Tom called. 'Then we're back through Bishops'

Gate and into the bustle.'

Back through the gate they went and on across the junction of Wormwood Street and Camomile Street. One street led to one of Lady Margaret's great closed London mansions, Wormwood in Jewry; and the other to another great house, St Mary's Papey, where Poley's mentor Francis Walsingham had set up his Secret Service, lived and died.

Between them, thought Tom darkly, the streets led from one end of this matter to the other.

Then on down Bishopsgate Street and into the press and bustle of the stirring town. At the well, where Bishopsgate widened as Threadneedle Street joined it, Tom reined in and let Ben push past. The gesture was not altruistic – it was to save his neck, for he had been craning over his shoulder twice in every instant as Ben gasped, groaned and threatened to tumble headlong. 'Straight on down into Gracechurch Street,' called Tom above the heads of the heaving crowd; and, as it was early and these the first horses to press on by, the crowd, hearing the order and seeing the state of its recipient, parted amenably so that the horse could follow its head.

Gracechurch Street led to New Fish Street and New Fish Street led to London Bridge. Here the bustle of the heaving crowds thickened, the noise intensified tenfold and the horses began to curvet uneasily. How Ben stayed in his saddle along the arcaded tunnel sections through the midst of the great houses, between the loud brightness of the shop-fronts, Tom could hardly imagine; but so he did, and was confident enough to rein in on the outskirts of a central open area while Tom swung down and hammered on a doorway there.

'What place is this?' demanded Ben, as though affronted that Tom should slow his progress south.

'It is Nonesuch,' answered Tom, as amenable as the crowd. 'Home to my friend Sir Thomas Walsingham and lodging to Kate and Audrey Shelton. I have a letter for Mistress Kate.'

This last was addressed to the serving-girl who opened the door to him.

'She's still abed, sir,' said the girl.

'Of course she is. Give it to her when she stirs.' He swung into the saddle as the door closed. 'Though I expect we'll be far down the Kent Road by then,' he added wryly.

And so they were, though Tom had no way of knowing it. They were past the Butts at Newington with its ramshackle little theatre where Philip Henslowe had transferred Will Shakespeare's play of *Romeo* last year so that its famous sword fights would tempt the crowds come to practise there. They were just coming south of Greenwich, in fact, and thundering towards the Roman road that led like an arrow's flight to Dartford and Gravesend.

They stopped only once, at the edge of the cobbled slope of the South Warke of London

Bridge, still under the shadows of the piked heads atop the Great Stone Gateway. Here Tom dismounted again and hammered on the door of the Borough Counter to rouse the Bishop's Bailiff.

The last time Tom had sped out to Elfinstone, he had caught the ferry to Gravesend and ridden down from there; and under most circumstances, the river was quicker than the road. This morning, however, things were different. They were not saddled with knackered jades, ancient and broken down from a rental. Instead they sat astride steeds that seemed close kin to Pegasus in the way they flew over the ground. The weather remained fine – and March had been dry of late so that the trackways that passed for municipal thoroughfares were mud-free and firm beneath their racing hooves. Where the roads sank into defiles between cultivated plots and hedgerows, or where they became busy with other travellers – on foot and snail-slow for the most part – it was easy enough to turn aside, up on to well-drained grassy slopes, and ride three-abreast under the broad blue heaven.

Even the Roman road, more than a thousand years old, by reputation at least, was overgrown – little more than a straight line over the rolling country, worn to a track by constant use rather than by maintenance or modern engineering; but it led them, as it had led the legions, straight towards their goal.

The only accident sufficient to slow their

progress came when Ben's horse cast a shoe and they were forced to linger, supping dark Kentish ale in the tiny hamlet of Wainscott – little more than an inn, a church and a smithy – while the local blacksmith repaired matters. Then off they rode again, and did not slow until the gates of Elfinstone's castle park loomed.

Tom found himself a prey to a disorientating whirl of conflicting emotions as he guided his black gelding's head beneath the arch of Elfinstone's great gate and past the empty gatehouse into the parkland that surrounded the ancient castle. The last time he had been here, the place had been in the hands of a hated enemy, who had been entertaining the Earls of Essex and Southampton – entertaining the Earls, who had been content to be entertained by a man so inferior to them in birth and breeding, each harbouring the hope that he would allow him access to his untold fortune, for they were both on the verge of ruin; entertaining them with the distant promise of Tom's murder and the immediate prospect of hunting Lady Margaret to death, at the very least, with horse and hound. And that had been no mere act of gratuitous cruelty, for the Lady, and the child gotten upon her by a rape seven years earlier still, were all that stood between the three of them and the fortune they so coveted. Indeed, the woman and the child represented, to the Earl of Essex at least, one of the few things that could destroy his standing at Court, in the bright sun of the Queen's favour, in support of which he had squandered his fortune in the first place.

In that little coppice over there, Tom thought, he had found her, all but naked, a wild, mad thing, as terrified of the snapping pack as the gentlest of hunted hinds; but silent, even then. He could almost feel, even now, the marble-cool weight of her as she rested on his saddle-bow and faced down a baron, two earls and their wild huntsmen with him.

And he remembered her, later, pulling from the ruin of her bodice the will that made her son the heir to all this land, all these riches, if they could only survive to claim them – a secret she had kept hidden in spite of all she had suffered, and that she revealed to him alone in the certain hope that he, and he alone, would save her and her boy. That certainty had made her fit for a mad room in Bedlam if nothing else had done, thought Tom with unaccustomed self-mockery.

He had hardly seen her since, believing – how naively, he now saw all too clearly – that the promised protection of the Council in the person of Lord Robert Cecil, Essex's deadly enemy, would hold her safe in the face of the mortally ambitious Earl's undying enmity.

The pathway across Elfinstone Park was better tended than the Roman road had been, though a good deal less direct. The three horses cantered down it towards the great grey fortress whose first stones had been laid by one of the Conqueror's barons. Over the brow of a hill they came, with the westering sun setting behind them and the great castle before them seeming to sink into a grey lake of shadows with only its topmost turrets aflame. The associations in Tom's mind added vividly to the brooding atmosphere of the place, and it was all too easy to envisage the Lady Margaret trapped within it, terribly aware of watching eyes, caged like a dove, mute as a swan.

Preoccupied though he was, Tom was using his eyes as well as his mind; and it was they that alerted him. 'Ben,' he said, 'do you see any lights?'

'No,' said Ben shortly.

'There should be lights by now. This is not some broken-down mansion chambering a family fallen on ruin, conserving their warmth and their brightness for an occasional guest. This is the home of one of the greatest fortunes in the land. There should be lights. And bustle.' But all remained dark and silent as they rode silently down to Elfinstone.

The roadway ended in an ancient entrance, turreted to hold a drawbridge but closed now by a great pair of black oak gates the better part of twenty feet high that met at the top in a Gothic point. In one gate there was a smaller, lighter door, more fit for the use of humans than giants, but still ten feet high – big enough for a mounted man to enter through, if he were willing to bow his head.

Tom rose in his stirrups and beat upon this door. The sound made by his pounding fist echoed across a courtyard immediately beyond and was then swallowed by the great maw of the building itself. The three of them looked at each other. They had little time to linger or to speculate. If the castle was closed and empty – for whatever sinister reason – then they had better turn away soon, for the night was falling fast; they were a small party in a great desolation, and once the dark was down, then the roads would fill with all sorts of deadly dangers. Tom knew the nearest inn and it was an hour's ride from here, through some notoriously lawless country.

Even before he could draw breath to voice his thoughts, however, Tom's sharp ears heard a door squeak open. Youthful, energetic footfalls clapped across the flags of the yard and the tall door was opened to them.

'My name is Tom Musgrave,' Tom told the young man who held the door. In his yellow brocade with its hastily fastened buttons askew, he was the very image of the messenger so lately removed from Tom's blood-boltered bed. 'Your mistress summoned me.'

'The Lady Margaret is no longer here. I had thought you must be...'

'Your brother, returned from London?'

'Indeed, and Master Mann...'

'Master Mann the castle's chamberlain,' hazarded Tom, thinking of the dark-suited, silver-bearded corpse from the Fleet: the

84

Council's eyes in the place.

'Indeed. The King of Elfinstone, he calls himself – when My Lady cannot hear.'

'They are not here. But do you know me, boy? By name or by sight?'

'By both, Master Musgrave. I was here to see you fight the Spaniard before the Earls of Essex and Southampton.'

'Then you will know that your mistress would want you to let me in. For I have much to do this night, and much to talk about.'

CHAPTER 8

Dead Mann's Kingdom

There was light enough in Elfinstone, and bustle too; but it was all in the dark bowels of the place, down in the servants' hall. Hither, at Tom's impatient prompting, the young man in daffodil brocade led them while the Master of Logic sought ways to break his tragic news and Ben Jonson silently wrestled with the leaps of logic underlying the apparently devilish knowledge his master had so thoughtlessly displayed. Talbot Law, old soldier that he was, followed his nose and hoped for provender.

'Since Lady Margaret's departure on Monday three days since, we have been but a small company,' the lad was explaining as they walked through the gloomy corridors, led by the dancing brightness of his taper-flame. 'Though when my brother and Master Mann return, we will, as ever, turn to the cleaning of the place. It is spring, so the castle must be cleaned. It has been ever thus. The New Year brings new brooms.'

'But if Lady Margaret and her family do not celebrate New Year here, then where do they do so?' asked Ben, still preoccupied.

'At Castle Cotehel in the far, foreign depths of Cornwall,' answered Tom as though the bricklayer were a buffoon; and only the dazzle of the logic again displayed distracted Ben's dangerous temper from the tone. 'We are on the right mission but have come to the wrong place. I knew it as soon as we saw no candles. Fool that I am! Blind, impatient fool! Elfinstone is the family's future, its bright and modern face, with the houses in London closed. Cotehel is its past, louring over the sea-borne trade routes that are the ancient foundation of its fortune. Where else would the family celebrate an ancient, traditional festival? Moreover, old Law, you know as well as I that Her Majesty's father's generosity always came at a price. If he added to Cotehel's fortifications, then he'll have demanded the family be there to defend it themselves as castellans during the raiding season; and what better time to move than this? But we have work enough here for an evening at least, if young James here will lead us on.'

'You know me!' The imperturbable young servant stopped, frozen with surprise; and the other three stopped behind him, scarcely less surprised themselves. 'You know my name!'

'A lucky guess,' said Tom. 'I have seen your brother – of an age with you and as like as two peas in a pod. Castor and Pollux seemed so unlikely for a pair of country twins, and so I thought James, perhaps, and John.'

'We have also seen Master Mann, your chamberlain, I think,' added Talbot, catching up with Tom and Ben at last.

The tone of their voices alerted young James to the weight of the news they carried, and he led them silently on for a step or two. Then he began to speak. 'I have perhaps spoken unfairly of Master Mann. He called himself King of the Castle only in jest, for indeed the Lady Margaret has no other lord to protect her...'

'And she needs protection, does she?' probed Tom at once. 'Who from?'

'From the World, I meant,' answered James, unease increasing in his voice. 'Not from the Flesh nor any Devil I can name. But my lady shows a lively affection for the man – as much as her station will allow. And she places an absolute trust in him as well.'

'As much as in young John and in yourself,' continued Tom smoothly.

'As much as our youth and inexperience will allow, indeed, though Master Mann has always been a powerful voice for our promotion to increased responsibility. The message John carried was entrusted to him on Master Mann's word, in despite of—'

The name of the person who did not trust the boys – or Master Mann's faith in them – had to wait. For on that very word, James stepped through a doorway and down into the servants' hall itself.

The servants' hall of Elfinstone was a large, open cellar-like room, combining kitchen, bakery and work area with a sizeable dining area for the servants. When the castle was full, the place was probably packed. Now it was all but empty, though their arrival caused a bustle of speculation amongst the people there.

Tom's practised eye swept over a range of servants here assembled for their supper while an ample under-cook and a couple of scrawny slatterns got it ready. These were castle staff, and the few extra needed to feed and tend them, people who lived here, required for the smooth running of an establishment such as this, and with nowhere else to go even when the mistress and the personal servants were all away: gardeners and groundsmen; keepers of stock, game, horse and hound; stable lads and kennel maids; cleaners and washerwomen – nobody senior; nobody apart from James with any brightness or intelligence in their eyes; honest country faces, not a little awed to find such gently dressed folk amongst them; none here used to dealing with the Lady Margaret and the family on a personal basis; all the body servants gone with the family to the wilds of Cornwall to celebrate New Year at Castle Cotehel, leaving only the most menial here to keep this place clean and ready against Her Ladyship's return, with Master Mann, James and John to lead them. Or so it had been planned.

'Ben,' said Tom quietly, 'I will address the servants here. You take young James aside and tell him our news man to man. And gently, mind!'

As Ben removed the boy, Tom turned back to the vacant faces. There were no ladies-in-waiting, liveried footmen, secretaries, advisors or factors here. Everyone of standing in the household, from the chief cook to the housekeeper in charge of My Lady's wardrobe, from the young Baron's tutor to whichever of them taught him self-defence, were all gone on the road – gone three days since on Monday, as James had said, with the coachmen and the master of horse and all.

Two days since – in the morning, when the dew called up enough mud to spatter off the dry roads on to legs, as Tom himself had observed – Master Mann and John had turned aside to come into London with messages for Tom and Robert Poley – turned aside in apparent expectation of delivering their letters and coming back here tonight at the latest; and someone had turned aside behind them – or had already arranged their reception and disposal. Then, while the messengers had died and the Master of Logic had chopped what few facts were left into a dog's dinner of misunderstanding, Lady Margaret's household had continued south and westward. The sun that had set behind Tom's shoulder tonight must have been shining in the Lady Margaret's eyes as she waited, desperately, for his reply.

Prompted by this thought, Tom pressed forward with brutal directness. 'I bring you heavy news,' he said, stepping forward with no further hesitation. 'Your chamberlain Master Mann lies dead in London, murdered by unknown hands – as does young John, who has shared his fate. Lady Margaret's letters – to myself and any others – have miscarried or been destroyed. I believe she stands in some danger or believes herself to do so. I am come here on my way to her side to seek for evidence that might support her fears and to ask amongst you some questions whose answers might start the men who killed your friends and stop the men who wish the Lady Margaret harm.'

'But first,' said Talbot Law into the shocked and cavernous silence, 'as we have ridden all day and stopped for neither food nor drink to get here, we would wish to send three of your number to stable, water and feed our horses while we join you in your supper now; and as we do so, my friend Master Musgrave will reveal to you the details of the case so far.'

'Pease pottage and small beer!' said Talbot

Law some half-hour later. 'Lenten fare indeed; as thin and unwholesome as the information you gleaned from those bumpkins in the kitchen.'

'It is Lent, old Law, Good Friday this Friday coming and Easter Day on Sunday. Besides, what else did you expect, with all the finer palates and sharper wits Cotehel-bound?'

'Aye, but pease pottage and small beer!'

'And there was more sawdust than flour in that bread,' added Ben disconsolately. 'I'm still picking trencher-splinters from my teeth. I note the boy was too wise to eat any of the poisonous mess.'

'Shocked to fasting, perhaps, by your dreadful news.'

'Perhaps, but I beg leave to doubt. He raised an eyebrow and said our arrival in their stead and the tones in which we talked of them had made him suspect the truth. It may be so. Or he may have caught Logic, like a contagion, from our sharper city wits.'

'Hush! He will hear you!'

James, still pale with shock in spite of what Ben had said, his eyes big and bright with tears, appeared in the doorway and called them forward. 'This is Lady Margaret's chamber,' he said. 'I have lit candles as you required but would beg you to make haste. That is almost our whole supply and it must last us until the household returns.'

'Or Lady Margaret sends another chamberlain with a well-stocked purse to replace

Master Mann,' said Tom bracingly. 'No. Stay with us, if you'd be so kind. We have need of your wits and your wisdom here.'

He exchanged a speaking look with Ben, but was immediately proved right. They needed James's knowledge – if nothing more – at once. The first thing of note within the room was a chimney-breast.

The room itself was remarkable only in that it was so small to house a countess, though of course well over thrice the size of Tom's own room in Black Friars. The ceiling was low and squared on white plaster with black wood beams. Black wood also was the panelling that reached almost to the ceiling itself – black wood relieved only by one portrait, that of the young Baron, hanging out of place and a little lonely to the left of the bed. The floor was wood too, but lovingly polished and blessedly splinter free – more so than the bread from dinner, at any rate. The furnishings were as modest as the chamber: a writing-table that stood breast-high with a cupboard hung above it; a clothes press and a wardrobe; no chairs, but the press's lid was worn, so the Lady Margaret must sit there sometimes – though, said the desk, never to read or write. There was the bed, and, opposite the bed-foot, the jutting chimney-breast, which, after one comprehensive glance, took all of Tom's attention.

The fire below it was low and deep-set, as befitted a bedroom hearth; but the breast itself, of broad red brick was strikingly unadorned. In a position such as this there should hang a mirror or ... 'A picture,' said Tom. 'I see the marks that must have been made by a gilded frame. What was it? Where is it?'

'The mysterious gift,' said James. 'Where it came from nobody seems to know, but it was a portrait of Lady Margaret herself, though she swears she never sat for such a thing. It showed her head and shoulders. She was painted in a fashionable bodice with a high lace ruff. I know nothing of such matters, of course – they are fit neither for my sex or station; but I heard Mistress Danforth talking of it once to Master Quin.'

'And who are these?' Tom needed all his concentration to follow the boy's words as his description brought the wounded portrait so vividly to mind.

'Mistress Agnes Danforth is Lady Margaret's housekeeper. She does for the family and their servants as Master Mann does – did – for the castle staff. And Master Quin is her master of horse. He oversees all her movements and transports. For all his mighty ways and his comings and goings he earns his keep but twice in a year: getting them all to Castle Cotehel and back from thence again.'

'And so, this portrait, that appeared so mysteriously but took My Lady's fancy and occasioned the comment between Danforth and Quin – how comes it to be absent now? Has Lady Margaret taken it with her for fondness of the thing?'

'Indeed no. I feel she never liked it much, in fact; but the young Baron took to it and asked that she hang it there. She did so to please him. But the chimney-breast becomes hot in the winter and so the picture was moved. Then, as strangely as it had come, it vanished, and no one any the wiser. Vanished more than a month since.'

'If the young Baron took a liking to it,' demanded Ben suddenly, 'why did he not hang it in his own chamber?'

'Oh no!' answered James, genuinely shocked. 'In the Baron's chamber hang the portraits of his ancestors in the title. No pictures but of the great men of the house of Outram must ever hang in there.'

'Models of historic perfection against whom the young man may model himself, no doubt,' said Tom, his interest in Lady Margaret's portrait and portraits in general apparently at an end. He looked at the Baron's portrait and the panelling opposite, frowning. Then he gave a little shrug and apparently forgot that matter too. He had turned to the bed.

Lady Margaret's bed was a large four-poster. In its size and shape lay nothing unusual, save that it was breathtakingly sumptuous. The brocade with which it was spread matched that which young James wore – except in one respect. It seemed to be, in fact, the cloth of gold that his clothing merely mimicked. There was an unusual element to the bed, however, at least to Tom's eye: the

94

four posts rose at the corners to within an ell of the low beam-squared ceiling – and there they stopped: naked. There were no rails, no hangings to dress them. Every such bed that Tom had seen or heard of was heavily dressed with curtains – not least because bedrooms, even bedrooms richer than this, in castles only half as ancient, were full of draughts and chills, especially in the darkest hours when the fire had died.

'It is Lady Margaret's years of imprisonment in the mad room at Wormwood House, perhaps,' said Tom quietly, 'that makes her fearful of tiny spaces – even within the hangings of a bed.'

'That may be the reason,' said James, seemingly much struck with the thought. 'Certainly she has never allowed the bed to be canopied while she occupies it. Not that I have any intimate knowledge of her wishes and directions, you understand. But I have listened; and I have observed.'

'Listened, indeed, to Mistress Danforth talking to Master Quin,' said Tom gently, 'and observed how things are done under those worthies and under Master Mann. And no more than that? Have you ever served in any establishment other than this one?'

'No, sir. John and I were born on the estate. Our mother and father were servants here before us. Indeed, they were sufficiently well thought of to accompany the old family to Wormwood House the year they all fell victim to the dreadful visitation. They went up with

Master Seyton, who was the chamberlain in those days. They all went up and left us here with Master Mann, who was his assistant, or deputy so to speak. Then the Plague came and they never came back. I myself have never been anywhere else – except for Wormwood House and Highmeet House in London, of course. Shut up though they are, they need visiting and tending once in a while. Master Mann would take John and me up there with him on occasion – training us up, he'd call it; and I was down at Castle Cotehel once, some years since, before the old family died. But I was no more than a lad then.'

'So, for a Kentish lad tied to a country estate and yet to get much experience in the matter of growing a beard, you've seen a good bit of the world.' As Tom talked, so he opened and closed the doors to the little book case above the desk. Then he opened the desk itself.

'Ah, at last. A paper. Writing. Writing scored over and corrected. What is this? Reigate scored through and replaced with Croydon. Croydon is in Lady Margaret's hand, I assume. I do not know the other. What is this?'

'It is the route of the journey, sir. And you are mistaken: the two hands are Master Quin's with Master Gawdy the Secretary's written over it, at Lady Margaret's direction I am sure.

'In past times, the family has made its progress over some seven to ten days, sleeping over at the places marked; but Lady Margaret is not for slow travel: the longer on the road, she believes – so I have heard – the greater the danger.'

'So if we follow the Lady's directions, if not her hand, we follow her footsteps, so to speak – her planned route south at least; to Croydon by Monday sunset, whence she must have despatched her messengers yesterday morning, while she set out for Farnham. She sleeps at Winchester tonight and then Salisbury, Sherborne, Honiton and Buckfast. An abbey town for Good Friday and another for Easter Day. She is moved by the spirit as well as by the will. Is this the way you went south to Cotehel yourself?'

'I can hardly remember, sir ... I remember the celebrations when we arrived, though. On the first of April we celebrate our own Feast of Fools down there – from time immemorial, as though it was January, in truth.'

'That's as may be,' said Tom, folding the paper into his purse and exchanging a meaningful look with his associates over the voluble boy's head. 'But you have spent the most of your time here – listening and observing, as you say. Now have you ever heard tell or seen sign of secret passages and priests' holes within these ancient walls?'

The question was so unexpected, and had been so carefully disguised as an *ambuscado* with Tom's apparently irrelevant chatter and the newly discovered list of Lady Margaret's destinations, that it caught them all off guard.

Young James's eyes glinted a little in the candles' brightness as they moved. Then he turned his head to disguise the tell-tale; then turned it back again, his gaze level and expression open. 'Yes indeed. I can scarcely believe you reasoned it without Satanic help, as you knew my name to be James amongst all the thousands it might have been ... but yes. I have been told of just such a panel. It is supposed to be somewhere over here. On the inner wall, I believe.' He crossed to the wall on the right side of the bed and began to tap the black-wood panels there.

CHAPTER 9

The Thirteenth Mouse

'Do you know what a sin-worm is?' asked Tom as they tapped the solid-seeming panelling where young James had indicated. 'Is the name familiar to you?'

'No,' said James, frowning. Ben and Talbot kept their stony faces and tapped at Tom's direction, listening for a hollow sound. One knew well enough, thought Tom; and the other would never willingly admit to ignorance.

'It is a man who loves to watch women. In secret – when they do not suspect he watches

98

– that he may see them doing things they would never do in public.' As he spoke, Tom eased his weight against the panel he was working on to see if it would give. Those built hard against the stone of a wall would sit firm. One backed by the tunnel James suspected would be likely to give way a little; but which one that might be was any man's guess. There must be more than fifty panels in the room, each square and edged with intricate designs of cats and mice, nutmegs and peppercorns, from the arms of the House of Outremer – the spices on which the family's fortunes had been made and on which they still so firmly rested; spices brought from all over the world in ships; ships famously well stocked with cats to keep at bay the mice and rats that could do such terrible damage to such delicate and priceless cargo; argosies of ships heaving in and out of the Channel under the frowning guard of Cotehel Castle, and home to safe haven in Plymouth.

'So a sin-worm is like the man called Tom in the old tale of Lady Godiva,' said James with a frown of effort as he strove to understand – or to hear a hollow sound under his wall-pressed ear. 'Tom who peeped and lost his eyes.'

'Indeed,' said Tom, at sudden pains not to think of Lady Margaret as Lady Godiva, particularly as he had seen her in the Lady's famous state. That would be calling himself a peeping Tom indeed.

Once they found a likely panel he would

have to seek a catch, he thought to distract himself at once. Lady Margaret would not take kindly to axe-work in her bedchamber, he suspected.

'Like Actaeon the hunter in the Greek legends, who saw the goddess Diana bathing in the forest and was turned to a stag then hunted in punishment,' added Ben, as he studied the wall from further back, looking with an apprentice bricklayer's eye, though no one had told him to.

'Indeed,' said Tom. 'But Actaeon as hunter, not hunted – Actaeon seeking the goddess out and watching her disrobe and bathe naked, all for his private pleasure.'

'Such men can be very dangerous indeed,' observed Talbot, 'particularly when they wish to change observation into action. To *touch* what they have been content to *watch*.'

'A chilling prospect,' agreed Ben, pretending more wisdom than he possessed. 'Even Ovid overlooked such sinfulness. There are no sin-worms in his *Metamorphoses*. A little to your right, master. No, another panel down. Yes. The wall above looks...' He fell silent, noting the frown with which young James was looking at him.

'If the man we met in London, whose actions there began this whole adventure, is the sin-worm, then he is preparing to take action indeed,' said Tom. 'But we must ask why? Why now? What has changed in his thoughts to prompt such a change in his actions?' As he spoke, so he followed the apprentice's directions and moved down until he was below a slight flaw in the white-painted stonework – a flaw so slight, indeed, that only the bricklayer's eyes would have noticed its existence or its implication. 'Why else would he have done all the things that he has done?'

'Even the lightest suspicion that takes you along such a dangerous route must make you fly to the Lady's side,' agreed Talbot Law heavily. He had stood back with James now, letting Ben's experienced eye guide Tom's wise fingers.

'It does, old Law, it does. But I will not go to her all ignorance, if I can help it. I will go armoured with knowledge and armed with sharp suspicion. Which is the point of our exploration here. Ah. Well done, Ben. I have it.' He knocked on the panel as he had knocked on Elfinstone's door and it rang with equal hollowness.

'Ben? Can your wise eyes see some flaw in design or strangeness in ornament that might conceal a catch of some sort? – other than the nail above, which I assume once held the mysterious and missing portrait when it was moved from the chimney-breast, for it is opposite the boy's on the outer wall. Here, too, I see traces of gilding from the frame. And Master James, have we reached the limit of your knowledge in the matter of this panel?'

Ben spoke before the boy could, alerted earlier in Tom's meandering soliloquy. 'There are twelve mice at the bottom but thirteen at the top. If you were to press the last of them...'

'Ah,' said Tom with deep satisfaction as his fingers, obedient to Ben's suggestion, caused the thirteenth mouse to move and the whole black panel four feet square to spring open and back.

Tom pushed it gently and it opened absolutely, flat back against a tunnel wall. Behind the panel in the wainscot was a tiny passageway four feet high and four or so wide, carved straight into the seemingly massive stonework of the wall. From the centre of its rough lintel, half-hidden by the width of the decorated edging, rose a crack that, four feet higher still, became the flaw in the wall that Ben had noticed. Tom was the first to stoop and enter it. Armed with a candle caught up from the nearest sconce, he stepped over the little ledge of wainscot edging that rose four inches from the bedroom floor then plunged a good foot down to the cold stone beyond. As soon as he did so, it became clear that the little tunnel had never been meant to contain more than one man alone. Even the open door itself seemed to crowd dangerously against his shoulder, like a braggart set on a brawl. In spite of the fact that there was a good step down from the modern, raised, wooden floor of the bedchamber on to the earlier stone flooring of the tunnel itself, it was cramped and tiny.

'Wait out there. I shall explore,' Tom

directed as he lifted his second booted foot high over the wooden step. 'James. Does your knowledge extend any further in this matter? You never answered when I asked just now. Come now, sir, be frank with us. A boy growing in a warren such as this must be expected to have explored – though only, I am certain, when the family was away.'

'No, sir. I know nothing more than that a panel was said to exist. Not even said – rumoured. Dreamed, rather. I hardly credited the legend with any truth and have never even discussed it with anyone else. And I have never, as you say, explored.'

'Admirable sentiments,' said Tom.

'In every situation except for this one,' added Ben in a low voice, 'for we could have used a guide.'

'But inevitable,' said Tom, who was very slowly turning round within the confines of the tunnel so that he could look out into the room again. To the others he looked strangely shortened, crouching with his legs seeming to end a little below his knees. 'For anything other than a hearty disbelief in the existence of such a panel in the Lady Margaret's bedchamber must have led you to warn Master Mann at the least. Would it not?'

'Of course. Just seeing the thing open now makes my blood run cold. When Lady Margaret sees it, we will all be out of her favour.'

'And out of work, as like as not,' said Talbot Law.

'And out of Elfinstone,' added Ben with

some relish. 'Faster than a Spaniard out of a fight.'

'Check the panel when I have closed it, Ben,' Tom ordered, 'and leave the boy alone. We have need of his good nature and his help. Do not use them up too swiftly with that bitter tongue of yours.' The last imprecation, however, came from behind the panel, for as he spoke, he stepped backwards, caught the makeshift doorway and swung it forward again until it snapped back into its place.

Alone in the little passageway, Tom slowly began to sink to his knees, holding the candle close to the rough inner surface where the panel stood untreated and unpolished. *Nearly as unpolished as Benjamin Jonson, apprentice bricklayer of Islington,* thought Tom. There were hinges on this side, cunningly placed so that the pins holding them fitted into the grain of the wood, the backs of them secured to the nutmeg-covered edging that ran up and down between the panels as the cats and mice all ran across; a little spring with a catch above it, a metal ring on the inside of the thirteenth mouse, no doubt – a simple system, of indeterminate age.

Tom had been in tunnels under London Bridge that had seemed almost of Roman antiquity – that had certainly been there since Will Shakespeare's famous Henry VI, cause of three whole plays, had been king. This tunnel also seemed to be that old – seemed to have been in place before the wainscot went in or the wooden floor had been raised. The system of catches and hinges, however, must have been of much more recent design. It seemed quite new; but that might have just been because it had been carefully maintained. Recently maintained, to boot; maintained and used, therefore, well within the year or so that Lady Margaret had occupied the room. Indeed, the tiny drops of wax on the panel immediately in front of his chin could have come there yesterday.

On his knees now, Tom pulled the candle to his lips and blew it out, adding, he knew, a few more drops of wax to the spray on the wood. In the sudden darkness, his eyes darted everywhere. The mysteries of Lady Margaret's fears, the missing portrait and the panel itself all turned around one thing in Tom's mind: around one tiny shaft of light. And there it was. Eagerly he leaned forward and pressed his eye to the hole in the wood that the light revealed. A knot-hole – like everything else in this elaborate system, too small to be readily seen; and yet, when his eyebrow leaned against the rough wood immediately above it, big enough to give him a good view across the room, to take in the whole of the undressed bed, and much of the rest besides. A man might kneel here in silence unobserved, all but unsuspected, and watch the Lady Margaret standing at her desk, reaching into her cupboard for pen and paper, ink or book; watch her come to bed, to sleep, to wake; watch her do everything a lady might do in the privacy of her bedchamber.

But what would the Lady Margaret actually do in there? Read and sleep, dream and wake; write her private letters – little more. No Diana at her forest pool, she would hardly disrobe herself in her sleeping-chamber; there would be a tiring-chamber for that. There she would don and remove her attire, don and remove any make-up with which she chose to adorn her cheeks; allow a maid, perhaps, to brush her hair, and one of her senior ladies-in-waiting to arrange it. He had suspected a mirror on the chimney-breast before the matter of the portrait had become more clear; but in fact there were no mirrors in the room at all. Unless the lovely lady favoured little hand-held ones – and then had taken them to Cotehel with her – she must certainly go to another room entirely to perform the secret intimacies of her attiring and toilet.

Deep in thought, Tom reached up and pulled the little ring that snapped the trap so that the panel jumped open. Light flooded in again and Tom shuffled back, eyes busy. The floor of the passage was clean and dust-free. Their sin-worm seemed a tidy soul – careful and meticulous at least. For an instant more he hesitated on his knees, calculating his next move. Remain here and look for details of the last man to occupy this strange location? Or light the candle, come to his feet and explore the tunnel behind him?

Carefully, he pulled himself erect and stepped out into the room. He found he was burning to explore – far too impatient for the minutiae of inch-by-inch search here; but first he had to check one thing. He swung the panel towards him with enough force to overcome the spring and, sure enough, it snapped shut once again. As soon as it had done so, he was on his knees again and looking for the knot-hole. Even though he knew where it must be, he still could not see it. Not until he slid his fingers over the slick blackness of the wood itself and felt the flaw like some dark lover's secret mark did he understand exactly where it lay; and there, precisely above it, on the next panel up, stood the nail that had held the missing portrait. Exactly on either side of it were the slight golden marks which told of the picture's ornate frame closing it off like an eye-patch – indeed, unless the sin-worm was absolutely confident that he could risk a good deal of noise and damage unsuspected, closing the panel itself as effectively as a lock and bolt. For even though the door opened inwards, only the most careful, crawling, exit from the tunnel could stop the precarious picture from tumbling off the wall; and swinging the door closed from the bed-chamber, as he had just done, must surely bring it down.

This, indeed, was exactly what had happened, before it had been smuggled to the house in Water Lane and at once worshipped and desecrated. The floor, although meticulously clean, was dented where the heavy frame had fallen; and his memory of the frame itself, though it lay now in his practice room in Blackfriars, was clear enough to bring to mind sprung joints and splintered gliding – things that had seemed of such slight account beside those chilling, calculated slits from throat to bodice, through lips and through neck, though all of them were gaining in weight and importance now.

Gaining and gaining, moment by moment.

CHAPTER 10

The Sin-Worm's Steps

To give himself more room in the tunnel, Tom took off his swords and laid them on Lady Margaret's bed. He laid his black doublet on top of them, in spite of the fact that the air in the secret passage was chill and the lawn and lace of his shirt designed for fashion, not warmth. Then, holding the longest candle as high as he could, he stepped back down over the ledge of wainscot and went into the tunnel again.

There was no turning around this time. Slowly, carefully, mindful of his head against the uneven roof, his feet on the slippery flooring and his elbows on the jagged walls, he went on. When the light around him died, he thought the door must have closed, but no –

it was his apprentice in his footsteps like the page in the legend of Wenceslas. It might as well have been the door closing, however. The bricklayer was as square and solid as the portal, and filled the tunnel as absolutely. The thought was distraction enough to bring a lump to Tom's head as he forgot to watch the roof. His mood darkened, only to lighten again as Ben's head caught the same hazard with the sound of a cannon-stone hitting a wall. 'Watch your head,' called Tom, quietly.

The sound of Ben's misfortune was still echoing more loudly than Tom's warning when the tunnel turned. The candle was giving little light and their eyes were not yet dark-adjusted, so the turning came as a surprise – or its closeness did: its existence was a thing of inevitability, as far as Tom was concerned.

Still apparently deep in the castle's internal walls, they went right with it, only to be faced with a junction after another half-dozen steps. The tunnel they were following ended with only a rubble-filled wall ahead. A branch went left while another went right. The left-hand path was wider, slightly taller, better made; the right-hand path a mean and narrow passage, rough-floored, rough-walled. After an instant's hesitation, Tom went left. The short tunnel they had just traversed must run parallel to the corridor along which the Lady Margaret's private chambers were situated. To turn right must take them back to the next behind the bedchamber. Logic dictated the tiring-chamber as he had suspected; but that was a conundrum to be considered later. In the meantime, to go left must take them somewhere new.

Within ten short steps it had taken them to another rough-wood inner surface. 'More panelling,' said Tom, feeling his companion crowding massively at his back. He moved the candle until another little ring, identical twin to the one behind the thirteenth mouse, appeared. 'Step back, Ben,' he ordered and waited until the uneasy sense of constriction had eased – and another cannon-stone crack announced that Ben had backed into the roof once more. Then, stooping, Tom stepped back again and pulled the ring. The secret door sprang ajar. Tom eased it wide and hesitated. All he could see was shadowy vacancy. The little candle flame did little to dissipate the dark. Tom eased himself forward, holding the little flame high – and, just at the last moment realized that what had seemed to be the low lintel of the doorway was the bottom of a picture frame. With all the slow purposefulness of one of Will Shakespeare's actors miming, Tom lowered his head still further and hunched his back, like Richard III. At the same time he took a great slow step up and over the raised ledge and stepped into the room.

Only when his shoulders were well clear did he begin to straighten, pulling his second foot up after him. He held the candle high and looked around the room he had just entered with such difficulty. He was immediately aware of eyes almost without number, all sternly watching him. Such light as the candle gave caught the gleaming whites of them, brought the liquid sheen of them to life. Disorientated, not a little disturbed, he turned, frowning. Wherever he looked, the eyes looked back down upon him.

A secretive scuffle of movement from behind him made him turn, and even as he did so, a half-seen figure pounced down at him from the very outer edge of his vision. He leaped back, raising the candle, putting the life of its guttering flame at deadly risk. How poignantly he regretted the rapiers on Lady Margaret's golden bedspread – but only for an instant. For, in the flickering near-darkness, surprised, disorientated as he was, he nevertheless recognized the man attacking him. It was a man he had seen dead at the Battle of Nijmagen eight years ago; a man he had last seen hanging in Highmeet St Magnus in London, in a portrait the twin of this one, a portrait of the current Baron's dead uncle, a hero of the Engineers, who had given his life to save the Earl of Leicester's army, mourned by the nation like Sir Philip Sidney had been.

The whole thing crashed to the floor. The raised boards shook and sounded like a drum-skin. Ben fell out into the room beneath the picture, whose frame had added yet another lump to his much-abused head.

The wind of the picture's downfall seemed

to have added some life to the candle, for it burned steadier and brighter now. Tom held it high again and looked around once more; and the picture itself had kindled understanding also in Tom's mind.

'It is the boy's bedchamber,' he said. 'It is exactly as young James described it: a fit place for a young baron to sleep, under the gaze of his ancestors.'

'Lucky I'm not a baron, then,' said Ben, rubbing the bristles on his crown. 'I could no more sleep with so many eyes upon me than I could dance a jig on the head of a pin.'

Tom laughed, and on the sound the door burst open. James led a fearsome-looking group of castle staff, but they all froze in the doorway, most of them gaping with surprise that two men closed in one chamber could appear in the midst of another. At least they brought more light.

'Thus is revealed the beginning of the matter,' said Tom a little later as he led Ben back into the tunnel. 'At some time in the more distant past, a passage was made so that a mother could visit her son at night without the bother of castle staff and household staff, of barons and countesses – just a mother looking to her boy; a secret thing, however, so done at the same time as the floors were raised and the wainscot hung; an innocent enough beginning, to ease the nightmares of some young baron in history with a soul as tender as yours, young Ben.'

'Though not a head as tender, I hope,' said Ben.

'But the good would seem to have been turned to bad. For the tunnel proved to be like any tree in a forest: it grew branches – one branch, at least.'

'But how? Why? And who would do such a thing?'

'*How* seems easy enough. The castle is ancient. The walls are solid, stone-faced and rubble-filled – even internal walls like these. The original passage moved sideways a little through that rubble filling – enough to give a lively mind a hint how the thing might be extended. Someone has removed the rubble little by little down to the floor, which seems to run solid at this level, and up to a low head height. And so they have made the second branch, a meaner, thinner brother to the first. Straight out of the side of the original and then in again, but this time at hazard, following gaps and flaws in the stone facing, making this smaller tunnel, which we are about to enter – being very careful of our heads.'

'Leading to a door again?'

'Logic suggests not. You see how the workmanship is much more basic here? The original, for all it was low and dangerous to your head, was journeyman-made. This never was. This has been done with stealth and in secret, by one man – I would judge – working alone. And, by extension, we find in the original tunnel well-fitted doors, craftsman-made – made by the men who fashioned the wainscot and the mice upon it, for only they could make both the doors and the mice that unlock them. But the man that picked out this meagre passageway could never have worked in wood like that. Therefore we look not for a door but for a knot-hole overlooking ... Ah. The answer to your second question: *Why?* Our knot-hole overwatches Talbot Law seated at ease in Lady Margaret's tiring-room well supplied with candles and admiring himself in a looking-glass. Here indeed might our sinister Actaeon discover his Diana disrobed.'

'Or Tom peep at his Godiva,' added Ben.

The four of them sat at the table in the servants' hall. They were alone, surrounded by shadows and hunched over one dull taper – James was so careful of the precious candles now, so many had been used in the investigation so far, particularly as the exploration of the tunnel had been followed by examination of the young Baron's room and the rooms of those most closely associated with him, Master Mann's room last of all. But apart from Lady Margaret's paper, they had found nothing more.

It was so late that dawn was almost threatening; but they still could not resolve Ben's last question: *Who?*

'If it must be someone intimate with the young Baron's movements...' said James.

'As would seem logical to assume, if he gained entry from the Baron's room,' said

Ben, echoing Tom's logic of an hour ago.

'Then we must return to the tutor, Dr Rowley.'

'None of his body servants?' probed Ben. 'Has he no steward, butler or dresser?'

'He has them all,' answered James. 'All and more.'

'Who is his tutor in defence?' asked Tom. 'This Captain Quin you have told us of? The Master of the Horse?'

'No. There is a bone of contention there, but the Lady Margaret maintains that Quin has enough to think on, overseeing his command of coachmen, grooms, ostlers and postillions. We use them but rarely, but they need constant watching; and when the household moves, as it is moving now, the quality and reliability of Quin's men is crucial.'

'But for most of the year his hands are idle, except that he is ape-leader to his equally idle men,' said Tom thoughtfully.

'Idleness breeds sin,' observed Talbot. 'It is an old saying rich in proof.'

'And there is another man that teaches the Baron his more bodily skills therefore?'

'Indeed: Master St Just. He sailed with Drake in the *Revenge* against the Armada, and had hoped to remain within his service; but he was wounded in the action at Portland Bill so that he fares to sea no more. Instead, he teaches the Baron the Sciences of Defence, Astrology, Astronomy, Navigation and Shiphandling. At Elfinstone this latter is all theory, of course; but down at Cotehel, they will put theory into practice, I believe. There are boats in plenty down there, of course. And that will all be to the good, I think, for Master St Just is young, growing stronger at last and increasingly active. He has found the post he holds increasingly irksome, I believe.'

'So his idleness weighs heavily too,' observed Tom. 'The tutor at least must rest content – the venerable Doctor Rowley...'

'Perhaps. He is a hard man to know. He and Master St Just spend much time in their star-gazing and their abstruse calculations that lead to obscure predictings. Master Gawdy joins them too, on occasion. He is the Lady Margaret's secretary, the son of a priest, they say. But none of these men is old, sir. It has been the cause of some comment in the hall and in the neighbourhood that the Lady Margaret surrounds herself and the Baron with new men, so to speak. The Captain has perhaps seen forty summers, but Master St Just had just attained his majority when he was struck down at Portland Bill, so he has yet to see thirty; and Master Rowley may be a Master of Arts and a Doctor of Philosophy, but he is only down from Corpus Christi ten years since and is no great age at all. I suppose Master Gawdy might be of an age with Captain Quin, but he is a slight and quiet man.'

'Ah,' said Tom, thoughtfully and almost to himself, 'but Rowley is a Cambridge man. Corpus was Kit Marlowe's college. And Robert Poley's, I believe.'

Later still, after James had gone to bed, exhausted by grief if nothing else, and Tom still sat with Talbot and Ben, though a chamber had been prepared for the three of them, Tom still could not rest. Ben rose to start another rushlight from the embers of the fire before the chill and creeping darkness claimed them all. Talbot poured the dregs of the small beer into a wooden tankard and supped, speculatively, his eyes on his young friend's brooding face.

'The Secretary has access – one man seeming to serve the Lady and the Baron. Two tutors – a Cambridge man who may be closer to Poley than merely a graduate from the same college. A seaman close to Drake. And to who else? To Raleigh? Lord Howard the Admiral? Possibly to one of the factions at Court. And St Just sounds like a Cornish man like the Master of the Horse, if the name is anything to go by. Like many of the household, brought up from Cotehel to Elfinstone after the death of the servants that died in the great visitation of the Plague on Wormwood House, when James's parents died with all the others, and all of Lady Margaret's family except the Lady Margaret herself. Is it of importance now that we know it was not plague that killed them but poison, placed by an ambitious cousin mad to claim the titles and the fortune for himself?'

'You'd have to wait and see,' said Talbot. 'Like all the rest, it's a matter like the abstruse speculations Rowley, St Just and sometimes Secretary Gawdy pull out of the stars. Only time will tell the truth of them.'

'Right you are, old Law. Let us return to the matters in hand therefore – the matters and the men. And Captain Quin himself, with his command ... Together with the castle staff, young James and John and Master Mann. Death does not automatically make them innocent of watching Lady Margaret. Mann, in fact, was doing so for Poley and the Council.'

'But,' said Ben slowly, sleepily, 'it must at least rule them out of any suspicion that they did murder in themselves – that they hired the footpads, dumped each other in the Fleet, met with the footpads' leader in the house on Water Lane, then fired the whole beneath us. Dead men could not do all of that.'

'The boy's got a point,' said Talbot.

'He has,' admitted Tom. 'You both have. We must look to the living for our sin-worm and our murderer. We must test our suspicions like St Just's navigation, in practice not theory. We must follow them to Cotehel if we are to solve the riddle and help Lady Margaret.

'To bed now, therefore, and off in their footsteps tomorrow – and betimes. We have far to go as well as much to do!'

As he spoke, he reached into his purse and threw across the table the folded piece of paper he had taken from Lady Margaret's writing desk, with its scratched and corrected list of names, houses and towns.

The long and dangerous road to distant, dangerous Castle Cotehel.

CHAPTER 11

The Portsmouth Road

Tom turned over in his bed. It was a huge affair of downy softness with new-fangled pillows like clouds. Although the blankets had an ethereal lightness equalled only by the silken softness of the sheets, his body seemed to burn. That anything so light and fragrant should contain such fearsome heat surprised him, even to the wonder of his sleeping mind.

A susurration of movement.

Tom's eyes opened fractionally.

A gleam of light. A candle passing outside the closed bedroom door. No. Not passing. Pausing. A breathless squeaking, like a secret mouse. The handle turned. The latch rose. The candle entered.

Above the golden brightness of its steady flame, the Lady Margaret's face shone like that of a goddess, all gold. Her hair fell free in gilded ringlets down to the shoulders of her simple shift. And that shift, of purest Flemish linen, half-laced and all transparent seemed to reveal more than it could ever conceal; to frame for him; to present to him – perfection in his eyes.

Tom watched, transfixed, as she crossed to his burning bed. With steady hand she raised the silken sheet and such a draught of coldness pierced him as almost made him shout with shock.

Even so, he did not realize that he was dreaming until his silent goddess whispered, 'I love you, Master Musgrave.'

Then he jumped awake to find himself seated at the servants' table with quill in hand and papers scattered across the boards. The last of James's precious candles was burning palely and a cold, grey dawn was washing in like a rising winter's tide.

It was time to move, he thought.

They stopped first at the White Hart in Croydon, hard by the Archbishop's Palace. They had set out soon after Tom awoke, leaving James in charge of the establishment in Elfinstone with a promise that they would send instructions back from Cotehel at the earliest opportunity. They travelled the thirty miles in little more than four hours, accomplishing what Lady Margaret's coachmen had done in the first whole day. They were hungry, having yet to break their fast and not well filled by last night's meagre meal. Even so, they were in a hurry and would have been content to eat in the saddle and go; but they had plans to finalize and information to gather. Therefore it fitted well with Tom's schemes that they give their horses to a couple of ostlers to walk while they took a private chamber and ordered the fourpenny ordinary.

In spite of the fact that he had not really slept at all, except for the moments when he had dreamed so dazzlingly – so dangerously – Tom was fizzing with energy; and he needed to be. This was a parting of the ways, for Talbot could not afford to take weeks away from his post. Southwark needed its Bailiff, chief law officer of the Archbishop of Winchester, who owned the land between London Bridge and Lambeth Marsh where the playhouses, bear- and bull-baiting, the taverns and the brothels gathered like dangerous barnacles on the keel of that great ship of London.

What Talbot took back with him now would be of crucial importance in the interim until Tom returned home; and, indeed, in determining the welcome he would get on his arrival.

There were letters, therefore, to Ugo Stell, about the School of Defence they ran together, about the portrait and what Tom wanted done with it; to Master Aske the Haberdasher about the premises he rented for the school. There was an urgent addition to this, for Master Aske was not only landlord but churchwarden in Tom's parish – who would be noting his absence from services during the crucial Holy Week – absence that in theory could put his back at risk of a whipping and his soul at risk of damnation.

There was a letter to Robert Poley detailing the case so far together with suspicions and instructions – neither one particularly well founded, in Tom's opinion. There was a letter to his closest friend and occasional employer, sometime spy-master Sir Thomas Walsingham, very similar to that he sent to Poley, for transmission to the Lord Hunsdon, the Lord Chamberlain, whose Man he was as associate with Will Shakespeare's players, in case things turned out badly; and with that there was an enclosure for Mistress Kate Shelton, whose contents were definitely not for transmission to anyone else at all. Finally, there was a letter whose direction only Ben could add, to his stepfather the bricklayer of Islington, explaining that Ben had not broken his indentures yet again and begging the indulgence of the lad's company for a month or so in Cornwall.

'He'll be glad to see the back of me,' said Ben, as though the other two would hardly credit this news as truth at all.

'Indeed,' said Talbot, deadpan. 'You surprise me.' As he spoke, he glanced up from the letter he was writing, for the mail was by no means going all one way. The pair of them would be passing through Winchester, where Talbot's wife Bess kept the Nag's Head Inn while he served the Bishop beneath whose cathedral walls the inn stood in His Lordship's properties in Southwark.

'To practical matters,' said Tom, swiftly, before Ben recognized the ironic tone. 'My letters ask that funds, clothing and other necessaries be despatched in my wake – to Cotehel, if they cannot catch me on the road. I have suggested some stuff of yours be added to my baggage, Ben. Otherwise we wear what's on our backs until the better part of May.'

'A fragrant prospect,' said Talbot, finishing his marital missive with a flourish.

'But it will do us no harm to seem a little down-at-heel and out-at-elbow as we travel the Portsmouth road and then the Plymouth road beyond it,' Tom observed. 'We are well supplied with coin and armed with the Council's passes – by the blessing of providence, general passes that will get us to Land's End as well as Elfinstone. Men such as we are ten-a-penny riding southward; and if we can be either minor messengers for some pygmy at court, or men with a naval swagger, bosom friends to Raleigh and Drake when in our cups, then we will pass unnoticed, I am sure. As there are but two of us, though our steel be true, we might not fare so well if we attracted the attention of the upright men, the footpads or the highwaymen who haunt our way.'

'They say Ratsey is abroad,' warned Talbot, naming the most notorious of the highway robbers.

'Then our progress should be the opposite of Lady Margaret's: secret and swift as shadows.'

Mention of Lady Margaret's progress

brought them on to the next point of their dismounting at Croydon. The White Hart was a large and bustling establishment, but for gentlemen who took private rooms mine host was always available – or his good lady wife was.

'Or, some say, his toothsome daughters,' observed Talbot dryly.

'It is information I want, as you well know,' said Tom severely, 'and we have no time for dalliance, even had we the inclination.'

Talbot shrugged and smiled. Ben looked a little crestfallen, however.

The host swept in and proved to be a cheerful man of a garrulous disposition, broad of face and full of belly. His innocent blue eyes twinkled artlessly above cheeks as red as beef. His smile was near as wide as the frontage of his hostel and Tom trusted him not one small part of an inch. But, with a combination of small-scale bribery, wheedling, fantasy and outright lies, he managed to extract something that seemed close to what he wanted to know.

Lady Margaret and her party had taken the whole of the inn on Monday night last. A servant of hers had come nearly a month earlier and booked the place, with details of numbers and requirements, plans of sleeping arrangements and victuals. For horses, men and women, high-born and low. This was an arrangement of long-standing with the Outram family who had been travelling from Elfinstone to Cotehel and back since the days of mine host's father's grandfather, for the inn had been in their family for generations. There were few that could accommodate such numbers, and the Hart had always been the first stop out and the last back. It was so convenient, after all. For most times the family themselves, and the most important household members, would be entertained up at the palace – for even archbishops were happy to invite such infinities of wealth beneath their roofs upon the slightest acquaintance.

So Tom swiftly built up the picture he had been seeking, which had only been half-drawn by the scrawled and scored itinerary he had discovered in Lady Margaret's desk.

For the better part of a century, one master of horse after another had sent out orders with military precision. They did so under the direction of Lord Outremer – or of Baron Cotehel, if he had not yet attained his majority and his investiture; or, in this case, of Lady Margaret Outram, the young boy-Baron's mother. And needfully so, for the movement of the household from one castle to another was the equivalent of a considerable military campaign. In the old days, it had only been the family and their immediate servants who had moved, for there had been full staffs in both castles, in Kent and in Cornwall; but, since the terrible death of the last Lord Outremer with all his family, things had clearly changed. They had changed perforce because all of the Elfinstone servants had died with the family in the tragedy at Wormwood in Jewry, and the confusion of events subsequent to that.

Only Lady Margaret and the young Baron had survived, and neither of them had been raised or trained to their great responsibilities. During the last couple of years, therefore, many of the family's most trusted retainers from Castle Cotehel in Cornwall had simply been moved in dribs and drabs up to Elfinstone in Kent; and now they were all being moved back down again at once, together with newly appointed people whom neither the Lady nor the young Baron could do without.

Indeed, it was not just the household that moved: there were men needed to transport them and protect them – and they needed housing too. The list was considerable. There were Captain Quin's coachmen, needed to drive the four great coaches; his ostlers to see to the horses as they went – and to act as link-boys lighting the way at dusk if the company was late; and, most importantly, his postillions, four to a coach and armed to the teeth, for it was they who kept such vultures as Ratsey the Highwayman from the soft and golden pickings Lady Margaret must represent.

According to Lady Margaret's itinerary, the whole army of them moved relentlessly south-westwards along the Portsmouth road – since the Armada, one of the busiest in all the realm. After Croydon, accommodation –

at inns and at local country houses – would have been arranged at all the towns on the list, as it had been done each year for generations and centuries: from Elfinstone to Croydon, then Farnham, Winchester, Salisbury, Sherborne, Honiton and Buckfast, down to Castle Cotehel itself. Throughout the whole of Holy Week, to Easter, the end of the old year and the start of the new with the Feast of All Fools.

Attended by all the danger that represented to the intrepid but silent woman in charge of all.

'It's time to move,' decided Tom.

Tom and Ben did not really join the Portsmouth road until they crossed the River Wey at Guildford. They could have ridden south to the shallow ford at Shalford, but they preferred to pay the toll on the Friary Bridge, which had lined the guild's pockets since they had taken control of the road and the ford itself in the days before Dick Whittington was Mayor of London, and make haste along their way; and, thought Tom, in due course and later on, it was a blessed chance well suited to the holy season that they did.

At the end of the hard-ridden day, as the sun began to set in their tired eyes, they cantered along the crest of the Downs, looking away across the purple-shadowed lowlands to north and south, spurring towards the still-distant village of Farnham and the hope of a bed for the night. The crest of the

Downs was high and sharp. It wound, dipped and rose as though a serpent writhed beneath. The countryside around was wild enough, and there was a reputation about the place sinister enough for the local villagers to give a part of it the name of the Devil's Punch-Bowl, a little to the south of here, in due time.

Woods gathered and gloomed along the narrow way, for all that the ground beneath them lay sky-coloured with bluebells, throwing down great spidery clouds of shadow through the blood-red dusky light, their myriad limbs thickened by the uncontrolled budding of new leaves for the spring. It was a balmy evening, fragrant with early blossom, a-stir with hares and rabbits and a-hum with the murmuring of early dumbledores. The thudding of their hooves and the jingle of their tack was all but lost beneath the evening cries of nesting birds – so that, as it had been at the beginning of the affair, it was only Tom's quicksilver-swift acuity and steel-sharp hearing that was able to distinguish the icy clash and slither of sword-steel on sword-steel in the heart of the darkness dead ahead.

CHAPTER 12

St Just

Tom pulled a budding branch silently aside and peered across the clearing. He moved the bough with his left hand, for his long, deadly rapier was drawn in his right.

'What can you see?' whispered Ben, crouching like a bear behind him, his voice ringing with ill-contained excitement. The master found himself distracted from the view for a moment by the thought that his young apprentice was far too fond of violence.

Tom gestured for silence and narrowed his eyes, focusing his intellect on the matter in hand again. In truth, he could see more than he had expected to see. The clearing before him opened on a shoulder of the Downs that fell away westwards above a wide smoke-grey valley; and so, while he and Ben knelt in darkness here, the men in the midst of the sword-fight were bathed in the last of the light. It was clear at a glance how things stood: one man alone fought three assailants.

The lone man was well dressed; the cast-away cloak and straying horse were doubtless

129

his, as well, thought Tom with the ghost of a frown, as the slouch-brimmed hat with its familiar feather. His clothing bespoke some gentility – some grasp of fashion and the funds to support it at the least. He was a master of defence, too, by the look of his technique, though in the traditional English school of old George Silver and his like – country-style, fit neither for London nor the fashions of Court, but effective enough for all that.

Tom felt Ben leaning massively forward at his shoulder and allowed the lad a clearer view, and a whisper of education.

'What we have here is a contest *al la macchia*, as we say – a rough and tumble. Literally – for the Italian means "in the woods".' He smiled at the little wordplay that had fallen so neatly. 'And it is on both sides a sword-and-dagger bout, for see, they are all armed left and right. The lone combatant is a master. Or has been very well taught. But in the old style. There. You see? He used the edge, not the point. Though the counter with the dagger was fine. And the fat opponent bleeds from the breast. Our man's falchion or bastard cutlass has merely wounded him, where our rapiers would have despatched him there and then.'

'Is not the cutlass a weapon such as common sailors might use?' demanded Ben. 'And sailors would not be so uncommon on the Portsmouth road,' he added as an afterthought.

130

'Indeed,' allowed Tom, to whom such thoughts came automatically, as though from the masters in the history of logical thinking. 'But this one, if a sailor, is by no means *common*. For see, he takes guard again. It is the high ward. And, from the look of it, what Silver would have called a *true guardant*. He will lead with the edge in a sweeping, downward ... There! See! And so the thin opponent staggers back. But once again, blooded. Not killed. Now comes their leader...'

'Polyphemus,' observed Ben.

'A Cyclops indeed,' agreed Tom, for the third ruffian wore an eye-patch.

'And a brave one to throw himself in like that,' suggested Ben.

'Or a foolhardy,' decided Tom. 'For see where our man has recovered from his stroke against the thin man and achieves a *molinello*, a near full-circle sweep across his face.'

'But he has missed!'

'The object was not beheading then. But see, Cyclops has started back to protect his last eye and ... Ah. I had not observed the whole ... You see? His bulk unsights the fat man, who has gone for a dag...'

No sooner had Tom made his observation than the little hand weapon exploded. The flat report was almost lost amid the confusion it caused, frightening every bird nearby into flapping and screeching panic. The footpad with the eye-patch was blown forward as the ball took him in the shoulder. And there, waiting convenient to his breast was the lone

131

sword-master's long-bladed *main gauche* dagger.

Tom saw at once, though, that all was not turning out as might have been expected. 'Cyclops is *armoured* as well as armed,' he spat as the slight figure in its gentlemanly garb was borne back abruptly, clearly taken by surprise. 'As one might expect a footpad to be.'

The last words were left on the air above Ben's head as Tom threw himself forward into the unequal combat.

'And the fat footpad has another dag, primed and ready to fire,' added Ben, almost to himself, as he too threw himself forward into the attack, suddenly bursting with simple glee.

He had no idea at all that he was howling like one of the fearsome natives of Raleigh's Virginia colony.

Tom had seen the second sidearm and he threw himself towards the fat footpad with all his considerable strength and speed. At the outer edge of his vision he saw the lone stranger falling backwards beneath the weight of the armoured but wounded Cyclops, dagger broken or gone, the heaviness of the body enhanced by the added pressure of both armour and ball-strike. But Cyclops, stunned by the attack by his own man, out of control of his ancient short-sword and his long poniard alike, presented no immediate threat beyond squassation – or, thought Tom, more accurately *peine forte et dure*, where the victim was pressed beneath with great weight on his breast.

Behind him, Ben came through the laurel like a bull through a gate, howling like an Irish banshee.

The fat footpad hesitated – whether in the face of Tom's shadowy speed or Ben's explosive entrance they would never know. The dag's short barrel wavered away from its primary target and never found another. Tom's rapier took the bloodied man exactly at the point where he had been wounded before, and deepened the shallow gash across his upper breast into a lethal well, plumbed by his rapier, reaching straight through his chest and out of his back. Clearly, only the leader of the band could afford any armour, thought Tom as he slid the two-foot length of his dagger into the footpad's heart and finished the business before disengaging and whirling away. The dag exploded in the dead man's grip and the ball did more damage to the local crows than to the combatants this time.

Ben had taken the thin man head to head, as though they were bulls in a field. Fortunately the scrawny footpad was much less than a master of his art, so that even the bricklayer's sword technique reduced him to confusion. No, thought Tom, given an instant's leisure to observe matters, not Ben's sword technique. It was Ben's approach to the battle that unnerved the gawky footpad. For Ben seemed in a very heaven of delight, his face aflame with blood-lust and his eyes agleam with joy. The footpad struck at him almost hesitantly and Ben hit the man's blade aside with his hand as though forgetting he held a sword at all. The weight of him hit the robber like a ram and blasted him back. He seemed to fly several feet before he hit a bush that was fortunately tall and strong enough to bear him up. Then he simply turned and fled into the shadows. Tom turned also, leaving Ben to huff and puff and shout a blood-curdling mix of threat and insult.

The man they had come to help lay alone. The Cyclops, like his lesser friend, had vanished during the melee, and it was Tom, as ever, who felt the weight of the matter. His mastery – and his alone – had claimed a life. However good the reason or the effect, he pondered darkly, he had put his hope of Heaven another step further away. How simple to be of the Catholic faith, he thought with a flash of shallow Protestant jealousy, to have confession, penance and forgiveness, to find a priest and obtain a snow-white soul; but then he sheathed his scruples with his rapier, as ever, and turned to the matter in hand.

Ben was crouching beside the man they had rescued, looking down with a frown. In the ruddy glow after sunset his face looked like a thing of brick – like one of the terracotta satyr masks Tom remembered from his years in Italy. Tom approached and knelt, thinking of his old saying – last used over the corpse of

the messenger who had started all this: Eyes
first...

'Is he dead?' demanded Ben almost hopefully, his blood-lust still up.

'I doubt it.' Tom's voice was distant, his
intellect engaged.

The man was young – younger than Tom, at
least. His clothes were of sober black, but
they were fastened with silver buttons cast as
nutmegs. He lay on his back on the grass as
though abed asleep, with his head turned to
the side, revealing, beneath a lock of fashion-
ably lengthy hair, a high forehead, a long,
straight, Greek nose that bisected a straight
brow like a Pythagorean diagram – a Greek
nose with a fine nostril that quivered with
breath; and, therefore, with life. A high cheekbone sat above a long, lean cheek that settled
into a long, fine jaw, saved from femininity by
a square, decided chin. And the face needed
some manly determination about it, thought
Tom, for it was a pattern of beauty. The
mouth was shaped like Cupid's own bow, and
the eyes, when they flickered open, were
wide, almond-shaped, framed with dark gold
lashes and violet in colour.

Then this young Adonis sat up, believing
himself still surrounded by footpads, no
doubt, and swift to continue his powerful
defence. Ben called out with shock, leaping
back in horror, and even Tom's massive equanimity was shaken; but not at the young
man's threatening action – at what his movements revealed of the left side of his face.

135

The left side of that beautiful visage was largely missing. Something – a falchion or a cutlass like his own, or some splinter of wood or metal behaving like a blade – had swept down that face, from cheekbone to jaw on the left side. Its edge had taken off the ear and much of the cheek – taken them clean off, revealing red muscle and pallid bone, a flash of white teeth, and, in the shadow beyond, a sinuous suggestion of tongue. And the horror of it was that the wound was by no means new, had not been inflicted in the recent fight.

The young man had been living with this face for some while, and would die with it, in the Lord's good time.

Tom remembered young James Hammond's words at Elfinstone last night as he had described the boy-Baron Cotehel's staff; and he put together the nutmeg buttons with the terrible scar that had taken so long to heal: the great scar earned at Drake's own shoulder on the deck of *Revenge* itself.

'We are friends, Master St Just,' he said quietly, just preventing another explosion of violent action. 'Friends to the Lady Margaret, at least.'

The distinction was finely made. For Master St Just was a hard man to befriend, as Tom and Ben learned well before the night was out. Long before disfigurement had come, the young man's character had been forged into arrogant and uncompromising lines – no doubt by his beauty and the indulgence it had won him from parents and peers alike. He was one of the *jeunesse doreé*, and no Spanish blade or splinter was going to change that, no matter what else it changed.

'Here'sss arrogance enough,' he said, starting up. 'Friendsss to the Lady and to nyself. I do not know you, fellow, and I doubt she does.'

He took it for granted that he himself should be known, and he spoke exclusively to Tom, as though Ben was below his notice entirely. His speech was slow, measured and slurred by his disfigurement. Without a cheek, he could make no 'm', 'p' or 'b' sounds, and unless he took great care, he hissed.

He was fortunate in current fashion at least, thought Tom, equably, watching him stride across the clearing past the gaping Ben to collect his cloak, hat and horse. The long locks made de rigueur by the Earls of Essex and Southampton went a fair way to hiding his wound. A cloak worn high on the shoulder and a hat slouched down over his eyes would disguise it altogether. Tom was hard put not to think of the stranger in the doorway of the long-burned house in Water Lane – disguised in exactly that way.

Yet he had misjudged his man, it seemed. For St Just swept his cloak into a rakish swash down off his left shoulder altogether, and his hat sat on the back of his head. 'Whichever of you nade this carrion should dury it,' he said as he swung into his saddle beside the dead footpad. It took even Tom an instant to realize he meant *bury it*...

'And you'll need to discuss natters with the Constatle at Farnham. If you get there defore the foot-tad's friends arrive to revenge hin.'

CHAPTER 13

Old Harry at Farnham

'Arrogant puppy,' huffed Ben, not for the first time, as they picked their way carefully along the last of the road towards the distant lights of Farnham village. They were on foot and taking it slowly, unwilling to risk the Lord Chamberlain's horses in the dark on unknown ground.

Tom, guiding his horse with the extra care dictated by the dead weight of the late footpad draped over its saddle-bow, spoke at last. 'Consider, Ben. Surely action is formed of an admixture of character and necessity. We each behave as we do because of what we are – what the Good Lord has made us to be – and because of what we are about.'

'Meaning?'

'Look at yourself. You were born a vicar's son, but chance has made you an apprentice bricklayer. Yet you behave like a scholar because you are working your way out of

Islington towards Cambridge.

'I was myself born the son of a blacksmith, but I too worked myself away from my destiny first to Carlisle Grammar School, then university at Glasgow, the battlefields of Flanders and the fencing schools of Siena. So I have become as I am through original design mutated through adventure and experience.'

'Your meaning?'

'Imagine if I were a young man forged by unblemished beauty and unalloyed adoration, given God's stamp to accept universal adulation as my right, climbing upwards to the very shoulder of the country's greatest hero at that hero's crowning moment; and, at that very instant, to have it all snatched from me. What changes on my character would the fires of bitter experience bring? Might it not add to my arrogance? Make me flaunt my destruction just as I once allowed my beauty to take every eye? And, were I rescued from a dangerous predicament by a well-intentioned stranger, might I not snap back at the helping hand...?'

'Like the veriest cur – even so,' said Ben. But his tone was half-hearted and his voice was thoughtful.

'Offering enmity in the face of friendship – especially were I, this piece of perfection, this sun of universal adulation, doing something secret, something unworthy; something dangerous at the time.'

'And consequently fearful of discovery.

Marry, that's well thought on. D'ye think it's likely?'

'Likely or not, I suspect we'll get to discuss the matter on further acquaintance,' said Tom. 'For we are bound to Cotehel as surely as the man himself; and we are bound to lodge beneath the same roof tonight, for I suspect there is only one inn at Farnham. And this is it.'

The inn was called The Harry, though in honour of which of the eight of that name who had graced the throne so far it was impossible to tell – an early one, judging by its age.

'We should call it The Old Harry...' opined Ben, squinting up at the sign by the burning bushel over the door, unconsciously prophetic. 'Surely the Lady Margaret and her retinue would never have stayed in such a place as this.'

'I don't doubt that some would have. 'Tis big enough to sleep a dozen and feed three. But there's the castle up the road for Lady Margaret and her kin. I don't know who owns it, but, like the Archbishop, they'll not be averse to the friendship of Croesus and his mother.'

They walked shoulder to shoulder into The Harry, stooping under the lintel and stepping down two stone steps on to an ancient earth floor. Tom's eyes swept over a dozen and more country faces, and St Just's still mask away over by the fire. The violet eyes met his, then slid away with no hint of recognition, let alone of gratitude.

There were half a dozen wooden tables, scattered with food and drink. Beyond, stood the low, brick-built open fire hung with pots and pans, spiked with spits, belching out welcome odours and a heat that was much less welcome on a warm spring night. Beside it stood the women of the place – mother and daughters by the look of it, full-figured and as fragrant as the chickens roasting on their spits. Beyond the fire, the recessed wall was piled with ale casks and wine butts, fronted with a low bar behind which stood a solid-looking man, his face as still as St Just's.

Tom met the stolid gaze and made use of the sudden silence occasioned by their entrance to say in his most ringing and commanding tones, 'Good even, landlord. We need food, drink and lodging for the night. But first, I think, we need the parish constable, for I've a dead man draped over my horse outside.'

'Should I ever turn playwright,' whispered Ben in the stir of shock the announcement brought, 'I'll have learned all I need to know of drama in the last few seconds, I think.'

The parish constable was a country cousin to Virgil Grimes; and, because the Farnham gaol was a cage built on to the back of The Harry, he was seated in the bar. There was, between the cage and the stables, an old stone store-room that served the fat footpad as a morgue. 'I'll warn the Justice in the morning,' said the constable, as they pulled the *corpus* in, allowing an ostler to lead their horses away. 'But it's Will Green, who's wanted along with One-Eyed Jack Sleaford. You'll only be held up over the matter if you want to wait for the price on his head – or if One-Eyed Jack comes looking for revenge.'

'How much is the reward?' demanded Ben.

'Nobbut a shilling.'

'Enough to bury him, perhaps,' said Tom.

'Ye'd have to ask the sexton that,' said the constable, closing the door on the dead man as though that was the end of the matter.

But the sexton was also in the bar and by the time that Tom and Ben were settled in the cooler shadows, over a table set with trenchers of chicken and pottage, tarred tankards of good ale and a bottle of sack apiece, the price of a decent burial had been settled at one shilling – and six pence, which Tom laid out at once.

Their standing thus established, Tom and Ben settled to quiet conversation as though they were as little acquainted with St Just as he wished to be with them – wisely enough on his part, perhaps, for the constable in his slow way came and went, checking their papers as their faces were unknown, returning with reports and affidavits to sign and witness, establishing their identities and business and recording Tom's version of the events leading up to Master Green's demise. A version that mentioned an assault upon a third party, but a man who ran away like his assailants and remained nameless, leaving Tom and Ben to bring the matter to an end.

'But why?' demanded Ben in one of their few private moments together, between the comings and goings of the constable and those of the landlord's wife and daughters with the food and the drink and the promise of so much more. 'Why not name St Just?'

'For the Lady Margaret's sake. I believe she would have me hold my tongue in this.'

'What makes you believe any such thing? We come close to breaking the law in this – by omission if not by commission. What makes you think a noble lady would have it so?'

'When you meet her, you will know.'

'That's as may be; but if you read the man aright, then your continued kindness to him – and this is kindly meant, you cannot deny it – will heap more coals of shame upon him and stoke the fire of his resentment against us.'

'Quite likely. You are swift of study, Ben. We'll make you master of your Toledo blade in no time. Then, perhaps, we'll make you master of yourself.'

Ben passed over that, much struck by another thought: 'And ye need no more enemies on this road, master, for ye've made one of this footpad Jack Sleaford...'

'Who looks a little like the landlord here, for all he has two eyes and is called Churt, not Sleaford.'

'A second cousin or some such. It's been known,' said Ben. 'They don't go in much for travel in these parts after all. Well then, master...'

Tom shrugged, but he remained adamant; and so it was done as he commanded.

The inn was spacious enough upstairs, and largely unoccupied. Tom paid extra so that Ben could have his own room, and he therefore slept alone – as did St Just. Apart from the room housing the Churt family – there were other children apart from those who served below – there were three more unoccupied. This was the Portsmouth road, after all; and the Castle might be expected to entertain more than the Lady Margaret on her twice-yearly ventures into the distant depths of Cornwall.

Alone at last, Tom stripped off his doublet and unbuckled his sword. In his shirt and galligaskin trousers he stooped over the bowl of water by his bed and washed. Face free of the grease of his dinner, he sat and removed his boots, considering for a moment whether to summon one of the landlord's daughters to complete the task for him. Then he washed his hands again and stood, stretching his weary body until all the joints between his long bones cracked and popped.

Then he caught up the saddle-bags he had packed before leaving London and put them on the little table beside the single candle that gave all the light he had, and opened them. Out of the depths of one he took the two deadly little dags the late Will Green had tried to use on St Just. Out of the other he took powder and shot. 'Your swords and daggers were hardly worth the salvaging, Will Green,' he said quietly as he worked. 'But these dags are another matter entirely. Now, once we are armed, we must watch and wait. For poor Ben is not quite quick enough of study yet to keep pace with his master...'

So saying, Tom closed his lips, but his mind ran on, picking his logic out thus: keeping St Just clear of the constable's investigation would do more than just pile coals of gratitude on his head and would make the risk of stoking up a wish for revenge in him worthwhile. For if kept clear enough of everything arising from the unexpected attack, St Just might well proceed with anything else he had planned to do between here and Castle Cotehel.

Tom had only the vaguest idea at the moment what such a thing might be, but he believed that he had arranged matters this evening so that all he would have to do to learn more of the arrogant puppy's plans was to watch the man. And wait.

As he always did at this time of his day, he cleared his mind of everything worldly then; and he knelt by his bed in the darkness and prayed – prayed until a balance was struck between the peace he was ever seeking and the wild galloping of the events he was riding to their terrible conclusions.

Tom turned over on his bed, alerted by a slight scrape of movement. His eyes were wide already.

A gleam of light. A candle passing outside his bedroom door. No. Not passing. Pausing.

A breathless squeaking, like a secret mouse. The handle turned. The latch rose. The candle entered.

Above the dullish brightness of the rush-light flame shone the plump face of the land-lord's eldest daughter, but the unsteady brightness lent it a kind of glory, and the hair that fell free in gilded ringlets reached down to the shoulders of the simple shift.

The shift was greying and grubby, but Tom had no eyes for it or for the form that it contained. All his gaze was riveted on her face: golden ringlets, deep-blue eyes, turned-up nose and decided chin, each with a little dimple at its tip.

Perhaps, wondered his whirling mind, it was simple coincidence that this girl's father looked a little like a highwayman after all; for on the sudden his daughter looked very like a countess. He tensed himself to move, but a hissing sound prevented him.

'No!' whispered St Just's distinctive lisp from further down the corridor, urgently replacing the m's he could not say with the n's that he could. 'Not there, Nargery. Here! Cun to ne *here*, ny lady...'

CHAPTER 14

The Nag's Head

Tom spent a restless night. Old Harry's inn walls were not thick and the lady by no means of a silent disposition, in spite of her resemblance to the Silent Woman and the whispered commands of her lover; but, thought the Master of Logic, in the small hours when stillness settled at last everywhere but in the whirl of his racing mind, surely the man who cut apart the portrait that currently lay in his fencing room – unless Ugo Stell had moved it already – would bring the girl who looked so much like Lady Margaret to cries of terror and agony rather than to those of ecstasy?

And St Just knew her name, calling her Margery familiarly, which spoke of a longer association than a swift liaison just tonight. So: no pain for Mistress Margery then; and no revulsion in her either. For even with the candle cold and his eyes tight shut to boot, St Just's face remained vivid enough to Tom, as it must to everyone else who saw it. But what did these things mean? Individually, they were hard enough to fathom. Taken together, they represented a knot of truly Gordian complexity.

Sleepless in any case, and fired by that immense energy that possessed his body sometimes when his mind was all awhirl, Tom was up with the chambermaids in the pre-dawn dark. He roused Ben well before sunrise and they set off with scarcely more than a crust and a tankard to sustain them. Off they trotted through a chilly, ghostly greyness on the road to Winchester with Tom at once deep in thought. He was still trying to balance the probabilities that the man who lusted after Lady Margaret and had spied upon her and cut her mysterious portrait could also be the terribly disfigured man who desired her so much that he slept with servants who resembled her; but he could see no immediate solution to the conundrum and so he turned his attention to other matters.

'We have made a good start,' he said to Ben.

'Aye.' Ben was clearly not at his best first thing. Or he was disgruntled by the whirl-wind speed of their departure.

'But there were only the two of us. Captain Quin would find it much more of a challenge to get the Lady Margaret's entourage upon the road. Even were the Lady herself up betimes and ready, as I suspect would be the case, there would be the others to move, half of them in one place, subject to the Arch-bishop's courtesy or My Lord of Farnham's, while the rest of them were in at least one inn.

There would have to be meetings, agreements, people setting forth early; people left behind...'

'Indeed. A man with any wit about him could come and go at his leisure and yet seem to be one of the group.'

'You have hit my thoughts aright, Ben. And that's allowing there may be others, like St Just *per exemplum*, who have actually arranged to be despatched about some business alone in any case – with or without the distractions of what must already be a more than usually violent passage. And the logic of the whole is rounded out by St Just's invisibility this morning.'

'Has he gone, master?'

'I could find no trace of him, though I did not put the whole of the landlord's brood to the question. Certainly, his room was empty and his horse is gone.'

'Then if he has gone, let us hope that he is not alone. I would wish One-Eyed Jack Sleaford well away from our path into the bargain, lest he decide to revenge Will Green that you slew yestere'en.'

'Marry, well thought on! But truth to tell, Ben, footpads and highwaymen are not noted for their early habits. We are not likely to see this Sleaford unless we accidentally ride over whatever ditch or kennel contains his bed.'

As the light gathered behind them and the low mist boiled away before them, they cantered easily side by side along the road, which led them past Alton and Alresford as they talked.

Tom established swiftly enough that Ben had slept through last night's liaison like the veriest babe and had no notion at all of St Just's affair or of its possible implications; but the slumber seemed to have cleared his companion's mind, for, as he came fully awake it became clear that he had taken strides forward in his attempt at mastering logic in the ways that, until now, had been peculiar to Tom. Their morning's conversation, covering more than three hours, which measured out another full day's travelling for Lady Margaret, turned around Robert Poley and his possible interest in the affair.

For it seemed to Tom that if such a man as Poley was taking such an interest in such a matter as the attempts of a sin-worm to play peeping Tom with Lady Margaret, then there might indeed be wider political significances that were almost impossible to fathom. Ben was quick to catch on to Tom's thinking, revealing as he did so an unexpected political acuity – and that, thought Tom, even before the extraordinary bricklayer knew that the Countess's son the Baron had been fathered in a rape by the Earl of Essex himself. It was a truth he had shared with as few people as possible – Poley, Kate, Law, and Will Shakespeare, who had been there when he had revealed the truth of the matter more than a year since after his miraculous escape from the Earl's black plans at Elfinstone. For it was a truth that put at risk the lives of all who knew it and would continue to do so while the Earl remained above ground.

Over and over the matter they went, through and through what little Tom knew of Poley's past, associations and likely preoccupations now; round and round and round the Earl of Essex and his equally sinister plans, but never naming His Grace at all, of course.

Yet the more they explored the wilder reaches of probability, where the strands of this great web of possibility and speculation were few and far between, the more Tom felt the urge to share that vital nugget with his suddenly insightful friend. For as it was with Will Shakespeare, so it was with Ben Jonson. Tom felt the Master of Logic within his racing mind raised to a higher plane as they speculated together along all the weary miles to Winchester.

They came into the city at noon, and followed the joyous sound of the bells through the heaving bustle towards the cathedral itself, for it was Good Friday and there were services all day; but Tom at least was not moved by religious prompting. For hard by the cathedral stood the inn owned by Talbot Law, Bailiff to the Bishop of Winchester, and resident of the Clink in Southwark. And that inn, the Nag's Head, foundation of Talbot's fortune and of his current standing in the Bishop's high regard, was run by his wife Bess.

Tom had never been to the place before and had rather imagined that it would be a small establishment crouching under the walls of the cathedral like a dwarf under the protection of a giant. The only thing he had known for certain about the place, other than that Talbot owned it and Bess ran it, was that its cages in the yard out back were the strongest and most reliable prison in the city. Relied upon by everyone from the local Justice to the cathedral court, that gaol had brought the man who built and ran it to His Reverend Lordship's personal notice; and the rest had been history.

But the place was huge. Three times as big at least as The Harry at Farnham, which had housed them last night, it filled the side of the cathedral square, seemingly half as big as the ancient church itself. Bright young ostlers took their horses at the door and led the tired nags through the arch to the stable yard. A promising tapster greeted the new guests and led them through into the main bar – though it was clear that this was but the largest room of many available on the ground floor alone; and tall though he was, Tom never even considered stooping as he strode through the massive doorway. Then he stopped, head and shoulders above the heaving crowd, struck by a simple possibility that had simply not occurred either to himself, or, seemingly, to the establishment's absentee landlord: If Lady Margaret's entourage had stayed in Winchester two nights since, then they must have stayed here with Bess Law.

'Tom Musgrave! Is it yourself, lad?' she

carolled as he caught her eye across the bustle of her huge establishment. 'My, you've hardly changed at all.' A moment later he was swept into her considerable embraces and, for all his worldly experience, he felt very much the boy again as he bent his cheek to a smacking kiss and handed over Talbot's letter.

'Bess,' he said, as she released him. 'But this place is huge. And such a bustle! I had no idea. Talbot—'

'Ha! 'Tis busier than usual, for this week end we have visitors from all over come almost on pilgrimage to the cathedral for the Easter worship. The Old New Year is due within the week. The whole of Winchester fills at this season with everyone south of London that cannot get to Canterbury. The best and the worst of them cheek by jowl here and in the cathedral – and all stations in between.

'But that scapegrace husband of mine visits only when the moon is blue.' Her voice was easy and indulgent. 'Has he many mistresses, or does he just pluck a goose from among the Winchester geese he protects for My Lord Bishop?'

'No!' Tom was honestly shocked: Talbot Law was everything he understood of steady faithfulness. He had never seen him look at another woman.

'Winchester geese is what we call the whores in Southwark that my husband guards as Bishop's Bailiff,' Bess explained to Ben. 'But Tom, tell me, who is this fine figure of a man? Not your apprentice surely, though

153

I see he is *armed* almost as well as you...' Her eyes fell roguishly below Ben's belt and his face turned to brick as he realized she might not be talking simply of his long Toledo blade.

'Aye, Lady Margaret was here two nights since. And she stayed here herself, for a wonder.' The three of them sat in a private room away from the bustle of the Nag's Head's public areas. The table before them was piled with fish in a gluttonously tempting range of states – spitted, roast, baked, boiled, jellied, marinated and raw; in pottages and pies, in stews and on trenchers. The only in-edible thing on the board was Bess's huge chatelaine of keys – for she was mistress of every door in the place, including those of the cages and gyves outside. As she spoke, Bess watched with motherly amusement while young Ben did his best to eat her out of house and home; but it was on Tom she focused her fearsome insight.

'The Bishop usually entertains Lady Mar-garet himself, but Easter has fallen badly for that this year. And so she stayed in my best chamber, with that Agnes Danforth, the housekeeper, close by. Which put Captain Polrudden Quin out of sorts, of course. He likes the best for himself and is full of lordly airs – when My Lady is not there to eclipse him. And then, when that stupid Percy Gawdy got into a fight and killed his man, Quin was happy to go off and leave him here

locked in my cage at the back! But that's
Captain Polrudden for you: always cheered
by another's misfortune. Left young Doctor
Rowley to watch and report.'

'So you've one of Lady Margaret's servants
caged at the back awaiting trial for what?
Manslaughter?'

'Murder. And waiting? No, we do things
quicker than that in Winchester! He was tried
yesterday and will be punished today.'

'Hanged?' asked Ben, awed. 'You said
murder...'

'Not for certain, no. He's the son of a vicar,
so he claimed benefit of clergy. Cost him
something to do so, for his father was a
famous martyr – burned at the stake at the
Rochester assizes in the last year of the boy
Edward's reign. The child was still in its
mother's womb at the time, but he can still
claim benefit now, so they say. The Bishop's
court sat yesterday and that was that.'

'Benefit of clergy?' said Ben thoughtfully.

But Tom was not to be distracted by legal
quibbles.

'What was the manner of this murder?' he
asked, feeling that here indeed was a most
unusually violent passage from Elfinstone to
Cotehel, with four dead men clustered
around it already.

'A tavern brawl. A dispute over the reckon-
ing or some such. No more, from what I can
see. Not in my tavern, thank the Lord. Gawdy
and Rowley both had crept out from under
their mistress's eye down to The Tun. A haunt

of thieves and whores, if you ask me; and that's what they found there – found thieves where they sought whores, like as not. And, Doctor Rowley says, a crooked game: one of the Green brothers – little more than foot-pads at the best and wanted men over the border in Surrey, so I'm told. Hot words became hasty blows and by all accounts Gawdy was lucky that Lean Green was drunk. And that was that. News of the matter came to Captain Quin. He may have discussed it with Mistress Danforth, for they are as thick as thieves, all *Mistress Agnes* this and *Captain Polrudden* that. But I doubt they told Lady Margaret. They moved her on in the morning and none the wiser, leaving the doctor as I say.'

'If they would not report to Lady Margaret,' said Ben quite scandalized, 'then surely they must tell the young Baron? They are his servants, after all, and owe him allegiance as any knight unto his liege.'

'Describe these people to me,' requested Tom, deep in thought, still refusing to be distracted.

'Ye can meet a brace of them in less than a moment – three if ye want to see Lean Green's corpse, for it lies in my store-shed awaiting a pauper's grave.'

'Aye, but before I do meet them, tell me: the murderer in your cage...'

'Percy Gawdy, My Lady's Secretary.'

'A university man?'

'Perhaps. Clever enough – and bachelor

enough even given his age. But no mention of a Bachelor of Arts. Secretary to great houses before this. Secretary to the previous Lord of Cotehel, I believe – to the Baron Cotehel, whom Talbot says you killed at Elfinstone a brace of years ago. He speaks fondly of Southampton House and knows your friend Will Shakespeare.'

'Hum,' said Tom noncommittally. 'I will weigh the implications of that in due course. And the other man I may meet on the instant?'

'The young Baron's tutor, Ezekiel Rowley, Doctor of Philosophy, graduate – as he is fond of pointing out – of Corpus Christi College, Cambridge. A steady, reliable man in my opinion, if more thoroughly churched than the vicar's son. Certainly a man I would be content to leave standing guard over Percy Gawdy until execution of his sentence.'

'Well,' said Tom, who clearly found himself with more to weigh in this plethora of information, 'let us glance briefly at the others. We have met St Just.'

'Poor lad. Did ye ever see such beauty so terribly defaced? But he was not here with the rest of them this time.'

'No. He was with us at Farnham, and we have lost sight of him since. But these other two: Agnes Danforth and Polrudden Quin.'

What Bess would have revealed about these two died stillborn on her lips, for no sooner had the names been said than a vigorous, muscular man came in through the doorway unannounced. 'Mistress Law,' he said with a forceful, educated accent that told Tom at least that this was Dr Rowley, 'they've come for Percy Gawdy.'

CHAPTER 15

Justice

Without a further word the three men follow-ed Bess out into the stable yard. Here a group of officers from the church court were wait-ing outside the cage door. The cage was a little lean-to, built against the back wall of the inn. It was waterproof and looked windproof as well – much more substantial than was the common run of such structures, thought Tom, betraying an unexpected humanity, an unheard-of consideration for the comfort of the occupants. For the structure itself did not need to be particularly strong. Everyone within it was restrained by heavy gyves of metal fastened at ankle and wrist, then chained to bolts driven into the straw-covered floor.

So it was in this case. The grim-faced murderer sat on a bench and blinked around them as Bess unlocked his chains. At first, all that could be seen of him, indeed, was his eyes, for they were large and strangely luminous, almost seeming to shine amongst the shadows. Secretary he might be – well-educated vicar's son and confidant to the Earl of Southampton, friend alike to Will Shakespeare and the Earl of Essex – but, observed Tom, here was a frightened man, fighting to stay calm in the face of death.

'Doctor Rowley, what will they do to me?' he croaked as the court officials pulled him up. *Though slight and youthful-looking, he must be the better part of forty years in age*, thought Tom.

'They have you for murder, Percy. Witnesses gave affidavits and the recorder wrote them down. Murder most foul.'

'My letters to the Earls?'

'Can hardly have been delivered yet, let alone answered.'

'Then I am helpless and friendless here. What will they do to me?'

Tom observed the tutor's demeanour with interest. After the first dry-throated rasp, his voice had settled, steadied. His conversation with Rowley had an almost disturbing calm about it. There was hardly even a tremble as the second part of the question was addressed to the stolid, silent officers, rather than to Dr Rowley.

The latter, apparently not counted among his friends and helpers, nevertheless went at Gawdy's shoulder out into the yard, then through the arch and across into the cathedral square. Tom and Ben followed. Tom at least was drawn by the coil that the conversations and what they had left unsaid had started in his brain. Ben, no doubt, with his love of violence, was drawn by baser things.

Lean Green, thought Tom, as he shouldered through the crowd between Bess and Ben, a wanted man across the border. And he himself had killed a Green last night: Will Green, a wanted man across the border in Farnham, Surrey. But the writ of the Surrey justice did not run here in Hampshire, where the Green brothers had thought themselves safe – the Green brothers and, no doubt, their leader, high lawyer, upright man and captain, One-Eyed Jack Sleaford.

The apparitors, or officers, led Gawdy steadily across the square to the platform beside the cathedral upon which stood the parish gallows. There was nothing strange that it should stand here. Beside St Paul's Cathedral in London stood stocks, pillory, cage, whipping-post and gallows all together; and all of them were rarely untenanted. It was fitting that those about their holy business there should observe the fate of those who had fallen from grace.

From the mid part of the gallows depended a noose that swung gently in the breeze – a breath not of Heaven, mused Tom, but born of the babbling bellow of the crowd. Noon service being done, the square would be alive with all-comers without the promise of public justice. Now it was packed and heaving. 'Look to your purse,' said Tom to Ben; 'and to your back,' he added, catching sight, out of the very corner of his eye, of a face with an eye-patch.

As gaoler, if not executioner, Bess got best view as of right. She had guarded the souls who came hither; it was fitting she see them despatched. In a voice as dulcet as that which had warned Ben beware, Tom asked Bess, 'Is there nothing we can do to spare him?'

She shrugged.

'I killed his brother Will last night on the Downs above Farnham,' he persisted. 'And there is no dancing on the *trining cheats* for me.'

'Farnham's a foreign country to us,' said Bess. 'There's no hope for the fiery Percy in what you did over there. But rest you calm, Tom, for I doubt your man Gawdy will dance on the gallows either. There's no executions allowed in a church court: they have to call for a Justice even to burn a witch. God knows who they had to call for permission to burn his father forty years and some ago.'

Bess, Tom and Ben stopped at the foot of the gallows steps, Tom in the lead, his foot upon the first one. Dr Rowley mounted a pair of them before the apparitors gestured him to stop and led the condemned man upwards. In truth he would hardly have proceeded in any case, for there stood at the top of the steps a fearsome individual. Naked above his black tights and old-fashioned breeches secured by a great thick belt, except for the black mask over his face, the executioner waited for Gawdy.

Still with back straight and head held high, the man stepped up to meet his fate. As the executioner's hands fastened on him, he turned and looked down at Dr Rowley. His strange eyes were distant, far removed from the horror of this place and predicament. 'How will you report this, Ezekiel?' he whispered, 'to Lord Robert and to Master Lane?'

Tom strained to hear the enigmatic conversation above the bellow of the crowd.

'I will tell them what I must,' answered Rowley, also in a frightened whisper. 'Enough to keep them from suspecting.'

The young man nodded once and the executioner led him to the midst of the platform, just beneath the swinging noose. Here he gave charge of his unresisting arms back to the grim apparitors and turned. He pulled into sight a solid table with a big metal crucible held in a stand upon it. Even in the brightness of the sunny spring midday, the crucible shone bright red.

'Kneel,' he said to Gawdy, but the secretary was so confused by this unexpected turn of events that the apparitors had to force him to his knees. 'Put out your left hand...' Again, the apparitors moved the unresisting limbs and the executioner fastened the wrist down with a steel gyve.

The Clerk to the Court and recorder of the church court stepped forward then and read the ruling about to be executed here.

'Percival Gawdy, son of the Reverend

162

Matthew Gawdy, late of Wouldham in the County of Kent, resident of Castle Cotehel in the County of Cornwall, servant to the Baron Cotehel, you are adjudged guilty by the court of My Lord the Bishop of Winchester of the wilful murder of Absalom Green of this parish, known as Lean Green, upon the night of Wednesday, the twenty-second of March in the Year of Grace 1595, being the thirty-seventh year in the reign of our liege lord, Queen Elizabeth, Sovereign of England, Ireland, Wales and France, Defender of the Faith...'

'Get on with it!' bellowed a raucous voice, which begat a wave of rough agreement, which drowned out the rest of Her Majesty's titles and degrees.

When things quietened, the Clerk was finishing the sentence. 'It is the sentence of this court, therefore, that you be branded upon the ball of your left thumb with the letter "T", by which sign all men may know that you have wilfully and illicitly taken a life. May God have mercy on your soul.'

In the stunned silence, the executioner pulled a red iron from the glowing crucible and pressed it into Percy Gawdy's imprison-ed hand. The spitting hiss the iron made seemed to trigger a bellow of outrage from some part of the crowd – which was fortu-nate, perhaps, for Percy, thought Tom, as it drowned the sound wrenched from him by the unexpectedly lively agony. So that Dr Rowley would never need to report them to

Lady Margaret – were she in fact the object to whom Gawdy had despatched his apparently final message; but in fact it seemed that Rowley would not be reporting anything in great detail, for at the spitting hiss of the iron on flesh and the smoky stench of braising meat – which Tom could smell even here – the good doctor turned aside and vanished, retching, into the crowd. It was as well, thought Tom, that he was a Doctor of Philosophy and not of Physick.

In fact this thought was Tom's last clear thought or observation for a while, because a section of the crowd suddenly broke into near-riot. Clearly either friends of the late Lean Green, or simple bystanders spurred on by frustration at missing out on a hanging, they set out to put matters right in the swiftest and most obvious fashion. As the fainting secretary was pushed staggering down the steps, the front few rows of the crowd nearest the gallows charged forward. Had there been anyone other than Ben, Tom and the redoubtable Bess there to meet them, rough justice would have been dealt out there and then; but as it was, things turned out a little differently.

Bess turned incredibly swiftly, pulling the chain of her chatelaine into her fist. With the huge bunch of metal keys on the end of it, the whole thing looked like a medieval mace in the hands of an English Joan of Arc. The first vicious swing came near to removing a nose, a jaw and an eye, each from a different rioter.

The crowd hesitated.

Tom stepped on to the lowest step and gave himself room to snatch out both rapier and long, lean dagger. Ben, slower to liberate his Toledo steel, nevertheless had the wit to grab the nearest likely-looking weapon. It was a hod, but none of them had leisure to appreciate the irony of that. The heavy angle of boards topping a short, stout pole, designed to sit on a man's shoulder as he carried bricks up and down ladders, made a worthy helpmeet to Bess's mace, and that was good enough for all of them.

'Should we stand and wait for help?' called Bess.

Tom was tempted. He could see a goodly crowd of servants, tapsters and ostlers coming out of the Nag's Head after their mistress; but he had counted without Ben's blood-lust.

'Stand?' bellowed the apprentice. 'Never! Attack or die, say I!' And, as good as his word, off he went. Bess, perforce, went with him.

'Bring Gawdy,' called Tom to the apparitors. 'We will see you safe to the inn.'

For a wonder, they obeyed. Half-carrying Percy, who was curled over the weighty agony of his hand like one of Bess's best freshwater lobsters, the two apparitors nevertheless flourished their short-swords manfully – and the executioner, armed with a red-hot iron in each mighty fist, closed in behind them.

They were a suddenly considerable force, but still they were all but lost in the maw of the mob. All around, just beyond the circumference of the arc described by Tom's glittering rapier, the disappointed citizens of Winchester bayed and howled. It was only a matter of time, thought the battle-hardened fencing-master, before someone came up with a pitchfork or a hook, or a scythe.

Before someone caught up a brick or a stone. Or a gun.

Cat-like, walking sideways, narrow-eyed and at battle-pitch, Tom moved. He knew what the men and woman moving beside him were doing almost by instinct. He could feel the will of the mob buffeting over him like a storm as the collection of men and women that made it up blew hot and cold. Did they want to start a slaughter? What revenges would be visited on them if they did? What justice would overtake them? Did they care?

'Come on, ye coward villains,' bellowed Ben in a voice that must have echoed in distant Islington, 'let's be having you. Do or die!'

'Get them!' came a strangulated shriek in answer. 'Kill them all!'

Tom looked back to the source of the sound and there, upon the empty gallows, stood two figures, with a third on the steps just below them. The screeching voice belonged to the scrawny opponent from the Downs above Farnham last night, brother to the fat corpse behind The Harry, and to the Lean one behind the Nag – last of the brothers Green. At his shoulder, holding on to the noose to steady him as he gestured, stood One-Eyed

Jack Sleaford. And on the steps below was the slouch-hatted, cloak-masked stranger Tom had last seen in the doorway of the fired house in Water Lane.

As Tom watched, helpless to do anything other than to force the retreat forward with all his might and main, the first missile sailed in from the back of the crowd to smash into an apparitor's shoulder with crippling force; and as it did so, the cloaked figure pulled out and levelled the strange and dangerous-looking pistol Tom remembered all too clearly from their first meeting. The distance between them was not so great. Tom knew they were all within the killing range, but even so it seemed that the barrel of the pistol became unnaturally large as it was pointed straight at him. What had Will Shakespeare made the dying Mercutio say in his play of *Romeo*? *As wide as a church door, as deep as a well...*

When the shot came, Tom's whole body flinched and it was an instant before the revelation came that he had not, in fact, been shot. He opened his eyes, thus discovering that he had shut them at the vital instant. The well-deep gun barrel and the masked man holding it were gone. Green the footpad was still there, but he was frozen with shock, looking at One-Eyed Jack Sleaford, who was held erect only because he had wound his arm through the noose to the shoulder. Across the suddenly silent crowd, the sound of the creaking rope came clearly as the highwayman swung slowly, turning until it became clear that he should be called No-Eyed Jack Sleaford – indeed, Half-Head Jack Sleaford.

Disturbingly similarly, suddenly, there on the edge of the crowd below Sleaford, Tom caught a glimpse of St Just. Then he was gone.

While over the sudden stirring of horse-hoofs close at hand came a coldly mocking, disturbingly familiar voice. 'Can I find you at Elfinstone? Can I catch you at Croydon or Farnham – though the corpses told me I was coming close.

'But the moment I discovered a riot under the walls of the cathedral in the very heart of Winchester on Good Friday, I knew exactly where you would be...'

CHAPTER 16

Dead Mann's Message

Tom watched Robert Poley narrow-eyed. He had expressed his thanks on his own behalf and those of the group that would have died, and had seen them shrugged away, even as the smoke from the powder lingered on the air above the stunned crowd.

He had watched as Poley discussed with the City Constable his right summarily to execute citizens engaged in the fomentation of riot, with the power and the authority of the Council and Court of Star Chamber. He had led him into the Nag's Head and introduced him to Bess.

He had seen him pick at the last Lenten fare of the fish platter – what little had been left by Ben; had seen him watch with distant disapproval the tending of Gawdy's branded thumb, the cause of the disturbance, by the green-faced Dr Rowley, recently reappeared.

Tom had watched all these things and waited for more. It was no coincidence that the spy-master had followed him – had sought him even at Elfinstone, indeed. As ever, Poley was up to some deep-laid stratagem of his own and Tom was content like a hunter in his hide to watch and wait to find out what it was; but he could not stop his mind from racing into speculation.

If Poley was here, then he had a need that Tom alone could meet. If Poley was passing through, then still, he had a matter he wanted Tom to clear up for him. Tom had left something undone in London or at Elfinstone. In London, most likely. Something undone, unobserved, overlooked. What could he have overlooked? Unless it was something more Poley had uncovered on closer inspection of the corpses Tom had left in his care.

The upper room in the Nag's Head was private and silent, even though the window stood wide to admit the cooling breezes of the warm afternoon. The cathedral square below was still, swiftly and forcibly calmed by the city authorities – legal and clerical – none of whom wanted the faintest breath of civil disorder to disfigure Good Friday's celebrations, or to put at risk the rich promise of the Easter Week end. Poley walked stiffly over to the window and looked across at the magnificence of the cathedral. The bells began to chime for afternoon services. He sucked in a great breath of spring-fresh air, in and in until the leather of his jerkin, pistol-belt and sword-swashes creaked. 'We should be in there, praying for our very souls,' he said, broodingly, 'and for Queen, Council and Commonwealth.'

'We should,' agreed Tom guardedly.

'But we do God's work in other ways. And that of the Queen, the Council and the Commonwealth. I am on my way to Plymouth, so I have not come out of my way in seeking you. They have a Spanish spy in the Plymouth Clink.'

'Should you not bring him to London, then?' asked Tom. 'Introduce him to Rackmaster Topcliffe, perhaps? Another swift confession and another hot story for Topcliffe to tell the Queen.' How swiftly God's work led men like himself and Poley to sup with the Devil, he thought.

'That is one of the decisions I must make when I talk to the spy. And it's not a *him*. 'Tis a woman. But in fact she has some services to render before I introduce her to Topcliffe or any of his acolytes.'

A little silence fell within the room. Tom very much did not want to think about what Topcliffe, the Queen's chief torturer, would do to a woman. The bells sank sonorously to stillness. Distantly on the breeze the carolling of a choir began. Poley closed the window and turned.

'You saw it,' he said, apparently changing the subject as swiftly as the flash of a dragon-fly's wing. 'When you realized why Mann was put into the Fleet river when he could have been left to burn anonymously with the house on Water Lane. You saw, but you did not quite understand the whole.'

'I saw that he was your eyes in Elfinstone and that his body was a message to you as well as to Lady Margaret.'

'If you saw that, was there nothing else to see?'

'That he had a message for you as well as for me – your message gone out of his wallet with mine.'

'Do you not understand it yet, Tom? He was a *secret* man...'

'Ah. Now that I *had* overlooked. And obviously I was not alone in doing so. If he was a secret man, then he may have been carrying a secret message...'

'Precisely.'

'A message you recovered at his post mortem, which I omitted to attend, having gone charging off on my fool's errand to

Elfinstone...'

'It was in the heel of his shoe,' said Poley simply. 'The heel was hollow – a device we used with some success in the matter of the traitors Babbington and Mary of Scots.'

'But it would need to have been a finely made hiding-place to have survived a ducking in both the Fleet and the Thames...'

'Precisely.'

'Ah. I see. So, you have a letter disfigured and defaced like the letter Lady Margaret sent to me, of which you understand enough to make you look to the south and your Spanish spy but the whole of which must still elude you. Surely Will Shakespeare could have helped you there and saved you lengthy rides out of your way to Elfinstone and Winchester.'

'I considered it. I even considered winkling Codemaster Thomas Phellippes out of Essex House; but in the end it would have been unwise. For after they translated it for me, like as not I'd have had to kill them.' Poley said it with calm, unshakable authority, and Tom didn't doubt he meant it.

'Perhaps I had better get to church, then, and make my own peace with God,' said Tom.

'No. They would have died for their associations, not their knowledge.'

'So it is Southampton and Essex you fear, for these are the men Shakespeare and Phellippes associate with.'

'You know it.'

'What do they have to do with Spanish spies? His Grace of Essex is fierce against the Dons, as you well know; and His Grace of Southampton like his friend.'

'And yet both consort with Spaniards when they feel the need. Remember Antonio Perez.'

'Has he published his memoirs yet?'

'He works and works.'

'Like a worm through a good ship's bottom?'

'As you say. But the point is made. For Essex and Southampton both, there are Spaniards and Spaniards.'

'But not for the Council? They have no such fine distinctions?'

Poley said nothing.

Tom continued. 'But whether you must needs kill me later or not, you were impressed by my translation of Lady Margaret's message. So I will do to pick out the meaning of yours. And preferably before you get to Portsmouth, in case...'

Now it was Tom's turn to fall silent, for it seemed that scales were falling from his eyes. 'But wait!' he breathed. 'This is a new game indeed, and a deadly-dangerous one. You wish me to find the sense in a damaged report from your spy watching Lady Margaret at Elfinstone before you talk to a Spanish spy in Plymouth. I can see at a glance how His Grace of Essex might figure in your concerns for the Baron – his bastard son – and Lady Margaret – the victim of his rapine

173

and subject of his plotting; but where in Heaven's name do Spanish spies fit into any of the affairs of Elfinstone or Castle Cotehel?'

'Perhaps if you look at the message you could help me discover the same,' said Poley.

'Indeed,' countered Tom. 'But you'll recall, no doubt, that a certain bricklayer helped me with the original. May I call upon him? Or will that lead to his untimely death?'

Poley hesitated, then he said, 'Call him. Let him see it.' And he cast upon the table before Tom a wrinkled, ink-stained rag of paper, the thinnest paper Tom had ever seen – near transparent, in fact – covered with the smallest, neatest writing he had ever come across. Tom gave it one glance and rose, crossing to the door. He opened it and bellowed, 'Ben!'

Neither man was in the least surprised when Ben arrived within the instant.

Tom made no mention of the lethal possibilities of the work as he gently spread the paper on the table. Indeed, his mind was far removed from Ben, focused fiercely on the matter literally in hand. The paper, carefully dried and preserved as though Hilliard himself had painted upon it, was nevertheless as fragile as an autumn leaf. It even had a voice of its own, which neither its writer nor its prime object had. It gave a whispery crackling as Tom unfolded it, as though it would breathe its message secretly into his very ear.

At last it lay unfolded so that he and Ben

could pore over it. They weighted the corners with the pommels of their daggers and – aptly enough – with the grip of Poley's pistol. Only then did Poley join them and look down upon the message that had remained wilfully dumb to him. It said:

... ... er Hogg I hv ... ... o rp't. Principal ... ongst them is t ... ... I rep'ted the ... ... tery of its arriv'l ... ... erious disappearance. Not ... ... from M L's private chamber. I have qu ... ... e legit ... ... ess to such a place but none of them ha ... ... ledge. You can see the danger of anyone *without legitimate access* getting to such a pl ... ... ly if we are ... ... some device of Essx's or S'mton's which is the sam ... ... This particularly ... ... – her certainty that she is being overw ... ... sing danger she fears to herself and the B.

... ... er stems from a secret source we do not yet su ... ... ting to a friend, requesting aid. Bu ... ... hell before he can be summoned. She relies up ... ... don or soon after and is ord ... ... amonds and I accompany the party unt ... ... ched thence with messages. She fears the journey but cannot do more than ... ... ted swiftly. Her insist ... ... ted Q, my opinion of whom you know, especially after his letters to Fra ... ... ain. ... She fears C ... ... tain she will lie beyond all hope ... ... down there in the ha ... ... es and as a playt ... ... est devices. This may be a fant ... ... act that she has never yet been th ... ... s, Q,D'fth, St J, even Gy and

Ry have much to do wi ... ... rs womanish. There is grave dang ... ... n Cornwall, to M ... ... ut perhaps also to the St ... ... There is something unho ... ... ious protector – can fathom and forestall it before it begins to claim our lives.

'The paper was folded and folded and placed within the hollow heel,' said Tom. 'Then, in the river, the heel began to leak, so that the water soaked into the paper. But the damage came from only one quarter. Where it became wet, the folded paper became blank, or the writing became indistinguishable. Where it remained dry – or nearly so – we have a word or two; but because the paper was folded half a dozen times, there are puddles of blankness that cannot be distinguished in the body of the whole.'

'Indeed,' said Ben. 'So that when we lay it flat there are circles of nothingness at the outer limits and through the heart of the thing. Well enough. It is no more complex a puzzle than the message we worked on a' Tuesday.'

'I'm relieved you think so, Apprentice Jolson,' said Poley ill-naturedly. And he paid for his bad temper at once.

' "... er Hogg",' said Tom with deceptive gentleness. 'Who is Master Hogg?'

'It is how Mann knew me. He never saw my face and it was not fitting that he knew my true...' He tailed off as he saw the pair of them looking at him. Much in their gaze made mute comment on the trust between a spy and spy-master who did not dare reveal his true name.

'Well, well,' said Tom. 'Let's leave that. What's next? "I hv ... ... o rp't." This, I would guess, says, "I have something to report"...'

'Some worries or concerns,' suggested Ben. 'For see, in the next bit there is a principal amongst them.'

'Indeed, Ben. Well observed. "Principal ... ongst them is t ... ... I rep'ted the ... ... tery of its arriv'l ... ... erious disappearance." He reports something that arrived and disappeared mysteriously.'

'That can only be My Lady's portrait that James Hammond told us of.'

'That Ugo Stell has reclaimed by the by,' said Poley. 'He is back and about your business.'

'Good,' said Tom. And then again, 'Good, Ben. Well reasoned. For see, "Not ... ... from M L's private chamber." That is where it went from – from My Lady's private chamber.

' "I have qu ... ... e legit ... ... ess to such a place but none of them ha ... ... ledge. You can see the danger of anyone *without legitimate access* getting to such a pl..." He has questioned everyone who might have legitimate access, but they know nothing. Consider the danger of such access by someone with no legitimate right...'

'Particularly,' added Ben, frowning, 'particularly if this were some device of Essex's. See where it says "... ly if we are ... ... some device of Essx's"?'

'Good,' said Tom yet again. 'And this is particularly important given her certainty that she is being watched: "... sing danger she fears to herself and the B. ... ... er stems from a secret source we do not yet su..." What is this? Increasing danger? That seems likely. An increasing danger that she fears to herself and the Baron. And from a secret source that you and he do not yet suspect. This is a very disturbing picture, Poley. A much more desperate danger than the one I had thought from the first letter. Was Mann given to wild speculation? Did he see monsters in shadows and bears in bushes?'

'No,' said Poley dully. 'The opposite: he was the most perfect spy of the time...'

'Then we have better cause to worry,' said Tom grimly, 'than did Caesar on the Ides of March.'

'But then,' said Ben, 'I believe that you have entered the picture, Tom. For see she is writing: "... ting to a friend, requesting aid."'

'That's as may be,' allowed Tom. 'But there's a fear. Look: "... hell before he can be summoned." That "hell" – it must mean Cotehel. She fears she will be in Cotehel before I can be summoned. A lively fear indeed; and one likely to prove true unless we cut free of this coil and ride.'

'In good time,' warned Poley; 'when your work here is finished.'

'Well,' allowed Tom, his discontentment sudden and severe. Then he read the next few phrases. ' "She relies up ... ... don or soon after". She relies upon what? Figuring it back from what happened as we now know, she must have relied upon me catching up with her at the place from whence she despatched the messages – to wit, Croydon, or soon after. A faint hope as matters chanced. But what next?' After the bitter question, he sat back a little, chewing his cheek.

Ben took over, giving no indication whatsoever that he sensed his master's bitter frustration and self-castigation. 'What have we here? – "and is ord ... ... amonds and I accompany the party unt ... ... ched thence with messages." And she is ordering that Mann and who? The Hammonds? Accompany the party until they are despatched thence with messages. That fits in with what you said, Master, and with what happened, does it not?'

'It does,' allowed Tom. 'But see. The plan was to take both the brothers James and John Hammond. James made no mention of going – or of expecting to go but being held back. I wonder why?'

"Tis all one,' said Poley dismissively. 'There are more things hidden here than are dreamed of in philosophy.'

'Well,' persisted Ben in the face of Tom's brooding silence: ' "She fears the journey" – that is plain – "but cannot do more than ... ... ted swiftly." What? Insist that it is completed swiftly? We know she demanded that, too.'

'Aye, but,' added Tom, stirring himself, 'there was a price to pay. "Her insist..." – insistence, we must prick it out – upset ... angered ... discomfited Quin: "... ted Q, my opinion of whom you know..." No good opinion, then?' He swung round on Poley who shrugged. 'Especially after his letters abroad to France and Spain,' persisted Tom. 'You think Quin, like Essex, sees Spaniards and Spaniards?'

'I do not like the Cornish,' Poley said. 'They are too like the Irish for my taste.'

'Papists, you mean? With a leaning towards Catholic France and Spain?'

'Philip of Spain has dreamed of putting an armada in Galway Bay and an army in Killarney since the defeat of the Great Armada seven years since,' said Poley. 'Why should he not dream of putting a navy in Mount Bay and an army in Portleven? 'Tis nearer to Spain and Spanish Flanders by far. And a good straight march to London.'

'But only if the Cornish are of an Irish mind in the matter,' said Tom, 'and content to let the Spanish come ashore. Is that what you suspect?'

'That's what I think the Spaniards may suspect,' said Poley. 'And that might amount to the same thing, might it not?'

'Hence the importance of your spy in the Plymouth Clink?'

'She fears Cotehel, as you fear the Cornish,'

said Ben, continuing his work in the silence that answered Tom's question. 'See? "She fears C..." And she is certain, as I think, here: "... tain she will lie beyond all hope ... ... down there..." '

'In the hands of her enemies,' translated Tom gloomily: "in the ha ... ... es..." And, what? As a plaything to their darkest devices: "and as a playt ... ... est devices." God help her.'

'But look,' said Ben bracingly. 'Mann believes that "This may be a fant ... ... act that she has never yet been th...": This may be a mere fantasy based on the fact that she has never yet been there.'

'But the others: "... s, Q,D'fth, St J, even Gy and Ry have much to do wi..." – with the place. And are her fears womanish? No. For "There is something unho..." – something unholy about the place.

'Let us hope the mysterious protector – "... ious protector": to wit, myself – "– can fathom and forestall it before it begins to claim our lives." '

Tom looked up and met first Ben's eyes and then Poley's.

'Aye,' he said bitterly. 'Too late for that.' He shook his head with anger and frustration. 'A world too late for that.'

CHAPTER 17

Buckfast

No sooner was Poley satisfied that Tom and Ben had hit the meaning of his near-ruined letter right than he was gone, planning to be at the Plymouth Clink as soon as he could. He travelled with a small troop of horsemen that reminded Tom irresistibly of the troops that had followed the big guns up Hog Lane. It required all of Bess's cunning to keep a decent pair of horses back for Tom and Ben, who would be leaving soon themselves. Gawdy and Dr Rowley elected to stay another night – recovering from shock at the very least, they said – and follow with what speed they could on the morrow; but, fired with a wild new urgency, Tom would not wait, and Ben perforce must follow his master.

Bess gave Tom the best horses left in her stables, a note for the innkeeper of the Antelope beside the abbey in Sherborne, for she knew well enough that if Poley and his men had passed there, good horses would be in short supply indeed.

Tom and Ben were gone at once, out into the rolling south country, pounding past Salisbury as the cathedral bells rang for evensong, and then past Shaftesbury at compline – though it was still illegal to call it by its Roman name – as the sun began to set in their eyes. Down the hill into the Stour valley they came, with evening gathering around them as they passed the Ship Inn in West Stour, already a popular resting place for sailors travelling between Plymouth and London. Darkness had descended by the time they trotted over the crossroads at Henstridge and it was too dark to see the sign of the new inn there; but the moon rose as they topped the rise at Oborne and its calm, silver radiance saw them safely down past the old castle and the new, where Sir Walter Raleigh and his Bess were at their housework, and into Sherborne at last.

They supped at the Antelope – past which Poley and his men had thundered some hours earlier, pausing only to annex the best horses they could find – and slept till dawn, guaranteed the best of service and of horseflesh by Bess's message.

'Best keep Missus Law's note and shew it anywheres along the Plymouth road,' the innkeeper at the Antelope advised them. 'It'll serve ye better than a pass from Her Majesty herself, such as that lean courier flourished yestere'en.'

And so they found, as they sped onwards through Easter Saturday, hurtling westwards and southwards at a steady fifteen of the Queen's new statute miles in an hour, relentlessly closing the distance between themselves and Lady Margaret.

They went through Yeovil with the early farmers coming in to the Easter market and used Bess's near-magical note to change horses at Crewkerne and Chard. They ate in the saddle at Honiton, where Lady Margaret had been last night while they lay at the Antelope and Poley had passed like a stormwind somewhere in between.

Tom had hoped to catch her at Exeter, but as they came down into the city, with the bells ringing for compline, it was after eight in the evening. Ben's horse was exhausted, stumbling over the cobbles of the cathedral square and so they stopped at the Clarence, showed the innkeeper Bess's letter and explained their business.

'Lady Margaret rested here at midday,' the innkeeper said. 'She planned to be at Buckfast tonight, from what she said. That's six hours distant for her and the best part of three for yourselves, with fresh horses and hard riding. Bestir yourselves betimes tomorrow and say your Easter prayers in the saddle and you'll catch her still at services in the abbey there before she leaves. I'll hire you the best of my horses then, but I'll not risk their legs in the dark – especially with riders as exhausted as your boy there on their backs.'

Frustrating though it was, Tom had to admit the logic of the argument. Ben was asleep on his feet – too tired to eat, indeed – and Tom was hardly in better shape. They climbed the stairs to the last vacant room in the place, which they were happy enough to share. They slept like the dead, awaking with the sun to discover that the landlord's daughter was hammering on the door – and that during the night their bodies had turned to stone.

'Dear God, Tom,' cried Ben in genuine distress, 'I cannot move. Is it the palsy? Is it the paralysis?'

'Neither,' said Tom. 'It is twelve hours in the saddle on two days running. Here. As soon as I can get off the bed I'll help you up.'

In fact they had to call the innkeeper's buxom daughter to help Tom before the pair of them pulled Ben on to his feet. The first peal of bells celebrating Easter dawn rang out as they did so – fortunately, for it spared the country virgin's ears from the bricklayer's unholy language.

The ostlers, with scarce-controlled hilarity, lifted Ben into the saddle like a French knight at Agincourt; then, with no more than a crust in their hands, they were off again. Allowing their wise, well-travelled horses their heads, they clattered through the gates before the cathedral watchmen could ask why they were heading away from church on the holiest of days. Away along the road south and west past the scattered hovels that comprised the villages of Hardcombe and Chudleigh, then on along the grassy track that was the

Plymouth road, as it led them under the wild and rugged shoulder of Dartmoor itself.

Like a great stone wave it rose before them, grimly forbidding even amid the spring-warm, sunny splendour of the happy, holy morning. Although the last week had been clement enough, the months before that had been amongst the wettest in living memory. Stream after stream came splashing down the grim granite precipices and the horses had to wade across the ford over the River Teign at Chudleigh Knighton. They pounded through long, thin Ashburton squashed against the moorside, and turned right at last, following the road along the bank of the lively River Dart. Up on to the Moor itself they cantered, towards where Buckfast stood on the ridge, and the abbey stood higher still, its tall steeples looking south to the Channel and north across the wildest stretches of moorland in the kingdom.

Even had they not known the road, the tuneful carolling of the abbey bells would have guided them like Ariadne's golden thread. 'I ache to get to services,' said Tom grimly. 'I was travelling all through Christmas Day and felt the lack of it then, but not so bad as this.'

'I just ache,' said Ben, grimly; but he was able to swing himself down from his horse with a great deal more agility than he had exercised in getting on to it at Exeter. Outside the ancient abbey's extensive accommodation stood a muddied travelling coach, its traces empty. Under the dirt on its door panel was a familiar crest of cats, mice and nutmegs. In the abbey's stables Tom found Lady Margaret's ostlers, preparing her horses against departure when the service was done, and Tom left his hired horses with them.

Then, slowly, almost shyly, of a sudden – all too vividly aware that he had not been barbered for days, that nothing he was wearing had been removed except to allow calls of nature for nearly a week, and that as much mud as bespattered Lady Margaret's coach also bespattered himself and his companion – Tom pushed open the door and tiptoed into the glory of the abbey church.

It was as though the very air was made of gold. Golden beams fell in cascades through all the windows until the stained glass above the altar rose in a jewel-bright glory of ruby, garnet, emerald and sapphire fit to rival the heavens themselves. Golden blades glanced and glimmered off the gilding on the fine, high columns that held the fluted roofing as though it were the floor of paradise itself. Golden sounds shimmered all along the nave, from chapels and choirs on every hand. Even the flags on the floor seemed to be running with gold as they trembled beneath the mighty chiming of the bells and the singing of the choir at Easter worship.

Tom was blinded by the light – light multiplied a thousand times by the tears that filled his eyes; but he would have been hard put to it to say with utter honesty whether his joy rose from the fact that he had completed his hard-won pilgrimage into the presence of his God – or into that of his Lady Margaret.

Not that there was, in the first instance, much to choose between them in his dazzled eyes. For when he discovered her at last, standing like a lily in the front rank of the congregation, she was, like all the rest in there, a thing compounded of airy gold. The lace that modestly contained her hair was a filigree of gilded threads, so fine, so burnished, that at first it was impossible to say what was headdress and what was hair. The curls the lace half-covered fell like glistering guineas to her shoulders, where a modest collar sat square before plunging into the bodice of golden silk. Even the glimpse of flesh the modest clothing allowed seemed cast of gold itself, like the works of the Italian metalsmith Benvenuto Cellini, whose work Tom had seen in Florence while he had been studying in Italy – seen and so admired.

Coveted, in fact; coveted most sinfully.

The word sprang into his mind unbidden. The idea was so sinful, so out of place with the rapture he had been enjoying, that it brought him up short, like a viciously reined-in horse. It cleared his eyes and mind alike. For was that not what he had been called here to prevent – the coveting of this golden woman? the secret worship of that golden flesh? the dangerous desire to possess it? – no matter what damage might be done to it in the process; no matter what further damage might be done to her.

He took Ben's arm and pushed him side-ways. There were no pews and the congregation stood, so it was easy enough to mingle with them – save that they were all fresh-washed and best-dressed, while the pair of new arrivals stank like stallions and looked like beggars.

Tom's mind was instantly very far removed from the ecstatic heights it had reached on first entry. Instead, his eyes swiftly narrowed against the glare until he could make out the individuals in the entourage around Lady Margaret and the wand-straight boy-Baron at her side.

There was no mistaking Captain Polrudden Quin. Had his bearing not born the stamp of a military swagger, his hair would have betrayed him. Tom was no Cornish-speaker, but it had hardly exercised his intelligence to fathom that 'polrudden' was likely to mean 'redhead'. So it proved. Tom had never seen such uncompromising copper in natural locks. Beside the gilded beauty of his mistress and master the man looked garish; his whole being seemed in bad taste. Red hair, copper ringlets in far too great profusion in South-ampton's style, or Essex's at Court. Beyond a ruddy cheek and jaw, barbed bronze tangles of moustache – curled up in the military style – and beard, if anything, redder still. In the light from the stained glass it looked as though he might have simply dipped his chin in blood.

Beside him, a different proposition again: a tall woman of indeterminate years but jet-black hair, dressed in similar style to her mistress – similar but cypress, black head-dress, lace collar reaching to black velvet bodice.

Ben coughed like a brick chimney, clearing his throat of the road's dust.

The woman – Agnes Danforth, surely – turned. Her gaze raked coldly over them but did not seem to see the newcomers. Tom saw sallow, olive skin, full and oily; an aquiline nose that would indeed have doubled as an eagle's beak; a thin mouth with a disapproving twist pulling down lines from the flare of her nostril to the first fold of her jowl; eyes like the fat black olives they grew in Sicily. Tom's eyebrows rose. He had seen women in the Alhambra who looked less Spanish than Mistress Danforth, he thought.

The man on Danforth's left glanced easily over his shoulder too and a strange murmur went through the congregation. Tom's eyebrows rose further still. How had St Just got here so swiftly? he wondered. It would be well to keep a close eye on someone who achieved with such seeming ease a feat that had come near to crippling both himself and Ben.

Dr Rowley and the branded Gawdy would be catching up with them in due course, he thought – unless they rode with the fevered speed of Poley or Master St Just; but this was the heart of the household, none of whom Master Mann had much call to trust, especially if Tom and Ben had translated his report to Poley correctly.

Tom closed his eyes briefly, seeing again that water-damaged list of initials: *D'fth, St J, even Gy and Ry* ... And, of course, *Q, my opinion of whom you know* ... Even before the matter of the secret letters abroad to France and Spain...

If Lady Margaret had any real reason for her fears, any true foundation for the letters she had written to him, then it must lie here, thought Tom. Would it not be neat to catch the sin-worm with his eyes fastened secretly but madly upon her – overwatching her, as she feared. Would it not make all the adventure so far immediately worthwhile and allow him to bring her, with his arrival, a full relief of all her terrible suspicions?

In fact it soon proved impossible for him to achieve anything of the kind; for even before the interminable Easter sermon began, it became clear to Tom that almost every eye in the place was fastened exclusively upon Lady Margaret.

CHAPTER 18

Cotehel

At the end of the service, Lady Margaret led the worshippers out into the noonday sunlight as was her right and duty. To do this, of course, she would have to turn and process along the full length of the abbey church.

As she turned to begin this procession, Tom frowned to see the lines of worry and fatigue that marked her elfin face. Beneath those huge blue eyes were bruise-dark rings. There were lines across that snowy forehead and astride the coral lips. The hand that she lowered to her son's hand trembled, but not as much as the other, which she laid with cool formality upon Captain Quin's forearm.

Tom's heart simply twisted within him. He had seen Lady Margaret, child and woman, in the uttermost exigencies, in the midst of being ravished, chained as a Bedlamite and being hunted with horse and hound; yet he had never seen such a wilderness of weary defeat upon her face. Like a lodestone pulled by its star, with scarcely any real control over himself at all, he pushed back through the congregation and stepped out into the aisle before her. Her eyes met his; widened. Their focus sharpened. Shock and surprise flitted over her expression like cloud-shadows over the moors. Disbelief followed. The huge eyes blinked. She hesitated. Quin, seemingly unaware, marched onward as to war. Agnes Danforth, a step behind, saw well enough, however, and her speed began to gather as she surged forward like a stately Spanish galleon to hurry her mistress by.

Lady Margaret's expression began to transform again. Cloud-shadow was replaced by simple, stunning sunshine. The worry and the wrinkles seemed to fall away. The most breathtaking, most dazzling, of smiles swept over her. She stopped. Quin strode on, then hesitated, foolishly, realizing he was alone and walking before his mistress, out of his place. Danforth crashed into her then stepped back stricken, off course and surprised, like the Armada under the guns of Howard, Drake and the rest.

The strange transformation was complete. With her son the Baron's hand still in hers, moving with swift determination now, Lady Margaret, every inch the Countess Cotehel, crossed the abbey church towards him; and again, scarcely in control of his limbs, Tom knelt to her – back straight and shoulders square but head bowed, down on one knee, as he had seen the Earl of Essex kneel to the Queen in the White Hall tiltyard last Whitsuntide when he had been victorious at a day of jousting and tourneying, playing Sir Lancelot to her Queen Guinevere.

And as Her Majesty had done to her knight in shining armour then, so Her Grace did to hers now. She settled her hand like a white dove on his shoulder and, as if by magic, pulled him erect again. There was a profound silence in the place. The whole household and congregation seemed held alike entranced, watching Lady Margaret and the travel-stained stranger. Their gazes locked, like equals in station and in height, for all she stood as far above him in one as he towered above her in the other. *'Welcome,'* said her lips, but no whisper of sound sullied the silence of the holy place.

Then her gentle hand was pushing him softly back, into his place; and she turned and gestured Quin imperiously back to her side. Her hand rested firmly on his forearm once again and she steered him decisively along to the doorway, out into the blazing noon as though she was utterly unaware of his beef-red cheeks and fiery looks.

Agnes Danforth disdained to look at Tom at all, as she swept past him, back on her course in her mistress's wake. St Just measured him coolly once again, and Tom's eyes met the gargoyle's square on without flinching. Then, as of right, as though they were also senior members of her household, Tom and Ben fell in behind Lady Margaret's entourage.

Tom calculated that it was thirty leagues

almost to the ell from the door of Buckfast abbey church to the main gate of Castle Cotehel. Lady Margaret commanded that the coach-drivers proceed along the road at five leagues or so in the hour, however, for she clearly wished to be home tonight; and they were able to obey, he observed, for the roads near Plymouth were better maintained than most. She sent the fractious Quin on ahead to prepare the way and warn the hostellers and their ostlers that they would be coming through even earlier than planned. The red-headed Captain went with ill grace enough, flashing thunderous looks at Tom as he sawed at his gelding's mouth with jerking reins and stabbed its sides with his spurs.

'The innkeepers and post-horse stablers keep good stock in and a weather eye out all along this stretch,' said Tom to Ben as they all set off together. 'They're well used to parties passing with little notice but at top speed, in each direction, day and night. We've seen the way Poley went with his troop. Earl Howard lives back in Arundel and Raleigh at Sherborne. Drake lives up at Buckland on the Moor itself, but also has a house in Looe Street in Plymouth. He is forever rushing between them – and up to London as well. They all wish to get themselves and their crews to their ships in Plymouth Sound swiftly and efficiently. And I observe the Lady Margaret is not above making good use of the systems in place for them.'

Even so, it took nearly three hours to get the

Cotehel coaches to Ivybridge and their first change of horses. On the other hand, thought Tom more cheerfully, they were able to make much better time afterwards. They changed again at Plympton and again at the Jewell in Plymouth overlooking the Hoe. Then they trundled down the hill to the harbour where, perforce, they stopped upon the very last of Devon.

Quin had booked the biggest ferry to take them across the Hamoaze to Torpoint and Cornwall, but the vessel could only manage one coach at a time. Of course, Lady Margaret's coach went first, across the glass-still waters on a gently falling tide. As the postillions guided the coach-horses aboard, the Baron's head appeared briefly and one of the burly fellows came back towards where Tom and Ben waited with the rest.

'You're to go with the Baron's coach,' he informed them.

St Just started forward with them as well, but there was really only room for one coach, six horses and two riders, so, in the face of his master's orders, he perforce remained behind. It was difficult to tell from his expression whether he was as discomfited as Quin had been; but Tom felt it safest to assume that he was.

'Apart from the Lady and the boy,' he said to Ben, as they stirred forward, 'look for nothing but enemies at Cotehel.'

There was just room for Tom and Ben to swing down as the ferrymen bustled about.

By no coincidence at all, Tom found himself standing at the door of the coach where Lady Margaret sat. She looked out through the open window straight into his eyes with almost disorientating intimacy. She put her hand out, but it was a moment before he saw that there was a tiny piece of paper in her fingers. He took it. When their fingers touched, a bolt of sensation passed between them that was almost too painful to bear. He opened the paper with shaking fingers, looking steadfastly down.

You are very welcome here, it said.

'You are very welcome here, Master Musgrave,' said a soft, dulcet voice.

Tom looked up again at once, stunned and disorientated. It was the voice from his dream of her – the way he had known in his very marrow that she would speak.

But no. The young Baron's face had joined his mother's at the window and was grinning down at him.

'My Lady,' Tom responded, a little stiffly, bowing his head from the neck almost in the German fashion. 'My Lord.'

When he straightened, he saw another face in the shadows of the coach behind them, and met the disapproving, Mediterranean gaze of Mistress Agnes Danforth. 'I have a great deal of news to give you both,' he said. 'But some of it is sad and some is disturbing, so perhaps it is better suited to some privacy.'

Lady Margaret's level gaze met his own, seemed to plumb the depths of his dark eyes.

A flicker of a frown came and went.

'But you will teach me how to fence in the new style, will you not?' asked the Baron, all boyish enthusiasm. Mistress Danforth tutted at such unseemly enthusiasm, but Lady Margaret smiled.

'Of course, My Lord.'

'You must call me Hal,' commanded the boy. 'Everyone does.' Then he leant forward across his mother's bosom, lowering his voice into laughing conspiracy. 'Well, the younger ones do. Captain Polrudden still says *My Lord* and so do Mistress Agnes and Master Martin the Chamberlain. But Gawdy and Rowley and Master St Just all call me Hal. 'Tis fortunate. *Hal* is one of the few names Master St Just can say. You should hear the trouble he has with *Master Martin* and *Captain Polrudden*!'

Only his mother's hand on his arm stilled the bubbling boy, Tom noticed; but at her touch, the child glanced up at her with such a look of trusting love that he felt his heart turn over again.

'Of course,' he answered. 'I shall be honoured to call you Hal, My Lord, and to teach you a pass or two, with the approval of your Lady Mother – and the leave, of course, of your own master of defence. I have seen Master St Just at swordplay and I assure you, sir, that there is little I could teach that he could not.'

'You have seen Ulysses fight!' said Hal, aglow. 'But how could that be?'

It took Tom but one beat of reasoning to realize it must be Ulysses St Just, and that one atomy of time to decide how the story must best be told. Modestly, therefore, he described his own poor part in Ulysses' battle with the Cyclops Jack Sleaford and the brothers Green; and by the time he was taxing his ingenuity for an outcome suitable to both the man and the boy, the ferry slid into Torpoint and they had to disembark.

Quin might have been disgruntled at being sent summarily on ahead, but he saw his duty and knew his job. Two link-boys riding ponies met them and then used their flaming torches to guide them through the gathering night out and round St John's Lake past Antony, with the bells for Easter compline ringing in the little church. Up and up their way took them until Tom saw all too clearly why Quin had taken such care. They turned south along a cliff path that seemed to teeter on the very brink, high above Long Sands and Sharrow Point up to the brooding castle high on bleak Rame Head.

It was not a beautiful castle. Even in the last of the light on a clear evening with the westering sun setting away behind the Lizard, the place looked squat and brutal. It had been carved there, chopped out of the grey rock of the place by an earlier generation of Outrams, the almost-pirates on whom the family fortunes were founded, blunt and brutal men who had taken their ships out of Plymouth after the exotic fruits and spices symbolized by those silver nutmegs now. The place was designed to watch the western approaches, and so it was built right to the very cliff-edge, extending an already dizzy height by more than a hundred grey-stone feet, augmented both in height and depth by Henry's engineers. It was designed to protect the anchorage and make kindling out of any ship seeking to slip into the Hamaoze unlooked for or unannounced. You could drop rocks on them, as blind Polyphemus had done on Ulysses; but there was no need: the most powerful guns in Henry VIII's great foundries had been put here fifty years ago. Then, since Armada Year, these had been augmented and updated with his daughter's best and most modern culverins.

Trotting along behind the coach with its torch at each corner and the link-men leading the leaders, Tom looked over the last of the cliff above Whitsand Bay, then up at the torch-hedged Main Approach that swept down to the gatehouse ahead. He felt he knew the place, though it was his first visit here. It was a building with its own place in the public imagination, like the Tower of London or the Palace at White Hall. Everyone knew something of the castle and its history. Tom, being Tom, would have known more than most even had that been all; but he had been involved with the Outram family in one way and another for seven years, the last two, by chance, more closely – if never intimately until now. Such a mind as his, in such an association, simply soaked up all the information he could come across – either by chance or on purpose.

Even Ben seemed awed as they trotted onwards, with the tall flambards blazing on either hand. 'Best-built edifice I've ever seen,' he said. 'Even more solid than the Tower, by the looks of things. Almost as old, I should judge, in parts, though I look forward to seeing the later additions ordered by King Henry himself. Those torches show off the stonework of the gatehouse a treat. I wonder does that portcullis work.'

'It should,' said Tom. 'They lowered it when the Great Armada came in sight. And they fired on the ships with those long culverins and cannons on the outer wall while Drake was finishing his game of bowls upon Plymouth Hoe. So the story goes, at any rate.'

They came under the portcullis then and their horse-hoofs echoed into the castle's main yard.

'What builders must have made this,' said Ben, awed.

Tempted beyond consideration, Tom said, 'Aye. It must make you proud to be a bricklayer.'

In fact it did make Ben obscurely proud to be associated with workmanship like this, so he huffed a little, but kept his temper under control.

The main keep of the castle rose above them, with two thick arms of grey wall reaching out to join at the gatehouse behind them.

Storey after storey the keep rose until its square top stood outlined against the rising moon. Its back was hard against the cliff, its back wall famously more than twenty feet thick at the base.

At the base of the keep on the inner side a great sweep of steps reached down from a main entrance a dozen feet and more above the ground. The balustrades of these steps, like the wide approach road, were all lined with blazing torches casting steady, golden light. The light itself, in such abundance here and jewel-bright within the castle keep itself, all bespoke one thing loud and clear: money. Only gold in great abundance could afford great brightness such as this; and were that message not well enough established, then the fact of it was driven home at once, like a dagger in a coup de grâce. For from the doorway, down the steps, to the heads of the stamping horses and to the doors of the new-stopped coach, swept the castle staff, Captain Polrudden at their head, beside a tall, dark-faced echo of Agnes Danforth – clearly Martin the Chamberlain, her brother. Even had he not already been described in the young Baron's gushing words, Tom would have known him from his black and sober suiting made pompous – in both senses – by his daffodil waistcoat and his matching cloth of gold cross-garters. Beneath this august pair there looked to be the better part of fifty people there, waiting to greet their young master for the first time and his Lady Mother their new mistress – though, after the much more modest staff of Elfinstone, it seemed to Tom that it was Lady Margaret and young Hal who were likely to be overpowered by this huge reception; and he would not have been at all surprised to find that this was the actual objective of the show.

Captain Quin strode with stately officiousness towards the horses' heads, while Chamberlain Danforth began to descend towards the coach door, cross-gartering gleaming impressively – clearly far too important and dignified to hurry.

Unobserved, ungreeted and impatient on the sudden, Tom stepped down and threw his reins up to Ben. Then he was in motion, striding across the last of the flagged yard to the coach-side.

Long before Martin Danforth condescended to negotiate the last few steps, Tom was at the door. He glanced across at Quin's shoulders and the back of his red head as the Captain of Horse took his charges. Then, paying no attention to the squawking of the sluggard chamberlain, he swung the door wide. Lady Margaret appeared, radiant in the golden firelight. The servants there burst into applause.

As though this was some kind of signal, the placid horses suddenly took fright and jumped forward, taking Captain Quin with them. Had Martin Danforth been at the door, Lady Margaret would have been thrown bodily from the coach and tumbled in the dirt; but

Tom was there in his stead, and as the Lady Margaret was thrown out and down by the sudden lurching of the coach, Tom reached up and plucked her from the very jaws of disaster.

Like the most courtly of gallants about the most elegant volte – Her Majesty's favourite dance – he caught the Lady Margaret at the waist and swung her safely, securely, to the ground.

'Welcome to Cotehel, My Lady,' he said quietly, holding her still until she recovered from the shock of near-disaster and steadied under his hands.

CHAPTER 19

Rage

Tom could scarcely remember having seen such rage in a man, let alone a woman; and it was all the more effective for being conducted in icy silence. Certainly Polrudden Quin and Martin Danforth quailed under the weight of it for all they both tried to bluster manfully.

Tom suspected that Lady Margaret might have been more given to charity had this not been a fiasco performed in the face of the whole household – with a much more serious consequence so narrowly averted; and he was certain that the mistress of Cotehel would have been more understanding – even of the pompous self-importance of the pair – had not poor Hal been so upset. Tossed about the inside of the coach and tumbled under the considerable bulk of Mistress Agnes, he had seen his beloved mother thrown bodily out through the door. He had no knowledge of the safe hands into which she had fallen. With a vivid certainty against which his own discomfort was as nothing, he had supposed his mother hurt and humiliated.

Consequently, when Tom had reached in and pulled him with almost fatherly hands from beneath the shaken Danforth, Hal had already been near hysterical. Only the strength of his aristocratic blood – amongst the purest in the land – had kept him in control as he walked with his mother through the crowd of servants; but there had been tempests and tantrums after that, and Tom, with ready sympathy, could well see why.

The other coaches had arrived to find Lady Margaret putting the tearful boy to bed herself, in the absence of any servants familiar or trustworthy enough to undertake the task. In her absence, the feast of welcome remained untasted and slowly coming to ruin.

When she did come down, like a whirlwind, it had not been to lead them to table. Agnes Danforth had been summoned. Some ten minutes later so had Tom, led by the shaken housekeeper to a private reading-room, where

Lady Margaret sat beside a low-banked fire with a pile of paper on a little table beside her, writing furiously – writing so furiously, indeed, that the little silver bell beside the papers kept up a constant, gentle, muted tintinnabulation. No sooner had Tom entered than the housekeeper was given two more pieces of paper and, glancing at them, she vanished.

Lady Margaret gestured Tom to a seat near at hand and he sat, uneasily. It did not feel right to him that he should sit in her presence; but if she so ordered, it would surely be a greater social mistake to disobey, and in her present mood it might well be very unwise to cross her.

Idly at first he watched her fierce writing; then he frowned. Even Will Shakespeare, when working full-speed on his plays, used quill and ink – though that was slow and messy; and, unworldly when concentrating, Will was apt to run out of ink at vital moments. But Lady Margaret was using one of those new-fangled pencils Tom had heard about. Up near Carlisle, where he had been born and raised, there was a graphite mine – so important that it was owned, mined and guarded by the Queen. For it was the only source in all the kingdom of the priceless columns of pencil-lead that were inserted into the little sticks. How much easier and more fluid was this new method of writing, Tom thought – how much easier, given that, apart from gesture and lip-movements, it was surely her primary method of communication.

No sooner had he completed the thought than she thrust a paper at him.

Thank you again, sir, it said. *You have done me very great service.*

'I hope to do more, Lady Margaret,' he began; but a knock at the door forestalled him.

She picked up a bell behind the pile of papers. She rang it clearly once. *Enter,* Tom assumed, for the door opened.

In came Martin Danforth first, still waistcoated and cross-gartered in daffodil. Polrudden Quin came behind him, face like a flitch of bacon. They stood before her like a pair of schoolboys caught scrumping the squire's apples.

'My Lady...' they both began together, comically, like a pair of clowns in one of Will's plays. Each looked at the other, mightily offended that he had been interrupted; and then each began again. 'My Lady...'

Up went My Lady's left hand, silencing their bluster as effectively as a slap. Unexpectedly, Tom was thrust another piece of paper with her right. He glanced down at it. He blenched; began to huff and bluster a little himself. 'Ah, the Lady Margaret wishes me to inform you...' he began, eyes scanning down the note a little desperately.

Her left hand rapped on the table, right hand busily scribbling. He faltered. She thrust another paper at him.

Read my words.

'All of your concern,' he read obediently, 'is to serve the Baron and myself, his mother. You have crossed us in our journey. You have slowed our progress. You have not worked to the best of your ability. You have welcomed us with pomp that would have made the Queen to blench and only Master Musgrave has saved us from disaster at your hands. You should thank him most profoundly, for it was only his swift thoughts and safe hands that have kept you in your posts. Good service I am swift to reward; laggard service I am swift to punish. If you fail again by the merest jot or tittle, I will send you packing, though your families have served mine since before this place was founded.'

Tom finished reading. As he had been the speaker, both men had looked at him, with outrage and no little hatred written on their faces; but as soon as he fell silent, Lady Margaret rapped upon the table and met their gaze with hers. Tom had not realized before that blue eyes could burn with rage.

But so, it seemed, they could.

Quin spoke first, his voice like a rusty hinge. 'My profoundest apologies, My Lady. It was an accident that will never be repeated.'

The burning blue gaze swivelled to Tom, and Quin turned, stiffly. 'I thank you, Master Musgrave,' he grated, 'for saving both my mistress and my employment tonight.'

'And I,' said Martin Danforth, his voice so thick with the Cornish tongue and manly outrage as to be impenetrable, 'apologize that my slowness allowed such a thing to occur. I, too, thank the Master of Defence for helping in the matter.'

'You have made two dangerous enemies there, Lady Margaret,' said Tom, as the door closed behind them. 'But you did well, I think, to spread some of their enmity to me.'

I do not fear what they might do to me was her hastily scrawled reply. *But Hal...*

'If you do not trust them, be rid of them.'

I seek only to winnow the wheat from the chaff. Many are very worthy.

'But all of them must have been employed by your cousin Hugh.'

That does not make them my enemies – just because he was.

'But still, My Lady, you are too good. And to run such a risk.'

No sooner had he spoken than there came a gentle tap at the door again.

The bell rang: *Enter.*

Agnes Danforth led in a couple of kitchen wenches bearing food and drink for two. They put the food where their silent mistress directed and, silently, left.

When we have eaten, said the next note, *I wish you to tell me all your news.*

Suddenly Tom found he wasn't all that hungry after all; but, under Lady Margaret's steady, unflinching gaze, he found he had no choice. So he started with the mysterious portrait.

You have seen it?

'I have it. Do you know whence it came?'

Essex. It came with a message which I returned. He wishes to mend fences.

'Don't trust him.'

She smiled a little and shook her head as though she had never considered it – which, of course, she never could, he thought. Only a man as arrogant as Essex would have supposed she might, in the face of the fact that he had raped her and tried to kill her more than once. He must be desperate.

Then Tom was forced to pull his wandering thoughts back to the matter in hand, with a mental admonishment. No matter what he spoke of next, he would upset her.

She was stronger than he could ever have dreamed, however. She accepted with grim equanimity his account of why the portrait had vanished from her chamber: because it blocked the spy-hole and made the secret panel impossible to open. Once over that hurdle, he described the second tunnel and the spy-hole in her dressing-room.

So. I must add another to the list of men that have seen me naked. Do you know who?

'Not yet. But you must have suspected something yourself. Why else did you write?'

I voiced a fear to Master Mann that I was being overwatched beyond reason and he suggested I do so. To someone I was sure would help me.

Tom hesitated of a sudden – not because he was chary of explaining how the note was delivered at last but because of that word

210

overwatched. It was a word he had taken most care in picking out of the original; and the phrase beside it – *Help me* – was the one phrase in all the missive that had been written whole. And they were not the same. Even with these being written in pencil and the other in ink, the handwriting was not the same. 'So,' he said quietly, 'you gave your message to your secretary and he made fair copies of it for you.'

Of course. Why else keep a secretary but to write my letters?

'You were not concerned that he should know your fears?'

Of course not. He knows all my business. I could not run my households without him. He reads and answers all my correspondence. I only see what he thinks is important enough to trouble me or I would be overwhelmed. I get letters from all over the kingdom – many of them begging. I have farms to run the length and breadth of the land as well as two castles to maintain. He writes to the factors of my estates. He even corresponds with the Rochester Assize for me. Did you know the Lord of Elfinstone is Justice to the court?

'So he wrote the letters Mann and John Hammond carried.'

Yes. Did you receive them?

Tom's deep breath warned her that his answer would be neither short nor pleasant.

It is a miracle, she wrote at last.

'What is?'

That you should have discovered so much from

211

so little. Have made such an adventure out of so few parts of words. Have come so far to aid me on such a slight summons.

'I would have come further on slighter, My Lady, had I thought to be of help to you.'

Gallantly said. The pencil hesitated. The hand withdrew. Returned. *What next?*

'We must get some rest. Tired minds will never fathom this coil.'

That's wise.

It is wise, thought Tom. But 'tis also a lie.

For he had no intention of sleeping tonight. Lady Margaret might fear the licence that All Fools would release within the great castle on Friday, but there was the potent promise of evil done long before that. And he would stand guard on her tonight – as close as ever he could – for were he the sin-worm or any one of the others confederated against her, he would be quick to consider swift action later this very night. Before he and Ben could explore the castle and its secret places; before the Lady could arrange her defences; while all was coil and bustle with everything out of place and nothing yet reduced to any order; and the lady almost as widely open to over-watching and abusing as she would be by the end of the week.

CHAPTER 20

Repose

There was much more they needed to discuss, of course – enough to keep them going through days, let alone nights; but Lady Margaret, shocked and distressed though she was, acquiesced. For Tom was right: tired minds make bad decisions; and bad decisions under these circumstances had already cost lives.

Lady Margaret rang the bell. Before its silver tinkling stopped echoing Agnes Danforth was in the room. The Lady's dimpled chin made a decisive upward gesture.

'Of course, My Lady. Your room has been prepared.'

She half-rose, then sat again, scribbling.

Hal?

'Asleep like a babe, My Lady. In the dressing-room beside your own where you put him. There is now a fire burning in both, as you ordered.'

Is he alone?

'Not tonight, My Lady. Young Gwennyth as he likes so much is sitting up with a candle in case he calls for something.'

Rooms for Master Musgrave?

'Prepared long since, My Lady. His, ah ... *apprentice* is safely bedded down. Master Martin has waited up himself to conduct Master Musgrave...' She glanced across to where Tom sat, watching. 'The rest of the household's abed, My Lady – except for the chaplain. He's celebrating the midnight services due to the season and the day. Maybe one or two there at communion with him – those that missed it at Buckfast.'

Lady Margaret nodded once and was in motion. Tom sprang to her side as she swept from the room. Agnes Danforth followed swiftly enough behind them, shielding the candle with her hand. Down a corridor they went, out into the main hall at the foot of the stair to the upper levels where Martin the Chamberlain sat in a hooded chair beneath a standard candelabrum boasting half a dozen steady flames. He sprang up as they approached and detached the largest of the candles, stepping up on to the lowest step of the staircase; but Lady Margaret stopped. Her eyes sought his and closed for an instant; her hands closed together as though in prayer.

'Take us to the chapel,' ordered Tom in the face of their confusion. 'My Lady wishes to join in the midnight services.' Without batting an eyelid, Martin Danforth returned the candle to the candelabrum and lifted the whole off the floor. Then, holding it almost theatrically high, he swept across the hall and

214

out before them with his sister Agnes, thin-lipped, behind and his mistress behind the pair of them, leaving Tom to close the great door once they were all through.

Martin and Agnes Danforth led them out through the main door, down the imposing outer staircase and into the great courtyard. The huge edifice of the castle hulked behind them, seeming to push them away with its black and absolute bulk; but the great court-yard was so substantial that there was room enough for them to feel easy – especially as the moon was high and filling, the sky was clear and all the stars were out. Though spring, it remained balmy and almost sum-mer in heat. All down the balustrades the flambards still burned – though low and guttering now – for it was easier to let them burn out. Through the gateway – open, with the portcullis up – the main approach was also still illuminated, stretching away along the cliff-edge above Whitsand Bay.

Agnes and Martin led the pair of them across the courtyard – though this was just service and courtesy, for it was clear enough where the chapel was. The little building nestled close against the inner wall, but tall and independent, with its steeple high and clear, though dwarfed a little by the battle-ments above. Dedicated to St Michael, it had been built here by the Conqueror's men, before the castle itself was ever dreamed of. The lights within it glimmered like fallen stars and, beside the flambards and under the moonlight, made Martin Danforth's gesture with the candelabrum quite unnecessary. This was a situation which, like the matter of the coach earlier, became compounded by misfortune. For, on the bottom step, he tripped. Perhaps his formal cross-gartering had come loose. In an instant he was reeling and the whole metal column of the candelabrum went spinning away to clatter across the courtyard like the crack of doom. Both Tom and Lady Margaret hurried to help him. They pulled him to his feet, tidied away the nearest candles and left him and his sister gathering the other precious white-wax columns and putting them back into their battered places. Then the pair of them crossed to the chapel door.

While Margaret hesitated on the doorstep, pulling up her lace shawl into a suitable headdress, Tom looked into the little church. Agnes had been mistaken, he thought. There was no one here except the priest kneeling silently at his devotions. Then he turned back to find Margaret waiting for him, hand raised. Down upon his forearm it came, resting there as naturally as it had rested on her master of horse's at Buckfast, seeming to burn through the thick black velvet like a brand into his flesh, even so.

As this was the private chapel of a rich and powerful family, there was provision of private pews at the front for their use, and Tom led Lady Margaret there, then stood, and sat and knelt at her side. Once in a while he glanced sideways at her, but she never took her eyes off the plain altar. Open in worship or closed in prayer, her eyes never stopped a gentle weeping as, he suspected shrewdly, she prayed for the souls of the good men killed in her service so far; and, he thought, after the sight of her rage against Danforth and Quin, she was probably also praying for the thorough damnation of whoever had caused their deaths. But his mind soon drifted away from speculation into other, darker reaches of its own. The power of her proximity was a powerful distraction from all thought. All too swiftly he found himself tempted into simple sensuality, listening to the steady whisper of her breathing, how it varied as she mouthed her silent responses. The warmth of her was transmitted over the cooling air to the back of his hand, to his arm, to the length of his leg. The scent of her filled his nose, a mysterious, nameless perfume, compound of some essence of her skin, sweet breath, and other, more personal odours. Only the sanctity of the moment, the holiness of the place and Tom's own iron self-control restrained his imagination from straying any further; and he prayed as he had never prayed before.

There was no interminable sermon tonight – and fortunately, for it would have presented Tom's mind with almost irresistible idleness and licence; but it was still nearly two in the morning when they softly thanked the Reverend Joses Wainscott and made their way back up to the back of the chapel where Agnes and Martin waited, dozing on their feet. This time Martin was a little more conservative – and a lot more careful – with his provision of light. Across the courtyard and up the steps they went, through the main doors, to hesitate while Martin closed them and locked them tight at last. Then on up the stairway to the first landing, where their guides separated. Following Martin up and to the right hand, Tom nevertheless strained over his shoulder to see Agnes's light – and Margaret's shadow – for as long as possible. For as soon as things were quiet, he and Ben would be off again, looking to stand guard on the Countess and the Baron as they slept.

The room Martin led him to was lost in a maze of corridors and staircases that made up this part of the castle; but Tom had suspected that it would be, for even if the strange behaviour he had seen so far was motivated by overawed affection for their mistress, logic dictated they would wish to lodge such interlopers as himself well away from her. And were their motives darker, their desire to be rid of him would be all the greater. However, though he did not know Cotehel, he knew many another castle like it, he thought. No sooner had Martin lit him to his door and shown him into the shadowed chamber lit by a single taper that seemed to tremble under the stentorian snores of its second occupant than he was planning how to return and explore.

The first thing he did, using the very last spark from the dying taper, was to light the wick of the great white candle he had stolen while helping Martin after he had fallen on the steps. He had slid it into the wide top of his boot, which he now removed, together with its fellow. Then, in stockinged feet and silent as a ghost, he crossed the shaking bed and shook Ben like a bear with a salmon until his apprentice came choking awake.

'Ben!' he spat. 'Stir yourself; we must away at once.'

For a man in such a deep sleep, the lad awoke bright-eyed and sharp-witted. 'I'm with ye, master. D'ye know where the Lady and the Baron sleep?'

'On the far side of the castle.'

'Now there's a surprise.'

'Irony. A classical tone, I assume.'

'Sarcasm, as well you know. Ciceronian in its effect, however.'

'I think an ironist such as yourself should play Lucifer, while I carry the iron of a different stamp.'

'A pleasing play on words, master. I will carry the candle, then; and you shall wield your steel.'

Tom suited the action to the word and slithered out his blade. 'Kick off your shoes that we may tip-toe,' he ordered. 'Open the door as silently as death. Then let us be about it.'

The darkness was absolute, but the candle burned still and clear, shedding ample light to guide them through the maze that Tom had taken such pains to remember. The ancient flooring was all stone, so it was easy to move in near absolute silence. They were slow and careful, however, both too well aware that the brightness that guided them would also betray them swiftly enough to any prying eyes.

Down the last set of steps they came to the upper landing, where Agnes had led Margaret away left and Martin had taken Tom to the right. Tom slowed them to their careful and most silent progress here, for the entrance hall was large. Galleries and passages – as well as stairways – led into it and out. There was no telling what eyes might be watching their star-bright progress ill-intentioned and unsuspected. For, after his greeting at Buckfast, his handling of the Countess's person and his entertainment subsequently, tongues would be wagging. A midnight visit to her chamber – no matter how necessary and well-intentioned – would be the undoing of her reputation if told by the wrong tongue – or recounted into the wrong ear. What work might the Earl of Essex, for instance, make of it in private gossip with Her Majesty. Enough to make her forget her irritation over his own marriage. Even that would be worth the risk to him.

Tom, though, sat squarely on the horns of the most terrible dilemma. For even a reputation stained and tattered would be preferable to a murdered Countess; or – and this was the deepest and darkest of his fears, one suited to the black watches in such a place as this – the Lady Margaret ravished once again, so that those malicious tongues in her enemies' employ might whisper, *But you see she must enjoy it. To have accepted it as a girl and again as a woman...*

'Straight on,' he hissed to Ben.

This side of the castle keep was much simpler in design than the one that housed them, thought Tom. Larger chambers made shorter passages. Public rooms filled entire floors – a great hall, a long gallery, a library and map-room; and in the very heart of the place, most unexpectedly, an armoury.

'A map-room I can understand,' Tom hissed to the awed Ben. 'Travel is the foundation of their fortune, after all. But there must be enough swords and armour, guns and spears here for an army. Can you see any powder?'

'No, master.'

'Thank God for that. Or the reduction of the Outram line to dust and ashes could be swiftly and completely achieved for certain, could it not?'

'That was probably a powder store I observed beside the church on the way in,' said Ben.

'You saw it too, did you? Well done.'

Such a man as Tom, even on such a vital mission as this, could hardly resist the call of an armoury. In he tip-toed, therefore, his eyes on the swords particularly. His movement caught Ben off guard and the light-bringer was slow to follow, therefore. The light went out of the room as the candle went behind Tom's back and for a moment he found himself in absolute darkness.

No. Not absolute.

His tired mind, distracted from its mission already, was distracted again. For right at the far end of the Stygian chamber there was a square of brightness high up on the wall: brightness laced, filigreed, with sinuous lines of shadow. Tom walked towards it, keeping his eyes fixed upon it even when Ben came into the room behind him with the candle. In the shadowy brightness of that one tiny flame it was just possible to see that, high on the wall, reaching right across the room was what looked like an internal window. Indeed, thought Tom suddenly, there should truly be windows in all of these rooms, for unless his sense of direction had been utterly confused, all the rooms on this side should be looking away southward over the star-spangled, moon-bright reaches of the Channel.

These thoughts took him to the end wall, hung with heavy tapestries like all the walls in the public rooms; but at the right-hand side, the tapestry was in a state of slight but constant motion. He lifted it and there was a door beneath it, let into the solid-looking wall.

'Have you seen the like of this?' he hissed to Ben.

'I've heard tell,' answered the bricklayer, taking the corner of the heavy cloth as Tom

222

knelt to the door's ancient lock. ' 'Twould not be such a wonder in daylight,' he said, 'for the inner window, barred or not, must let in some light. But aye, 'tis a double wall. I wonder what's behind it...'

'Cannon,' said Tom, working now with his dagger. 'This is the place where King Henry's builders added new defences to the old castle and put in the cannon and culverins that fired the first shot at the Armada, and famously so. 'Tis the only explanation for such a strange design.' At the last word, he opened the door, which swung back flat against the wall into a little lobby at the bottom of a flight of steps.

Ben followed him into the stairwell, careful of his candle; but he need hardly have bothered, for the stairwell was bright – and short. No sooner had they stepped up than their heads were above the floor level above; and it was as Tom had said: behind the wall of the armoury was a kind of balcony, strongly built and stone-floored, walled on the outer side but with two gaping embrasures in which sat a pair of long cannon, pointing southward across the restless waters near three hundred feet below.

On the left side of the place was the foot of a ladder leading upwards and on the right, a square hole in the floor containing the head of a ladder leading down. The open-sided chamber was tidy, well supplied with shot and coiled ropes. Pikes stood beside the cannon, ready to vary their field of fire. Barrels of match sat ready; rams and swabs beside them.

'But still no powder,' whispered Tom. When he received no answer, he turned to find Ben peeping through the grille behind, which looked over the shadowed well of the armoury, behind and below them now.

With no further hesitation, Tom led Ben up the ladder on to the next gun platform. Here, even in the moon-brightness, it was possible to see that the inner grille was glimmering with golden light. Silently but curtly, Tom gestured Ben to wait at the ladder's head and he crossed on silent tip-toe to check the platform. The flooring looked solid enough – stone except for a wooden trap in the corner by the foot of one ladder; solid stone wall at the back, except for the opening. He sank down on one knee, holding his breath and straining to see. It was Lady Margaret's chamber, never a doubt of it. For there was an uncanopied bed, untenanted to boot, and a fire banked low in the grate. A candle stood on a paper-strewn table and a door into the next room stood ajar. The bedchamber was much smaller than the armoury below, the larger areas of the old castle walled and partitioned as they had been in Elfinstone. If he strained, he could hear a whisper of low voices; but no sooner had he recognized young Hal talking to his silent mother than the Lady herself returned. Even in the shadows the glory of her undressed hair seemed to shine. She wore a golden un-dressing-robe, its stiff material open to reveal a simple sleeping-shift beneath. With unconscious grace, even as she came in through the door, she pulled the robe off and cast it over the foot of the bed. The thin stuff of her simple shift seemed to cling to every womanly curve of her as she moved; and in that fatal instant before Tom could tear his eyes away, she crossed in front of the fire and there, imprinted in his eyes, as indelibly as the brand on Gawdy's thumb, was the picture of her form perfectly presented, as though stark naked, as the firelight shone through the linen.

Tom tore his eyes away and turned to find Ben gesturing at him silently but fiercely. Tom rose and crossed to his friend's side.

'What?' he spat.

'Look!'

Tom strained his eyes again, blinking the lingering vision of Lady Margaret away. The sea crawled away towards France like a great swathe of creased grey silk, stirring under a breeze. Above it, falling from the height of Heaven down to the restless wrinkles, fell the stars. The moon was setting behind the castle, so its brightness was diminishing. In from the Western Approaches a milky skim of high, high cloud was spreading across the heavens, making the stars all pale and ghostly.

So that it was easy to see what Ben was talking about: down below in the distant waters lay the black shape of a ship. It was big and broad with high castles fore and aft, like the pictures Tom had seen of the ill-fated Armada galleons. Its sails were furled and its masts nodding gently as though it sat at anchor.

Someone on its high forecastle was signalling: a bright dot of light, clearer and more insistent than any star, was blinking in their direction.

CHAPTER 21

Secrets

Tom and Ben glanced at each other, sharing the same thought with the same look. If there was a signal, then there was someone being signalled to. Tom leaped on to the ladder and began to swarm up it with all the speed he could manage, pausing only as his head came past floor level to look around. The next level was empty, and so was the one above that.

Tom came out on to the top level, still only half-aware of the layout of the castle through whose secret labyrinths he was climbing. Such was his tension, excitement and tiredness that he paused, glanced and continued without allowing the information from his eyes time to register on his mind. So it was that he leaped out on to the very battlements themselves. There were no crenellations, merely a hole with an open trap-door beside a short-barrelled culverin. The culverin stood on the very edge of the place, its stubby barrel jutting over a sheer stone precipice. That stone-built cliff joined a rough rock cliff over one hundred feet below and then fell more than two hundred feet more to the breakers whose whispering roar was lost in the buffeting of the wind. Suddenly dizzied by the closeness of such an awesome depth, Tom staggered over to the solidity of the gun itself as Ben threw himself upwards as well.

Disorientated though he was, Tom was looking around. They were alone – and again, fortunately so, for any enemy with an ounce of fortitude could have pitched the pair of them to their doom in the next few seconds, he thought grimly. Then Ben joined him clinging to the cannon as though the weight and solidity of the thing were all that would save them from being blown like gossamer over the edge.

The plain roof of the great keep stretched inwards from the vertiginous chasm apparently featurelessly, like a square, monolithic pinnacle atop some legendary mountain. The flagstones of which it was made were set smooth and square and reached in series inwards from the absolute angle of the edge as though Euclid or Pythagoras had laid them out. The moon, shining exactly across the place, as though they stood level with its declining crescent, showed hardly any irregularities before, away on the inner side, an absolute black line defined the other edge square-cut.

Tom looked away to his right. The line of culverins stepped away in series, each jutting its stubby barrel out over the precipice, each with the solid little wheels of its trunnions rolled up to the very edge, each with a tub of powder beside its tub of match. Beyond the last of them, the lip of the platform became the top of the wall. Tom turned. Behind him, beyond Ben, a couple of culverins separated him from a second edge, where the platform once again became the top of the outer wall, which circled solidly round until it joined the top of the battlements above the gatehouse. Apart from the wall-top, nothing came near the elevated platform; apart from the church tower, nothing overlooked it – and only the inner shafts led up to and down from the place.

Tom let go of the solid metal and stepped inwards. Of course, the platform he was crossing could not be as featureless at it had first seemed. There was another opening three cannons down, with another ladder leading back down into the gun emplacements they had just explored. Further in, near the centre of the area, there was a series of trap-doors. All of these were locked or stuck – except for one. Tom eased that one up for an inch or so, allowing the moonlight to flood into the shaft it capped; his nose twitched, then he replaced it silently and rose.

Everywhere was empty, silent, but for the restlessnesses of wind close at hand and far-distant waves; except for the waning light of the setting moon, dark. But for Ben, Tom might have been standing alone at the utter edge of all the world.

Then why, he wondered, was he certain that there was someone watching him? 'Ben?' he called, his voice low.

Ben turned from his inspection of the vessel far below. 'Master?'

'Do you feel that secret eyes are on us?' His voice only just carried to his thoughtful assistant.

'No, Master. But I have been watching this ship, so I have paid scant attention. It has stopped signalling and is setting sail.'

'Very well,' said Tom, loudly, after a moment more. 'Then let us return to our post. There is nothing more for us here.'

So they passed the night, with Ben sitting beside the cannon and Tom leaning against the inner wall beside the metal grille.

Tom, particularly, kept his eyes out to seaward, as though watching for the mysterious ship's return. In fact his eyes were closed, allowing only the sensitivity of his most acute hearing to venture in through the grille into the dark room – where, as the night passed, the fire crackled and settled; the errant draughts whispered in papers like autumn leaves; the candle guttered and hissed into silence; and his lady's even breathing was punctuated with the whispering sound of her night clothes and her bed clothes as she tossed and turned restlessly in the grip of her silent sleep.

★　★　★

Only when both she and Ben were safe and sound did Tom stir. Silently he climbed back up to the square-cut roof. Out of the pouch at his side he took the tinderbox that rarely left his side and, easily in the dead calm of moon-set, he lit the candle once again. Then, with the steady star of light in one hand and the late footpad Green's dag loaded and ready in the other, he explored the roof again and tried the trap that had been open before. It was closed and bolted now, but still the tell-tale stench given off by a dark-lantern lingered; and still in the hinge of the thing, as he had noticed in the moonlight earlier, was a scrap of lace torn off the cuff of the secret signaller – hopefully unnoticed as he made good his escape down here.

Awoken before dawn by the breakfast feeding of the local gulls, Ben and Tom crept silently back to their chamber and – flesh having its limitations even in such as they – slept until the early afternoon. Both men were old soldiers, used to maintaining their clothing even in battlefield conditions; they invested the first hour after awakening in brushing and washing, in spitting and polishing. Then, while various garments aired and dried, they fell to barbering, trimming and shaving, with Tom's long razor-sharp Solingen steel daggers. Then, having made themselves pre-sentable with Tom's fearsome armaments, courtesy dictated that the swords and daggers

– all but one dagger apiece for use at table – be left in their room.

They made a creditable show of cleanliness and courtly fashion in person, linen, boots and beards, when they swaggered forth in search of late luncheon, therefore, but were swept into My Lady's bustling orbit before fashion or famine could be addressed.

'Master Musgrave,' called Agnes Danforth the moment Tom stepped down into the entrance hall. 'My Lady asked me to call you to her the moment I saw you myself.'

'What's toward?' demanded Tom with a frown of worry. He turned on her heel and gestured Ben to follow.

'Something I daresay you'll dismiss as a trifle, but it's upset her.'

Tom manfully demurred, but the fact was that when the Lady Margaret told him of her latest trial he was hard put not to laugh aloud. The expression on his face as he read her note, however, caused a flash of fire in those warm blue eyes, a frown and a decided stamp of her foot.

'You do not understand,' said Agnes with infinite superiority, resuming at last her rightful place as both woman and housekeeper over him, mere man and passing visitor that he was. 'Percy Gawdy's continued absence is a serious matter to My Lady. At least the Baron can continue his education with Master St Just in Doctor Rowley's absence, but without her secretary Her Ladyship is most sorely tried. You do not comprehend the weight of her responsibilities, sir, nor the delicacy of her position. It is expected that she will host a party for all the local people of the first rank within the next two days and yet without Secretary Gawdy she cannot even issue invitations...'

'What!' said Tom. 'Is Gawdy the only one of you that can write?'

No! answered the Lady, neatly proving her word by her action. *But these things must be done in a certain style and form...*

'And in clear handwriting, as like as not,' allowed Tom.

'You have it right, sir,' admitted Agnes. 'There are proud families hereabout that would be mortally offended if someone such as My Lady were to send out a missive of any kind that was less than perfectly presented...'

'I see,' said Tom thoughtfully. And of course he saw more even than Agnes would tell: that the most educated here, those with the best writing and the grasp of the correct forms, were every bit as proud as the local lords and ladies. Somehow he could not imagine Master Quin or Danforth being willing to demean himself and cover his cuffs and fingers in humiliating ink-blots. Nor St Just, come to that. He had particularly long and fashionable cuffs: he would hardly risk his standing in the household, even to spend an afternoon cheek by jowl with his too-beloved mistress. The secretary, after all, like the schoolmaster, was necessarily of high education but eternally of low esteem.

'Well I can go in search of them, I suppose,' he said after a while. 'Or ... No. I have it. Fear not, My Lady; I think help is at hand. And from the most unlikely source of all.' For into his memory had flashed the original note that she had sent him – not the bloodied version, fading even as he looked at it, but Ben's transcription, bold, clear and beautifully written.

No fool, and no willing scribe either, Ben was halfway out through the door by this time, but Tom was too quick for him. At least, to sweeten the deal, Tom arranged to have food brought in to him while he worked.

With Lady Margaret's most pressing need satisfied for the time being, Tom took his nose for dark-lanterns and trouble together with his one torn clue of lace and explored the castle. He went everywhere the notion took him. If there were places in the castle kept intentionally secret, he did not find them then. Every place he wished to visit was opened to him as he worked his slow, thoughtful way upward through that Monday afternoon. It was not always done with good grace, nor was it always done at once – for his desires often ran counter to the usual routines and both Martin Danforth and Polrudden Quin had good reason to resent his inquisitiveness; but it was done, because the Lady Margaret ordered it – and her word, silent though it might be, was law.

He began in the deepest medieval dungeon

in the place and climbed level after level. Through centuries and cellars, store-rooms, wash-rooms, laundry, shambles, butchery, smoke-house, bakery, brew-house, smithy, chapel and powder-room up to the defensive works scarce fifty years old; out into the bee garden lined with spring-busy hives, through herb garden and kitchen garden, both a-buzz with honey bees, back into the kitchen. Then on to the servants' quarters, dining-rooms, and through private rooms and family rooms to public rooms and bedrooms, back to the areas he knew from last night, right up to the still-awesome gun emplacement on the roof.

Here, being the man he was, Tom began to test himself, savouring the rare taste of his diminishing fear of the place. Thus he was standing on the very edge, looking down past a toe-cap that actually projected from the edge when the young Baron found him.

'Master St Just is taking me out in my boat. Would you like to come?'

'Does the Lady Margaret know of this?'

'Oh, we need not tell her everything, need we?' sparkled the excited boy. 'My Lady mother has enough to worry about, even though I hear you have lent her your brick-layer as a secretary! Hurry or we shall miss the tide!'

Between the chapel and the powder store there was a sally-port or secret gateway in the wall. It led out on to a solid rock balcony that gave on to a combination of steps and sloping

pathways that swooped under a beetling overhang and away down the cliff to a little bay
and a big stone jetty. At various points on this
vertiginous way there were more balconies,
many of them backed not with solid rock but
with great iron-bound doors set into the cliff
face; and down the steepest paths and stairways ropes hung convenient for use as banisters. It was at once a surprise that the sea, so
distant from the castle battlements, should be
so accessible; and yet it was somehow
inevitable, thought Tom, for the sea and the
ships upon it were the reason for the castle's
existence in the first place.

The bay was private, the jetty solid – large
but by no means huge. Tom turned and
looked upwards. The ropes that proved such
useful banisters were attached to a series of
pulleys reaching up beneath the castle walls,
which seemed to reach out into the very air,
standing on the overhang at the top of that
vertiginous cliff. He could see how in the
early days of the Outram family's rise to
fortune, a goodly fleet of trading vessels could
have come and gone from here, sending their
cargoes up the cliffs easily and swiftly –
almost secretly – before the fleet became so
large and the vessels themselves so massive
that they had been forced to move round the
corner into the larger anchorages in Plymouth itself.

Certainly, there were no large vessels here at
the moment. All that bobbed by the jetty,
held by a single line, was a little open boat,

scarcely more than a rowing-boat. If it was a dozen feet long Tom would have been surprised. The mast stepped through the forward seat seemed little taller than he was himself. There was a simple foresail secured to the bow without the addition of a bow-sprit. There was a triangular mainsail held at the mast-top and on a simple, stubby boom. A pair of oars and a boat-hook lay in the bilge, which seemed sound enough and dry. It was very much the type of boat that Tom had played around in with his big brother John and their friend Hobbie Noble on the Lakes and on the Solway Firth close by.

'See, Master St Just,' called Hal as they arrived, 'I have brought Master Musgrave. He shall see me take the tiller too!'

St Just looked up from where he was untying the line. 'I saw ye on the cliff,' he said. *Cliff* hissed a little, but it was clear enough – clear also that he had had time enough to school himself out of any resentment he might have felt at Tom's sudden inclusion in the expedition. 'Can ye sail?'

'Not like you,' said Tom courteously. 'Never with the likes of Drake.'

'In then and take the tiller. Nind the doon.'

It took Tom a moment to translate: *Mind the boom.*

Tom stepped down and sat with the tiller under his arm, his spare hand on the ropes that held the boom. The liveliness of the little vessel flowed into him with the same shock as he had felt when touching Lady Mary's hand.

236

A fist closed on his shoulder and Hal climbed down.

'In the dow till we're out in the day,' ordered St Just, and the boy obeyed with unsteady care.

The line slapped into the bow in front of him, then St Just stepped down beside Tom. His fist too closed briefly on his shoulder, revealing to Tom's quick eye a long lace cuff – with a piece of it torn away. 'You nidshits. I take tiller.'

Tom moved on to the midships seat at the foot of the mast, careful lest his weight set the little vessel rocking too dangerously. St Just took the tiller and the wind took the sails as though their strange skipper had whistled it up. But no, thought Tom: whistling was something else lost to him with 'b's and 'p's and 'm's and any hopes he may ever have harboured of winning his Lady's heart. He looked at Hal and received Lady Margaret's sunniest smile with a twinkle from the Earl of Essex's eyes.

The little vessel skimmed across the bay towards the open sea, but before they came anywhere near the bigger waters out in the Channel proper, St Just turned once again, using the headland to protect them while the wind came steadily over their shoulders. Tom's wise eyes read the water and he began to understand what Hal had said about missing the tide. It must be slack water now, sitting lazily on top of the flood. They would have to watch out when the ebb set in, though, or they would be swept out into dangerous waters very swiftly indeed.

Tom's thoughts were interrupted by a terse command in St Just's peculiar accent. Hal rose obediently and made his careful way back down the boat. Soon he was seated at St Just's side and the sailor began to instruct him on how to take the tiller and steer. 'Renender,' he said gently, 'the doat's head will go the other way to the way you hush the tiller. *See?*'

The tiller was pushed right a little; the bow began to swing left.

'And as you go, ratch the doon. Over it cones! Duck!'

Round she came and over came the boom, the sail filling on the other tack. Tom found himself leaning backwards with his shoulders seemingly just above the hissing surface. He looked ahead. They were skimming along parallel to the shore of Whitsand Bay, with the cliffs reaching out to the castle on Rame Head still protecting them, seeming to swell, indeed, towards their highest point, such was the speed of their passage. The boat gave a little skip as St Just gave the boy full control and a handful of foam slapped Tom in the face. Laughing, he dashed it away and blinked his eyes clear, thinking, *He'd better be quick to come about at the end of this tack or we'll be away out to sea with a vengeance.* And so he did. The little vessel danced around well enough under his increasingly confident hand. The two men relaxed a little as the boy concentrated.

'Why would someone want to be signalling from the castle in the dead of night?' asked Tom conversationally. 'Someone with a dark-lantern?'

St Just's face came round slowly, until his violet eyes rested on Tom. He was so controlled that it occurred to Tom at once that he had been waiting for the question all afternoon. 'The coast's alive with snugglers,' he hissed. 'Across to France and out to the Scillies. There are those in the castle have deen signalling to snugglers since the first of the Outrans cane here.'

'And before then,' added Hal excitedly. 'Smugglers have been signalling here since long before my ancestors arrived, though I would wager my forefathers were as good at smuggling as they were at exploring.'

'And you, Master St Just – are you following in an ancient family tradition?' asked Tom, holding out the piece of lace as he spoke, to see if it would fit in St Just's torn sleeve.

The squall came round the headland then, so fast that it took them all by surprise. It was just a sudden flaw in the wind, a counter-draft. Tom saw it most clearly as a sudden darkening of the sea just in front of them as a counter-set of wavelets came with the new wind. The wind slapped him in the face harder than the foam had done; and again, more purposefully. The foresail slammed across from a swelling in front of Tom to a

hollow on the far side. The little boat hesitated, came upright, seemed to freeze at the
point where all the forces were, for an atom of
time, in balance.

Tom looked back over his shoulder. Then
over she went the other way, at the mercy of
the sudden headwind. The mainsail did
exactly what the foresail had done and slammed across on to the other side of the boat,
taking the boom with it. Sea-wise and quick-
thinking, even with the distraction of Tom's
sudden accusation, St Just ducked automatically so that the heavy balk of wood skimmed
over his gleaming curls.

Hal, confused, hesitant, literally taken
aback, was too slow. The boom took him
squarely on the side of the head and batted
him over the side.

St Just took control of the vessel at once,
hauling the tiller round so that the new wind
spun the boat almost on her heel. Tom knew
better than to move, but his eyes were
fastened on the circle of ripples and the
column of bubbles at their centre where the
lad had gone in. Round they came with every
line and joint groaning with the strain.

'Can ye see hin?' bellowed St Just.

'No.'

'I can't sin!' he called.

Tom's whirling brain couldn't make it out.
He forgot what he had been thinking earlier
about St Just's missing 'w's and 'm's.

'I'n a sailor. I can't sin!' shouted the desperate man.

Then, as they came thumping back across the first ripples of that terrible circle, Tom understood what St Just was saying.

I'm a sailor. I can't swim.

CHAPTER 22

Life and Death

Tom hit the water head-first with no further thought – with no thought at all, in fact, or he would have taken off his black-velvet doublet and his boots. At the very least he would have put the tell-tale scrap of lace somewhere safe; but as it was, he simply sucked in a massive breath, rolled sideways over the gunwale and began to swim vigorously downwards, following the column of bubbles into the darkening heart of the bay.

He very nearly lost his precious lungful when the water temperature hit him, but by then he was in fearsome action and was able to pull his mind and will away from the trembling shell of his body, like a soul on its way to Heaven. Always a strong swimmer, he grabbed great handfuls of water and hurled them back past his sides as his booted feet kicked tirelessly. The weight of the sodden wool, velvet and leather he was wearing helped him dive deeper and deeper, allowing him to keep the precious air in his chest. His mind, focusing with fearsome concentration, sought the boy and noted how the weight of the clothing was helping now. Quite what would happen if he found Hal and needed to swim upwards with him again was something that remained in the realms of distant speculation – with other such distant worries as what would happen if the squall that started this had brought a rogue current with it; or what would happen if they met a shark down here; or what he would say to Lady Margaret if they didn't find her son.

The bay was not deep, but the bottom he was heading for with all his might was disappointingly lacking in the white sand that gave the place its name, against which Hal's outline would have been clear; and the lack of some distinguishing feature was growing more of a problem by the moment, for the last of the bubbles he had been following so far glittered past his face and still there was no sign of the body that had made them. The departure of that last little piece of air seemed to signal something to Tom's lungs too, for the first spasm of real pain ripped at his chest then so fiercely that he might as well have been between the jaws of a ravening shark.

But he was simply not going to give up.

One more great convulsive heave of his leaden arms. One more kick with his aching legs. One more fevered glance from his burning, half-blind eyes. And there he was.

242

Hal's white face and snowy shirt were outlined against the black rocks just beneath, as though the lad were an anchor that had simply plummeted straight down from the point he had hit the water. The sight was enough to galvanize Tom into even more convulsive action, as though the sheer desperation with which he wanted to hold the lad had been fed directly into his limbs. Down he went through those last few icy feet, as though he were plumbing the frozen depths of Hell itself.

Better get used to it, Tom, suggested an ironic part of his mind.

The clarity of the water was deceptive, however: Hal lay further away than it seemed. Another series of increasingly desperate movements was needed to pull Tom right down until his numb and clumsy hands could wrap themselves like clawed clubs in the stuff of the boy's shirt.

Tom pulled the white drowned face to his own, feeling his heart twist agonizingly in his breast. As though the lad had been his own son, he pressed his lips to the boy's cold mouth. Air poured from Tom's lungs into Hal's and, as it did so, Tom felt the young body flinch.

That one convulsive movement was enough. Tom turned and began to fight his way upward, buoyed by the dizzy, burning hope that the boy still had a spark of life left in him and, if he could gain the surface swiftly enough, he might fan it back to life.

He could see the shifting, liquid mirror of the surface, with the shape of the boat like a water-beetle squatting on it. *Dear God*, he thought, but how far away it was. One-handed, he clawed upwards again, kicking against the dead weight of the boy.

And the most unexpected thing happened: a harpoon came down, striking at him as though he were some kind of whale. He saw it coming, in a strange slowness of movement, slicing down through the crystal heart of the water towards him. He saw the white iron point of it with the cockspur of the hook behind. He saw the shaft of it, smooth as a broom-handle, straight as a spear. He even noted that a line had been secured to it – a line of rope that led snaking up to the water-bug of the boat above. He had time enough to notice all these things as the spear made its stately way through the thickening, choking element towards him. He even had time to think what a perfect way the harpoon would be for a guilty man caught signalling to smugglers – or to Spaniards, indeed – to be rid of an importunate accuser. But he did not have time to move out of its way.

It struck him on the shoulder, grazed past and continued downwards for a little. Then it jerked to a stop and began to slip back upwards.

Distantly – very distantly – it occurred to him that if he could somehow grasp the harpoon it might help him to float upwards too. The thought registered; he understood it.

Reason told him that if he were going to try this then speed was of the essence. The white-wood handle slid up past his face again.

I should grasp hold of that, he told himself. Indeed he noted that his hand was convenient to it; but his hand was just floating there as though it had become detached from the rest of him. The wood knocked against it as it slid on upwards relentlessly and with gathering pace.

Then it occurred to Tom that the boat-hook might not, in fact, be floating upwards but that Hal and he might be sinking downwards once again, and that the next thing he was like to feel after the numbness gripping his body was the flames of Hell searing his soul. Sheer naked terror flashed right through the whole of his frame. So terrible and over-whelmingly powerful was it that it made him achieve the most difficult feat of his life: it made him close his fist. He jerked with all his might and felt the line tighten abruptly – and saw with distant satisfaction that St Just, so equivocally on the other end of it – was pitched out into the water above them.

The next thing Tom knew for certain was that he was hanging against the side of the boat, puking like a baby and trying to sum-mon up the energy to follow St Just into the rocking little cockleshell. Distantly, he heard a strangely accented voice saying monoton-ously, 'Cun on, Hal, another dreath, Hal. That's it, get rid of the rest. Duke it ut...' The next sounds set Tom off once again, but they were also amongst the most beautiful sounds he had ever heard in his life. He looked up to see the torn cuff again, and this time there was a strong and steady hand within it, reaching down for him as it had reached for Hal a few moments earlier.

A few moments later still, they were off again. Tom and St Just were both soaking from their ducking, bruised and bleeding from where they had scrambled back into the little boat and shivering in the cold evening wind. Hal was green and shaking, but strong enough – and determined – to take the tiller once again and con them back to the jetty. 'They're watching from the castle,' he said through chattering teeth. 'They must see what a sea-dog you have made of me, Master Ulysses, must they not?'

St Just climbed ashore looking as weary and battered as Tom felt, and secured the line before collapsing on to the jetty. Then the three of them just sat there, grinning at each other, laughing in the face of death.

'What shall we tell your mother?' asked St Just after a while, speaking, to Tom's adapting ear, more clearly than ever before.

'As little as possible. That's what I'd advise,' he gasped. 'Though if Hal was right about someone watching us, then she'll have heard the worst already. God, what a wilderness of trouble we'll be in when the Lady Margaret gets her hands on us!'

That started them all laughing properly and the laughter seemed to clear their lungs.

'She's going to be fit to burst,' choked Hal. And that set them off again.

Really, it was only the coming of the shadow-laden evening breeze, and the way the falling tide called in a persistent, chilly wind hard upon its heels, that got the three of them to move. One after the other they toiled up the cliff path with Tom leading and St Just bringing up the rear. They looked seasick, cold and bedraggled, but echoing upward before them went the sound of their manly laughter – which sound no doubt made it so easy for Martin Danforth to find them and inform them that Lady Margaret had been looking for them for some time past.

They went into the little library Lady Margaret was using as her office together and faced her, shoulder to shoulder. Ben was seated at a newly supplied table at the back, scribbling away in a world of his own. The Lady faced them standing, with pale cheeks and dark eyes, her mouth a thin, angry line.

They were men of their times and aware of the standing of their gender in the face of the weaker sex; but they were men and each one too well aware that they had brought the promise of outrage, sorrow and deadly tragedy into Lady Margaret's life – and that, perhaps for the first time, hopefully for the last and only time, they must lie to her by omission, if by nothing more.

Are you well? This to Hal, first.

'Quite well, Mother, though a little chilled

and seasick. Master St Just has taught me how to sail a boat; and Master Musgrave helped – somewhat. We fell into the water, I'm afraid, and went for a little swim.'

Are you mad?

This probably to St Just, but Tom spoke before he could.

'There's no harm done, My Lady. Master St Just has taught the lad a useful skill and one that might well guard his life in the future. The price was a wetting and a little seasickness.'

Lady Margaret looked at them, her eyes thawing, perhaps, just a fraction.

And the ruin of your wardrobe, she observed. *All of you.*

'Indeed, My Lady. I must into Plymouth on the morrow in the hope of a tailor and boot-maker. Or a cobbler, at the least.'

'And I,' added St Just. 'The cuffs are gone off ny shirt entirely.'

I will to market there myself. Tomorrow. And we will dine privately tonight, so that your apparel will cause none offence.

'We thank Your Ladyship,' said Tom. When he bowed, he dripped on to the floor.

I suspect I need to thank you more than you will allow, she wrote at last.

'You will need to expend a good weight of coin, master,' said Ben, almost awed – probably by the utter fullness with which Tom had ruined all the clothing he currently possessed – 'if you are going to hold your head up on

248

Thursday.'

They were walking slowly up towards the room they shared, getting ready to prepare for the promised private supper.

'I have written, I think, to every family of the first rank in this county and the next,' he continued. 'Everyone of consequence south of Dartmoor and Bodmin is bidden to dinner in the castle then. Most of the letters went out by rider as I finished them, area by area, all afternoon. The last go out at dawn, I understand. Hence Lady Margaret's need to go to market on the morrow. She'll be taking Cook with her, and perchance the *boutellier*, though he says the cellars are well enough stocked.'

'They are,' said Tom. 'I looked in on them this afternoon before I went boating with the Baron.'

'You know she had you watched – well, not *you*, precisely: her son.'

'Logic suggested it – logic, and her last note.'

'Agnes Danforth did it. She has the sharpest eyes in the castle. She reported a drowning and there was much concern. I overheard some of what she said, for although she whispered, she was mightily upset. There was a good deal of to-ing and fro-ing.'

'Hum,' said Tom.

'Master,' continued Ben, frowning, 'must we watch again tonight? My head pounds with all that penmanship; and I must observe, Master, that, drowning or not, you look as pale as milk – as a mixture of curds and whey, indeed.'

'Well, we'll see,' allowed Tom.

In the little room they shared a fire had been lit then banked low. Immediately before it stood a bath made of half a barrel, filled with fragrant, steaming water. Tom lowered himself into this at the earliest opportunity, folding his knees up until they touched his chin as he sought to bring the warmth of the water up to his very shoulders. No sooner had he done so than there came a tapping at the door and Ben let in two servant girls. The first had come to remove Tom's sopping clothes to see what restorative magic the castle's washerwoman could exercise upon them. The second came laden with what little from the castle slop-chest was of sufficient size and fashion to serve Tom through the rest of the evening.

The rest of the evening passed simply enough, however. Tom had supposed that the private supper proposed by Lady Margaret meant that Ben and he would be fed in a room alone; but no: by that deceptive phrase Lady Margaret had meant that she and the immediate members of the household should eat privately with her guests.

Thus in the family dining-room – rather than the main hall, where full formality obtained – were seated at seven the private family party. Lady Margaret and the young Baron Cotehel were there, of course; Agnes Danforth, though not at first Martin, who oversaw the service and organized the removes; Captain Polrudden Quin; Master Ulysses St Just, resplendent in new shirt and replacement clothes from the wardrobe he kept in the place; the Reverend Joses Wainscott; Tom; Ben. There were two places laid for Dr Ezekiel Rowley and Percy Gawdy, in the vain hope that they might arrive.

It was a festive board, most obviously marked by spring lamb, but well served also with mutton, beef and pork as well as a wide selection of fish. The occasion was, perhaps, a little more muted than it might have been, for Lady Margaret seemed thoughtful, and young Baron Henry said little and ate less – the bright and bubbling Hal of this afternoon seemed snuffed, for the moment, like a candle, either by his near-acquaintance with death or by his mother's upset. Spirits were raised by the *boutellier*, who tried some of his better vintages out in preparation for Thursday, but by and large it was a quiet affair where most of those seated around the table were physically, emotionally or spiritually exhausted.

At the end of the meal everyone went to bed. Last night had been a late one and tomorrow morning would be an early start – and not just for the last few messengers delivering the final half-dozen invitations. Tom and Ben retired to their room, somehow higher in the general esteem and supplied with candles instead of a taper. Miraculously, in the interim Tom's tub had been emptied

251

and removed. His close brush with death this afternoon had drained even his great strength, so that when Ben repeated his request that they replace watching with resting – just for tonight – he acquiesced.

The pair of them clambered into the big bed, half-dressed, therefore, in shirts and hose. No sooner were they down than they were sleeping.

And, it seemed, no sooner sleeping than awake.

The hammering came upon their door some unmeasured time later. The hammering was repeated and the door burst wide. It was Polrudden Quin, white and wide-eyed, his face above the candle-flame like a skull. 'She is dead,' he whispered. 'Dead and murdered. Come. For God's sake come!'

Dazed with the depth of the sleep that had overcome him, Tom struggled up, riven with simple horror. Too stunned to speak, he caught up his sword and staggered after the distraught man.

Out along the little corridor they went and down the stairs and passageways into the great entrance hall; down the steps towards the main door – though Tom had hesitated, looking up towards the passageways that he and Ben had followed to Lady Margaret's rooms last night; down the staircase, across the hallway and out through the doors on to the steps where Danforth had fallen the night before; down the steps and across the main yard, staggering over to the church.

At Quin's shoulder, Tom burst into the little church, to be confronted with the Reverend Wainscott, white and trembling, his pallor accentuated by the light of the candle he was holding.

'Here,' he whispered. 'She is here.'

He turned and opened a little door that Tom had hardly noticed when he had come here with Lady Margaret last night. Tom followed him, but froze in the doorway. Wainscott was standing at the bottom of the bell-tower, looking upward, shaking.

Above the little globe of light cast by the flickering flame the tower rose in a column of utter darkness; and there, on the upper edge of the trembling brightness, attired in a gold undressing-robe, little more than white toes dangling below the glistering hem and a form fading eerily into the darkness above, the figure of a woman was hanging.

CHAPTER 23

Post Mortem

The impact of seeing Lady Margaret alive was nothing compared to the impact of seeing her dead. Only the strength that had allowed him to pull her son back from the very jaws of death this afternoon held him erect now. He stepped forward, jerkily, like an Italian puppet moved by strings. He reached over and touched the toes hanging from the hem of the golden undressing-robe he had last seen sprawled across the foot of her bed when he had been guarding her last night. The foot was cold. He hesitated there, holding it, not knowing what to do next. He was finding it as hard to breathe as he had done at the bottom of Whitsand Bay.

Wainscott and Quin stepped forward with him, the light of their candles creeping up the statue-still, gold-clad form; but her face remained in shadow. 'What should we do?' quavered the Reverend Wainscott, sounding as old, frail and desperate as he looked.

'We must take her down, prepare her,' whispered Quin.

'Wait,' said Tom. 'We should call the justices and crowner from the nearest town. There are forms of law to be observed.' *And I should warn Poley*, he thought. *What will Poley make of this?* 'Who is the nearest justice?' he demanded.

'The Baron is,' said Quin. 'When he is in residence, he is justice to the local assize and crowner too, when inquests are to be held.'

'We cannot call the Baron,' said Tom. 'Well, I will do the crowner's work and report to him as witness when this comes to any court.' *For I will have to report to Poley too*, he thought.

'But we need the help of the law in this,' quavered Wainscott. 'Can no one ride to Plymouth?'

'Plymouth is across the border,' said Quin roundly. 'We are in Cornwall here. Our nearest law in Cornwall is in Liskeard. And Justice Pinnock will be here with Lord St Keane on Thursday in any case, invited to the Lady Margaret's festive entertainment and hardly likely to get here any sooner than that, short of witchcraft.'

'Liskeard's the nearest by road, mayhap,' said a new voice, decisive, hissing. 'Saltash is the nearest by water. And there's a searcher at Torpoint.'

'She's not dead of the Plague, man!' snapped a second new voice. 'We don't want no strangers poking around in this!'

Tom rounded on them. 'We want someone to poke around on it, Master Danforth,' he snapped. 'For 'tis murder – murder sure

255

enough.'

No sooner had he delivered himself of this than Tom stopped, as though turned to stone himself. Over Quin's shoulder, he could see the glimmer of a single candle-flame coming across the courtyard; and above it, a most ghostly cloud of golden ringlets. There seemed to be no body – just a head floating through the air, the head that was hidden by the bell-tower's shadows on the body up above him, floating closer across the courtyard as he watched.

As Tom observed the spectral vision approach, he quite forgot to breathe until it settled silently at the door and he realized it was not a ghost at all. It was a fleshly woman wrapped in a black travelling-cloak; and the woman hanging in the belfry was not who he had supposed her to be, after all.

Lady Margaret stood for just a second, looking past their gaping faces; then, as silently as ever, she fainted dead away, her vital spirit snuffed out as abruptly as the flame of the candle that she dropped as she fell.

Tom, taking a great, tearing breath, turned back and raised his candle to the highest stretch of his considerable height to reveal the mottled, staring death mask of Agnes Danforth gaping down at him – Agnes Danforth, dressed in her mistress's golden robe.

When he turned back, St Just was sweeping his fainting mistress up into his arms. With no further word he strode off towards the castle keep. Tom crossed to Martin Danforth, who was standing riven with the exact opposite to the emotion that sang in Tom's heart. Quin, unexpectedly, put an arm round his shoulder and, with Wainscott, led him into the chapel and down to the family pew, where he sat silently, shaking, apparently at prayer.

Ben arrived then. 'What's to do?' he asked, his eyes huge.

Tom told him.

'So you'll complete a crowner's quest yourself?' asked Ben.

'As best I can. For there is no doubt that we have murder and more.'

'What more?'

'The woman is dead, Ben, and would appear to have been dead for some time. Dead people do not suspend themselves from bell-ropes.'

'They do if they're trying to hang themselves.'

'Then where, pray, is whatever she was standing on to achieve the height? And why did the full weight of a strangling body, convulsing into death, fail to ring the bell and alarm the whole of the castle?'

Ben's mouth opened. Closed. Opened.

'Stop playing the codfish, Ben, and help me look around.'

Side by side by candle-light they searched the floor on hands and knees.

'This is a waste of time,' said Ben after a while. 'What is there to see on dusty flag-stones as hard and impossible to impress as

257

the Devil's own heart?'

'Those round marks and the specks of black immediately beneath your candle-flame to begin with. And take care: the specks are not dust, as you suppose, but powder.'

'Powder?' Ben frowned and lowered the flame, still not understanding. One of the black specks flared and spat in the heat. Ben reared back as though stung. 'Oh. That sort of powder. D'ye think she was *blown* up there, then?'

'Hush!' The order came with the shuffling sound of footsteps on flagstones.

Polrudden Quin led Martin Danforth past Agnes's body and away across the courtyard. The Reverend Wainscott lingered in the doorway.

'Get to bed, sir,' Tom said softly. 'There's no work here for a man of God. I'll send for you when 'tis time for prayers and preparations.'

Alone at last, the pair of them continued to quarter the floor, but by now it was clear that Ben had a point. There was little more to be found.

'Well, we have found enough to proceed to a little proof. We know *how* if not *who*, yet.'

'Or why,' added Ben, getting into the way of the grim game.

'Why? Because she was wearing My Lady's robe. Perhaps. Or perhaps that is too simple. Let us go to the powder store.'

'But, master; it is Agnes Danforth. How could she be confused with Lady Margaret, even in the golden robe?'

258

'In the dark – or near-dark. And from behind. We will see. Ah, here is the door, and unlocked. For pity's sake be careful with that candle. There are ten thousand thousand atomies in here like the one you ignited on the floor. But I see we do not have to search too far...'

There was a powder-barrel just inside the door and it took the pair of them only an instant to tilt it and to roll it past the little doorway that opened on to the cliff, and over to the church, for it was empty and easy to manage.

'You see?' said Tom, settling it in place, 'how well it fits the marks.'

'And showers forth powder,' acknowledged Ben.

'An easy step up, and...'

'That's how it must have been done, master. I calculate there's enough room for a second man to stand up there too...'

'Ah. You see that, do you, Ben? Well observed. One very strong and agile man, perhaps, might have achieved it, but...' He paused, holding the dead woman gently, as he reached back for his dagger. 'Two normal men working together is much more likely. Get ready ... There!'

As Tom spoke, he sliced the bell-rope as high above Agnes's head as he could reach and lowered her to Ben. Sharp though the dagger was, the process was difficult, and sufficiently violent to swing the bell. It rang just once as Agnes came free.

By the time Tom had descended and helped Ben to lay the body on the floor of the church, both Quin and St Just were there. This was a fortunate thing as far as Tom was concerned, for it was easy and quick for the four of them to move the body on to a ladder from a nearby workshop and carry her into the keep.

They laid her on an old table in a small storage cellar at Quin's suggestion, and, while he and St Just went off to comfort Agnes's broken-hearted brother, Tom and Ben lit all the flambards and candles they could get.

'The more light we cast upon the situation, the more readily we will see the answers,' said Tom grimly.

'I can already see more than I would wish,' said Ben. 'Her face will haunt me for a while, I fear.'

'If ye don't want your face to look like that, Ben, then don't get hanged.'

'I'll try and avoid it, master.'

'But still and all...'

'What?' Forgetting his unease at the staring eyes and protruding, purple tongue, Ben craned over to see what Tom was looking at, mindful of the brilliance he had shown when looking at the body of the messenger at the start of this.

The Master of Logic was easing the bell-rope gently away from the dead woman's throat, revealing beneath the thick hemp an area of livid bruising and, opposite, the tell-tale swelling that spoke of a broken neck.

'Been to many hangings, Ben?'

'A few.'

'Ever managed a close look at the body afterwards?'

'Never this close!' *And would never want to!* said his tone, though Tom, well aware of Ben's predilection for violence, was not so sure.

'Well, let us dispense with the Socratic method, at least, for there is no *a priori* knowledge to plumb with my questions. Observe instead; and learn. The eyes and tongue tell us the woman died of strangling, as is usual in hanging; but she was not hanged by this bell-rope or we would have heard the bell – as we did when we cut her down and raised the alarm, indeed.'

'I see,' said Ben. 'So she was hanged somewhere else. Then why in Heaven's name...'

'What is also usual in hanging is that the Adam's apple is crushed. But women have no Adam's apple – therefore we should find the windpipe crushed instead. And do we? Feel here.'

'No. That seems sound enough to me, though I'm no doctor...'

'Good. Strangled, then, but not hanged. Certainly not hanged where she was found. And then there is the broken neck.'

'I have seen necks broken at hangings.'

'As have I. But only when the victim's friends have caught him at the heels and pulled him down a-purpose to snap his neck and ease his suffering.'

'Could not that have been done here?'

'I can conceive, with some effort, of a situation ... But let's not waste our time. The final proof of death by hanging is the rope-burn. It is a most distinctive mark, as though the weave of the rope were branded into the flesh of the neck. And can you see it here?'

'No.'

'No. No mark, no crushing, no pulling by the heels. No hanging, then.' Tom straightened. He took the dead woman by the shoulders and lifted her. 'Hold her, Ben, while I lift her head. I want to ... Ah...' As Ben accepted the weight of the woman's torso, Tom eased her head over a little so that he could inspect the knot in the bell-rope. 'An added proof,' he said. 'Such a simple knot was held in place only by her dead weight. Had she struggled or been pulled by the heels to break her neck, it would have come undone – easily. There, you see? And with the rope out of the way...'

They laid her flat again and Tom leaned down over her throat. 'What do we see? Finger-marks. You see them? Four fingers across the throat. Note that: fingers, not thumbs. Strangled from behind, therefore. A struggle, leading to a broken neck – and fortunately for the killer, for he seems only to have one hand; or to have only had the chance to use one hand. For see, there is only one set of finger-marks.'

'Perhaps he was holding something in the other hand? A dagger?'

'If he had a dagger out, why not use it? But

the thought is good. Perhaps he held her wrists. No. There would be bruising. And look for a scratched face, for there is blood beneath her nails. Any bruising on her head or face?'

There was none, but as Tom's examination proceeded to the body beneath the golden robe, there were more bruises – sharp-edged bruises and larger, mottled areas, ill-defined.

At last, as a high window up at the roof of the cellar was revealed by the glimmering of dawn, Tom declared himself satisfied. 'I know how it was done and, I think, where.'

'And why?'

'Still the golden robe, Ben.'

On that answer, Tom led the pair of them out of the cellar and up into the great entrance hall. Then, with none of the guilty secrecy they had used on the night before last, they ran up to Lady Margaret's chamber.

'But why the bell-rope?' asked Ben, as they pounded up past the armoury.

'A message. This man – these men – like sending messages, Ben.' Tom's steps slowed as he came to the foot of a flight of stairs. The flight was narrow and quite steep. Tom crouched and brought his candle low, studying each step before placing his foot up on it. Halfway up, he struck the wall on either side quite hard with his fist. At the top, there was a long corridor. It was dark, for there were no windows here – the double walls held the cannon out on the balcony beyond and the only grille that gave light from that looked into Lady Margaret's chamber beyond.

'But to whom is this message addressed?' demanded Ben, following Tom along the corridor to an apparently solid wall at its end, beyond Lady Margaret's tightly closed door.

Then, as in the bell-tower, Tom raised his candle to the full reach of his great height and saw much more than he had expected. 'Who knows?' he said thoughtfully, lowering the candle. 'But the last one was to Robert Poley.'

'*Poley!* What in God's name can the likes of Poley have to do with the murder of a housekeeper in the depths of Cornwall?'

'At the very least,' said Tom, leading his apprentice back down the narrow stairwell, 'it can tell him – tell us all, in fact – how easily it could have been the Countess.

'Which is what we have been warned about all along, have we not? – in the picture, and in the secret passage at Elfinstone, and now again with Agnes – how easily it could have been the Countess. Time and time again.'

CHAPTER 24

Markets, Meetings and Mysteries

'The letters have been sent,' insisted Tom, gently. 'It cannot be cancelled now. I feel it would be a serious mistake to change your plans in any case, My Lady.'

'He's right, My Lady,' said Martin Danforth quietly. 'It would hurt poor Agnes's soul more than the terrible manner of her death to know of the damage such a cancellation would cause – no matter how good the reason.'

'And if the feast continues a-Thursday, preparations must be made today as you had planned,' insisted Polrudden Quin. 'Cook and all her helpers are primed and at the point for action.'

'And we must therefore to market,' concluded Tom.

Is there no more you can tell me of her death?

'Of the manner of it? No, My Lady. It is as I have said. Whoever killed her came in silently through the trap from the gun emplacement and jumped down into the end of the corridor that runs past your rooms. He came up behind Mistress Agnes at the top of the stair and took her from behind, trying to choke her. She fought and they fell. There was no sound of alarm, for he was too swift to give her a chance to scream. There was no sound of falling, for the stairs are stone and set between two thick stone walls; moreover, they lead from one stone passageway to another, all within the very fabric of the place. You could hunt a stag down those stairs without anyone hearing a sound.

'When they came to the foot of the stairs, Mistress Agnes was dead of a broken neck and the man that had killed her was bruised and perhaps scratched; shaken, but well enough to proceed.'

This does not answer all of our questions.

'Nor all of mine, My Lady. But it tells us all we need to know for the moment. I must urge that you do not change your plans but that you proceed ever watchfully. And we will have our eyes at all times riveted to you.'

And to Hal.

'And to the Baron of course, My Lady.'

'And it is at Saltash Narket,' added St Just, 'where we nay alert the nearest justice.'

'There will be a watch constable there,' insisted Quin. 'Perhaps a sergeant, or even a captain on market day.'

'If there isn't,' said Tom, 'I can take the ferry into Plymouth and see the watch captain there – there's a permanent watch on the docks, I know – and he'll tell me who next to contact – other than the Baron, of course.'

And there we can look for news of Percy and Dr Rowley. Lady Margaret acquiesced at last. *I have sore need of my secretary if you are resuming your tutelage of Ben.*

They set out in two coaches – one for the Countess and the Baron and the other for Cook and her helpers. The men rode – Tom, Ben, Quin and St Just in the lead, the castle's butcher and two of his boys on ponies behind. Anything worth buying at the market in the way of particularly promising lambs, sheep or calves they would drive back on foot this afternoon. The beef had been butchered long since and was hanging ripening in the castle's shambles with the game, the game-birds and the bigger fish and dolphins already caught and prepared. Chickens, ducks and geese beyond the castle's own supplies would be basketed atop the cook's coach. Fine-woven baskets sat beside them, waiting to contain blackbirds, larks and doves that would be baked in pies and dipped in honey and stuffed or used as stuffing. Fish and eels, freshwater and salt, would be bought fresh and wrapped in straw before being packed in the long box above the back axle of either or both of the coaches. In the largest there was already a big compartment prepared to take the oysters. Fruit, vegetables and herbs that took Cook's fancy would ride inside with herself and her girls.

The castle was in all respects self-sufficient, and much of the land through which they were driving down along Rame Head was the old demesne designed to bring it all the supplies and provisions it would need; but this was a special occasion, which required just that little bit of extra preparation.

It was fortunate indeed that Agnes Danforth's lengthy absences at Elfinstone had caused Martin to train up an assistant housekeeper upon whom he and Lady Margaret could rely to prepare the rest of the castle's accommodations almost as effectively as Agnes would have done – as effectively, in fact, as the feast itself was being prepared, though it was typical of Lady Margaret that she was busily involved in the practicalities of both. Where many another, more languid, countess would have been content to stay all day abed preparing for the exigencies of party-giving, Lady Margaret rolled up her sleeves and got down to work with the rest.

Saltash market was set in the square on the corner of Fore Street. The weather was clement, so that only a few of the stalls were set inside the Market Hall. All the clamour and bustle echoed cheerfully, therefore, under the wide blue sky. No sooner did they arrive than they split up. Tom went through the market in search of a tailor with some grasp of London fashions and a stock of shirts, hose, waistcoats, doublets and cannions or galligaskins. Also a bootmaker well stocked with Spanish leather – though this was less important, for Tom's own boots had not yet been declared beyond all help though badly stretched. This he was willing to accept, particularly as a looser fit was coming into fashion.

Though Tom had promised Lady Margaret that he would seek out the local watch, he had been less than honest in this, for he had every intention of slipping across on the ferry and seeking out the dock watch at Plymouth for news of Robert Poley and his Spanish spy.

It was typical of Tom that he should seek out the tailor first. He found one hard by the church of St Nicholas and St Faith. Master Moss proved surprisingly well stocked – even in sizes fit for Tom's tall frame; and the tailor's eye for fashion had been schooled by local seafarers who often had business up in the City or at Court. The only compromises Tom had to make were in the matter of colour, accepting dark russet slashed with tobacco – which was, at least, all the rage as a colour as the weed was all the rage for smoking. On the other hand, there were only breeches loose at the knee instead of the tight galligaskins he normally favoured; but then, as an enquiry and a cursory survey discovered no bootmakers, it looked as though loose breeches and stretched boots would have to do as the newest fashion in any case.

'What now?' demanded Ben, hopeful of a tavern and perhaps an ordinary.

'The Plymouth Clink,' said Tom roundly, heading down towards the ferry.

The Clink was a big, solid half-fortified building that frowned down across the Sound in silent and disapproving warning to all the stout sea-dogs aboard the tall ships nodding there. It was of a size and in a place where it was most immediately needed, thought the Master of Logic.

However, Poley was not within its dark and iron-barred bowels. Nor, indeed, was his Spanish prisoner. Tom spoke to the watch captain himself, who had time to indulge him because the docks were quiet and the market – and the trouble – was over at Saltash. Tom enjoyed their conversation, gleaning advice as well as information over a mug of ale and a pipe of the new tobacco, which he swiftly passed to Ben. As with the matters of boots and doublets, it was the information that he really wanted.

'Ar,' said the watch captain. 'Master Poley's been here with his passes and his troop; but he was sore disappointed, as I understand it. His hopeful Spanish spy was no more than a smuggler in from The Isles of Scilly, some half-starved fishwife from St Mary's Port as has lost her man but not his boat, fallen in with tobacco smugglers and desperate enough to be shipping the weed under the noses of the men from Custom House. Swept her away with him he did, and her chained like a slave in one of them Spanish galleys that's forever cruising along the coasts of Spanish Flanders hard by. And he's like to return, with her or without.

'Whither he's gone in the meantime and when he'll be back is more than I can say, but he expects to be in Plymouth through the rest of the week, so he tells me. He comes and goes as he pleases and at the pleasure of Her Majesty and the Council, but my writ only runs across the border into Cornwall in the case of national emergency. I've not been over to Torpoint or Saltash since Armada Year – not in the way of business. You must needs report your murder to Trematon Castle, and ye can do that right enough if ye take the long road back from Saltash to Castle Cotehel. Though I think His Lordship's away from home as well.'

'Very well,' said Tom. 'I'll tell the Countess. Thank you, Captain.'

'It's not much to have come all this way for,' grumbled Ben as they boarded the ferry back to Saltash. The tobacco had made him queasy, and the ferry ride was not helping his constitution or his disposition.

'No,' said Tom, leaning against the rail and looking out towards the distant Channel; 'but it is worth much to know where the players are positioned.'

He turned and looked Ben full in the face – perhaps for the first time in their brief friendship. 'We are in the midst of a strange game of chess here. We know where the Queen, Lady Margaret, is – or we think we do, for the time being. Let us call her the White Queen. We also know where the White King, her son, is – to the extent that he acts alone and without undue influence.

'We know where the White Knights are, for

we are the White Knights – you and me, and peradventure Robert Poley, if I read his messages aright; and the Castles and the Bishops – as long as we can trust them to be what they appear to be.'

'And the *black* pieces?'

'Ah. The black pieces. Who they are and what their plans may be ... These things are still...'

'For us to discover?'

'For us to *prove*, perhaps.'

'But, master, how will we ever achieve such a thing?'

'Because, apprentice, if we do not, then we will be dead by the end of the week, together with the Lady Margaret, the Baron, and all the other white pieces on our chessboard. Checkmated, slaughtered and dead.'

Tom reported to Lady Margaret who, busy and distracted, sent him on to Tremanton to report Agnes's death as the watch captain at Plymouth had advised; but this too proved something of a fool's errand for, again as the captain had warned, His Lordship was away from home and not likely to return until the morrow.

Side by side, and wearying at last, Tom and Ben trotted along the road to Landrake and Tideford before cutting across country down to Polbathic and then along the gathering spine of the land up towards Rame itself. It was a long ride, and to begin with they were content to continue in silence, for the afternoon was warm and the way full of shadowed pathways giving suddenly on to increasingly spectacular views.

Tom mused on the abstruser aspects of the situation and tried to see ahead far enough to make some simple plans. As he had said to Ben on the ferry, he really thought that if they had not solved the matter satisfactorily by the end of the week, then they would all likely be dead; and this was Tuesday afternoon. He hardly considered his apprentice in the mastery of Logic at all – let alone what Ben was thinking.

Until, winding away south of Polbathic, Ben suddenly said, 'Master, the only thing I cannot fathom is why Agnes was dressed in Lady Margaret's undressing-robe.'

'The only thing of what, Ben?'

'The only thing of all, I believe.'

'So, the entire matter lies before you as plain as one of Master Camden's Classical texts at Westminster School; and the only phrase in all this transliteration that remains stubbornly Greek to you is My Lady's robe?'

Ben bridled at Tom's gently mocking tone, but he was learning humility and self-control with all the rest and so he shrugged amenably enough. 'I believe so, master.'

'Very well, apprentice mine, expound your explanation. Tell me what all this matter means and I will translate the last of it for you so that we may approach the Lady Margaret tonight with everything laid plain.' ·

'Well, master. We know that someone in My

Lady's household watches her constantly and closely; that he is what we have called a sin-worm, such as the Tom that peeped at Godiva in the legend; that he did so at Elfinstone and hollowed out an extension to a secret passage in the wall so that he might do so; and that he uses the system of gun emplacements in the outer walls at Cotehel to do the same. And, we assume, it is he that signals in secret while he spies on her.'

'Very well, apprentice. Expound further.'

'We know that the Earl of Essex sent Lady Margaret a portrait of her as a mark of – shall we say, affection? Certainly an apology for past wrongs. She reacted coolly but kept the gift. By chance she hung it in a place where the sin-worm spied on her from and so he stole it. He horribly defaced it and left it to burn. We rescued the portrait, however, as we plan to rescue the Lady, and you have directed your friend Ugo Stell in the matter of its restoration as you have requested him to send moneys and clothing after us to Cotehel.'

'Well remembered and well reasoned again. Continue.'

'But Lady Margaret became aware of these eyes upon her, grew fearful at the extra licence isolation in Cotehel and the tradition of the Feast of Fools might offer, and sent to you for help; but she was unaware that there were more legitimate eyes upon her: the eyes of the Council, as arranged and overseen by Master Poley. Not so the sin-worm. He also became aware that Master Mann watched

274

both of them. And therefore, when he heard of the letter asking for your help, he arranged to have both missives and messengers stopped.

'In these dark ambitions he was only partially successful – because of your ingenuity twice exercised on near-destroyed letters; and so it is at this point that we enter the story. The tables are now turned, therefore. He is no longer the master of the game. Now he finds he is not the hunter but the hunted instead. And yet he still has his plans and can vary but not change them. He is tight in the grip of his own devices. Thus, desperately and more desperately still, he begins to take more risks, to do things perforce that he had not planned to do, to take actions whose consequences he has not had the leisure to think through.'

'*Per exemplum?*'

'For example, master, his attempt to kill you at Winchester. How much more effectively could that have been achieved had the riot not distracted, had he chosen some other moment than that in which Percy Gawdy was branded.'

'Thus,' Tom summated: 'on the road to Cotehel, he was distracted by our pursuit. He had planned to be with Lady Margaret, perfecting his plans – for the Feast of Fools we surmise – but instead he has had to leave her unwatched and instead pursue his pursuers – to wit, ourselves. Is that what you believe?'

'Is it not self-evident? Now that we are safely ensconced at Cotehel, he waits and watches and continues with his plans; but his control continues to slip away relentlessly as long as we remain alive. He cannot trust himself simply to watch and wait. He is beginning to take reckless action, as he did last night.

'For a reason that I cannot explain, he saw a figure dressed in gold and supposed it Lady Margaret. He snatched his opportunity and killed her on the spot. Then he discovered his mistake, removed her from the place where the crime had been committed and hung her where we found her.'

'Good. And when you tell me who the mysterious murderer is, then I shall tell you why Agnes Danforth was dressed in Lady Margaret's robe.'

'Well, let us first see who it was not.'

'A logical place to start.'

'It cannot have been her own brother. Martin Danforth has been here in Cornwall all the time; we have no reason to believe he was ever in London or was ever at Elfinstone able to watch the Lady Margaret. Besides, he is Agnes's brother. I do not even consider the Reverend Wainscott, for he is a man of the cloth and again, like Danforth, was never at London nor Elfinstone, as far as we can tell. By the same token, it cannot have been Doctor Rowley the Tutor or Percy Gawdy the Secretary, for neither of them has been at Cotehel since we arrived.

'Quin or St Just must be our man, there-fore. And there is a strong case to be made against St Just, is there not? We know he has unnatural desires that are aimed at the Lady, for he has taken as lover a girl who bears her a striking resemblance. We know he would have drowned the Baron yesterday, had you not been there to stop him. We know he has been at both Elfinstone and Cotehel – and that, while Lady Margaret went down from one to the other, she gave him leave and freedom so that he could have been at the burning house in Water Lane and the cathedral square in Winchester with equal ease. Finally, we know that the man who sought twice to kill you wears hat and cloak to hide his face – and St Just has more reason than any man alive to do that. St Just is your man, therefore, master. Now, can you explain to me why Agnes was in My Lady Margaret's robe?'

'Alas, Ben, I find I cannot,' admitted Tom, his voice quietly amused.

'Master! Is it because I have overlooked some detail in my own poor exercise of logic?'

'You have overlooked surprisingly little, Apprentice Ben.'

'Then, master, why? Surely it is not that you do not know why yourself?'

'That's as may be, Ben. But the real reason I cannot tell you is because we are just about to be joined by two of the suspects whose names you have just discussed.'

Ben craned round to see that two riders had

very nearly caught up with them as they had talked. Seeing their hesitation, the riders spurred on apace, one of them waving a bandaged hand, coming right up beside them, even as Tom called. 'Doctor Rowley! Master Gawdy. Give you good evening, sirs! Are you bound, like us, for Cotehel?'

'Indeed we are, sir,' came Dr Rowley's cheery reply. 'Where else? Percy's thumb is near-mended, as you see, and I am myself in much more hearty spirits. We could not miss the feast tomorrow!'

'Nor,' added Gawdy with a broad grin and a broader wink, 'the Feast of Fools that comes after it!'

CHAPTER 25

Preparation

The return of Rowley and Gawdy brought a frenetic air to Cotehel through Tuesday night and Wednesday. For, as the others were all involved with the readying of the castle for the guests tomorrow or the preparation of the feast that would greet them, the doctor and the tutor seemed primarily concerned with semi-secret preparations for the castle's special Feast of Fools.

'It is as well these two are but lately returned,' huffed Ben on Wednesday evening, 'for
their presence would have added a touch of
simple madness to the doings of the last two
days.' He was secretly satisfied to have Gawdy
back, however, so that he stood in no further
danger of soiling his hands or his cuffs with
secretarial work.

Though to be fair, he observed, nor did
Gawdy – even though his lightly bandaged
branded hand was not his writing hand. Lady
Margaret was far too busy with her silent
regimentation of the new housekeeper and
her myriad minions, and with equally silent
but exacting oversight of cook, butcher, *boutellier*, baker, candlestick-maker – that worthy
especially busy preparing light best suited to
so many honoured guests, and all the rest.

Ben perforce made this observation unto
himself, for as Lady Margaret and the two
new arrivals seemed to be everywhere, so
Master Musgrave himself suddenly seemed
to be nowhere, except, in the night, on guard.

This upset the Apprentice Master of Logic,
for he ached to get his mentor on one side
and complete the conversation Rowley and
Gawdy had interrupted. So absolute did the
impossibility of achieving this aim become,
however, that Ben began to suspect darkly
that Master Musgrave must be avoiding him
on purpose – unable, as like as not, to fault
his pupil's explanation of the case and to
explain as promised the significance of the
golden undressing-robe Agnes Danforth's

corpse had been wearing when they found it. And was still wearing now, in fact, as she lay stiffening on the old table in the locked and little-used cellar that remained her resting-place until the full weight of the local law came into force.

In the face of his master's irritating invisibility, Ben did the thing that seemed to him to be the most logical: he fell to watching the man he most suspected of being the sin-worm and the murderer. Inevitably, therefore, he also watched the young Baron, for although the boy's academic tutor had returned, he had other business elsewhere.

Idly at first, Ben watched St Just teaching the boy with blunts the rudiments of fencing. All blade-work, edge against edge, showy but old-fashioned, thought Ben, from the superior heights of his new-learned knowledge; none of Master Musgrave's vaunted point-work at all. Then to the castle butts beside the powder store. Here, at the foot of the straightest section of wall, the lad practised with his longbows and his crossbows. He did some brisk work with pike and quarterstaff. Then St Just disappeared into the powder store – only to reappear with Master Musgrave at his side, deep in conversation.

'Aye,' St Just was saying when Ben hurried up to them, 'there is cellarage deneath – all the way along the outer wall as far as the gate.'

'With tunnels?' persisted Tom.

'Aye. O'ening out in the cliff face on the ph'ath and stets we went down for the sailing lesson.'

'The iron-bound gates on the level sections open into them?'

'Indeed,' lisped St Just. 'Fron the days when the castle ceased deing a defensive estadlishnent and was ada'ted as store-house to the Outran family's cargoes. Ye can cun down to look again in half an hour. We'll have finished shooting then and we'fe a sailing lesson to finish.'

'Is there no other lad in all the castle you can take as crew with you?' asked Tom easily. 'One that can sail and help you show His young Lordship? One that can swim?'

'Kit Newman the butcher's boy,' called Hal, overhearing this.

'Ben,' said Tom at once. 'Go to the shambles and bring the butcher's boy.'

Ben didn't hesitate, but when he returned with young Kit and handed him over to St Just, Master Musgrave was gone again. So Ben spent the next hour outside the sallyport gate under the overhang that held the walls here, watching the little boat tacking safely and steadily this way and that across Whitsand Bay as the Baron became a confident helmsman. After the hour he got bored and wandered away.

At the stroke of six, as though by magic, for there was no castle clock, therefore no actual audible chime, and – without the rope – no bell to summon worshippers, Lady Margaret came to evensong. She brought a fair number of the household, including the Baron, lately returned from his second sailing lesson, safe and sound. Master Musgrave did not appear, however.

It was cold cuts and catch-as-catch-can for dinner. Everyone in the kitchens was full of the needs of tomorrow night, and ordered by Lady Margaret's terse notes to let tonight take care of itself; but unsatisfactory though the meal might have been, at least it brought Master Musgrave out again. At a table in the great hall which seemed like a piece of flotsam miraculously strewn right-side-up in the storm-wrack of the preparations, Ben sat down at last beside his master, far enough removed from all the rest to allow a secret whisper.

'So, master, of the golden robe...'

Tom looked down at the eager face with its slightly bulbous, fiercely clever eyes. 'Ah yes,' he said, airily waving a chicken drumstick as he talked. 'The importance of the golden robe. It depends entirely – does it not? – on who was murdered.'

'But, master! We know who was murdered. Agnes Danforth was murdered.'

'You fail to follow close enough, Ben. Agnes Danforth died; but who was *supposed* to die? That is where the importance of the robe lies, is it not?'

Tom took a bite of the cold chicken and chewed reflectively as Ben wrestled with this conundrum; but before the apprentice could deliver any further thoughts, the master continued.

'For if Agnes was wearing the golden robe when she died, then it was Lady Margaret who was being murdered. There was little light in the corridor, but the robe would have glistered, and our sin-worm would have known that sheen. If, therefore, the woman was wearing the robe when he struck, then he was murdering the Lady Margaret – which is what we have been led to expect, is it not? That Lady Margaret will be murdered? Defaced, perhaps, burned conceivably, ravished almost certainly and finally murdered.'

'But, you are saying, master,' asked Ben at last, 'that if Agnes was *not* wearing the robe when she died, then maybe it was she herself and not the Lady Margaret who was designed to be the victim?'

'A thought quite worthy of you, apprentice mine.'

'But who would want to murder Agnes Danforth?'

'Someone she had seen doing something of terrible danger or deadly moment...'

'Yes! She saw St Just and the Baron with you in the boat yesterday. In it and out of it, by all accounts – perhaps even more clearly than you might have done yourself, if my observations this afternoon were anything to go by; and she had famously sharp eyes, did Agnes Danforth.'

'Well, there you are, Ben.'

'But why take a dead woman, dress her in a

robe and hang her in a church tower?'

'To do what has been done, Ben: to stop us asking *Who would want to kill Agnes Danforth?* And to keep us like chickens following a line drawn on the ground, only ever asking *Who wants to harm the Lady Margaret?*

'And to stop us asking *Why? Why?* is the most important question of all and yet we have hardly asked it in a week. For there is no need to ask *Why?* in the madness of such a creature as our sin-worm.'

'So,' said Ben slowly, 'the sin-worm is a creation? A madness assumed to mask some deeper stratagem? Is that what you are saying? Our murderer comes amongst us like Ulysses returned, in disguise until he can perfect his terrible revenge?'

'Perhaps,' said Tom thoughtfully. 'Or perhaps matters run even deeper than that. Consider a creature given to such predilections, but with cunning enough to use his own vices as a mask to cover something deeper or darker still. What would we make of that, Ben? What would we ever make of that?'

"'Tis a horror beyond imagining,' said Ben: 'a madman able to use his madness as a vizard over his evil cunning. Such a thing cannot exist outside the bounds of Hell itself – Can it, master?'

'Perhaps,' said Tom weightily, 'the Good Lord might allow the circumstances to exist where such an abomination walked amongst us.'

'And watched the Lady Margaret ever,

planning to do her nameless ill?'

'We are come full-circle, Ben, are we not? Now all we can do is prepare to face it in all its cunning and sinful evil when the mask comes off.' He threw his naked bone aside and rose. 'Come on, apprentice mine, let's to the armoury.'

The armoury was dark but there were candles enough to give them some brightness. Although the walls were cluttered with cabinets and cases, overhung with weapons both ancient and more modern, the midst of the room was clear. A well-polished *piste* had been made here, where the edged weapons on the walls at least might be tested out. Tom brought Ben here and here they fell to practising. Tom took off his Solingen rapier and they used the short falchions from the walls first, while Tom instructed Ben in the basics of attack and defence with the edge, as though one or the other of them needed to be ready to face St Just; just the swords at first, then basic sword- and dagger-work – then sword and buckler. After more than an hour of this wide-swinging, shoulder-wrenching exercise, Ben felt the need to enquire, somewhat breathlessly, 'But what of my Toledo rapier, master? Why do we work with the edge like bumpkins when we have the lethal point at our command?'

'Fetch it,' ordered Tom. 'I will remain and exercise here until you return.'

With Ben gone, Tom took out his rapier and began to work up and down the *piste*, as though he needed to re-accustom his arm and eye to fighting along a line; and indeed, the change was considerable. The stance was much more sideways-on. The wrist replaced the shoulder as the power-house of the strokes. A twitch of finger and thumb made more momentous difference than a twist of forearm with a falchion. Impetus from ankle replaced heave of hip and back. Bodyweight and speed replaced armweight and power.

If Ben understood any of the subtleties when he returned and fell into the new style, he said little. He was given scant opportunity, to be fair, for he was plunged immediately as far out of his depth in the matter as Tom had been in Whitsand Bay yesterday afternoon. Nothing he could do, even under Tom's most careful tutelage, could keep the Toledo blade on line or even in his grasp; and he was fortunate indeed that the Spanish swordsmith who made both blade and basket had left the grip simple. Had he been possessed of a complex basket hilt like Tom's, which seemed to fit around his whole hand like a glove, Ben began to suspect, as his sword spun across the room for the third time, that the glittering steel would have taken his fingers away with it.

After a further hour, Tom stopped, much to Ben's relief. For the last half-hour at least, by the young man's computation, his master had been elsewhere in any case, his face closed and his body working while his spirit quested far away from this place – far from the armoury, but still well within the castle walls, reckoned Ben.

'Back to our room,' ordered Tom abruptly. Once there he crossed to his saddle-bags and opened one. 'Ben,' he said, 'keep your rapier handy. It is yours and you should guard it; but do not use it. I will find a falchion better suited to your style and we will complete your mastery of the point when we return to London. In the meantime...' Tom turned and Ben realized that he was holding one of the deadly little dags he had taken from Green, the footpad in Farnham. 'In the meantime, keep this primed and ready. It will serve you better than any blade; and I will tell you who to use it on tomorrow.' He looked out of the bedroom window and judged the time by the height of the moon. 'Tomorrow at this very hour,' he said. 'For if I judge right, it is close to midnight. Within the hour, therefore, it will be Lady Margaret's feast day. And all too soon after that, the castle will be lost in the madness of its own peculiar Feast of Fools.'

CHAPTER 26

Traps and Tunnels

Tom again stood guard through the final hours of darkness, as he had the first night, on the balcony beside the culverins outside Lady Margaret's chamber. It was here that Ben found him next morning so deeply asleep that he was oblivious even to the feeding gulls; but he did not stay sleepy for long, for the apprentice came with news that was as welcome as it was unexpected.

'There's a Dutchman at the great gate asking for you,' said Ben rather breathlessly in the first light of the momentous feast day. 'He says he's a friend.'

Ugo was more than a friend: he was something of a saviour. He led a laden packhorse whose bulging saddle-bags would have tempted many a footpad on the Portsmouth and Plymouth roads – had Tom and Poley not disposed of most of them along the way; though, to be fair, had any footpad attempted to relieve him of anything he carried, the result would have been as final as anything Tom could have delivered. Even seated

288

apparently at ease by the great gate, Ugo held a short-barrelled dunderbus across his horse's withers, and he did not put this aside until he had given both his charges safely into the hands of a sleepy stable-lad.

Up from the stables Tom, Ben and the taciturn Ugo carried clothing – for both of them, by a miracle; more weaponry – both bladed and barrelled, for Ugo was a famous gunsmith; personal items, such as soaps and perfumes and a letter from Kate Shelton; money – very welcome, for the tobacco-slashed doublet had used the last of Tom's travelling funds; and, most carefully of all, a great square bundle wrapped in clean sacking and bound with hempen rope.

Up in Tom and Ben's room, as the two of them packed their necessaries away and Ugo swilled the dust of travel from his hands, face and throat, they fell to talking.

'Plymouth's all a-bustle,' said Ugo. 'Poley's there, so I heard, though I didn't see him. Has this anything to do with you, Tom?'

'I'd wager it does, though Poley's being secret and I haven't fathomed all of it out for myself as yet. They say he has a smuggler's wench in tow.'

'So they say.'

Tom shook his head. 'I cannot see it, Ugo. Poley's a spy not a Custom House man. He works for the Council and the Star Chamber, not the Revenue or the Exchequer.'

'Perhaps they all lap over each other,' suggested Ben.

'Lord Burghley signs both the Exchequer warrants and the Council orders,' admitted Tom thoughtfully. 'But still and all, this does not feel like a matter of smuggling, though I dare say there's smuggling being done, right at the very heart of things – right here, for instance, at Cotehel itself.'

'What could that have to do with the Lady Margaret and young Hal?' demanded Ben. 'With all the killing and the rest? Especially as so much of it was done in Kent and in London?'

'Oh I don't think we should ever under-estimate how important Kent and London are in this particular puzzle,' said Tom. 'Though as we said when we were in Plymouth ourselves, Ben, all the players seem to be down here with us now; and preparing for the final contest.'

Ugo glanced across at the frowning Ben and a ghost of a smile crinkled his long, lined face. 'Don't worry if his riddles seem obscure, lad,' he said in his flat Dutch tones. 'They'll be clear as day soon enough.' But having said that, he glanced at the distracted Tom and fell to sorting out the little armoury of guns he had brought with him.

And so the day proceeded. Lady Margaret, though distracted by a dozen calls in every moment, was gracious enough to receive Ugo herself – for, like Tom, he was known to her – and appoint that he be given bed and board. Consequently a trestle was brought into the little room Ben and Tom were already sharing, which, though crowded, was convenient enough.

Lunch was little better than dinner last night had been, and was taken on the run in the servants' hall beside the kitchen, for the great hall was nearing perfection and must not be put at any risk at all.

Soon after lunch the castle was declared ready. Everyone of consequence within the walls withdrew into their private quarters to ensure that they were equally ready, for in one way or another, this was the high-point of their year; and through the afternoon the guests began to arrive. They had all come a good distance, and none of them were travelling in their best attire. So as they arrived – with or without their own body servants – they disappeared into their assigned quarters according to the plans laid down by Martin Danforth and his late sister, and began to prepare in turn. The castle filled rapidly and soon it became obvious that even three to a room was something of a luxury tonight. A dozen pairs of guests brought the better part of fifty servants with them, from footmen to wardrobe girls, from postillions to ostlers. Local people travelled lighter, and those who knew the castle better were generally content to use Lady Margaret's staff, who consequently bustled about breathlessly from one chamber to another, seemingly at everyone's beck and call.

Tom hesitated at the end of the bed, casting a thoughtful eye over the finery, the selection and packing which Kate had overseen at Ugo's side. As none of it included new boots, Tom must perforce wear the stretched and wrinkled ones he had gone swimming in. Therefore the galligaskins from Black Friars were useless and the wide-bottomed breeches from Plymouth would have to do. He was able to discard the tobacco-slashed doublet in favour of one with a boat-bottomed belly, however, of black velvet slashed with crimson silk – together with the black boots and breeches; and a modest belt to carry one sword at his left hip, as etiquette demanded even at dinner on such an occasion, balanced by a long, lean dagger at his right. Then, with the rubies he habitually wore in ear-lobes pierced clean through during his first duel with a rapier, he was complete and, as he ever strove to be, right at the very pinnacle of fashion. The only thing he added, before he dived into the swirl outside, was a pair of Ugo's best dags, primed and ready to cock – one in each of the so conveniently loosened boot-tops.

Ben, in his brown bricklayer's breeches, cut a much less courtly figure – until Tom recommended the tobacco-slashed doublet he no longer needed himself; and, for a miracle, it fitted perfectly, even allowing room for one of the late footpad Green's guns tucked secretly under its short skirt, into the belt, which bore the all but useless Toledo sword. Ugo favoured plain black broadcloth with a simple white linen collar and ended up looking even more priestlike than the Reverend Joses Wainscott, though the reverend vicar of St Michael's Within Cotehel was probably not armed to the teeth beneath his jacket.

The three of them had no duties to perform, of course. They had no guests to greet, and were not due to be introduced to any until the official start of the feast at six. They were content to vanish into the whirl of activity, therefore, hoping to remain unobserved amid the distracting frenzy, like cunning salmon running deep beneath a river in spate. Ben had thought that Tom would first lead them down to the cellar where Agnes Danvers lay, to explain to his friend his theories about her murder – but no. Instead he took them out of the castle keep altogether into the last place Ben would have thought of: the powder store. Here Tom led them into the dark recess of the cold room, behind the piled barrels, to where a trap-door was set in the floor. Without a word, Tom reached down and raised this. If Ben had expected anything of the rooms beneath, he would have supposed a cellar of Stygian gloom where the need for light would ever be at war with the danger of a spark – but again, no. The room beneath the powder store was long and low, and, for a wonder, well lit.

'It runs to the first ledge of the way down to the bay,' said Tom to Ugo as they climbed down. 'There is a door at the end here which opens out on to the cliff-side and into this very room. It is strong and iron-bound, but it lets in light in surprising amounts. Even when securely locked,' Tom concluded.

'A safe and secret place,' said Ugo, looking around.

'Not that safe,' inserted Ben, pointing at a line of unevenness in the floor. 'It rests upon an overhang.'

'You noticed that too? Well done, my apprentice bricklayer; but more than that,' said Tom grimly: 'it is the beginning of a series of stores and tunnels that interlink and lead all about as though the whole ground between the top of Rame Head and the bottom of the castle keep had been mined and engineered by moles and rabbits.'

'Like the walls of Elfinstone, indeed, from what your message said,' observed Ugo dryly. 'Were there rabbits there?'

'Rabbits need no lanterns,' said Ben, catching up a dark-lantern that stood right at the bottom of the ladder to the powder store.

'No,' allowed Tom, 'but we shall. So, well found, boy. Let us explore. And do not fear for your finery,' he added, seeing Ben hesitate; 'there has been many a tall and lusty lad through here of late. They'll have swept away the dust and cobwebs for us, I'll be bound.'

They found the truth of this assertion in the third chamber they came to, for the place was piled with small bales and little barrels. Under the light of the dark-lantern, its shutters set at their widest while he worked, Tom inspected these.

'Who knows?' he ruminated, apparently thoughtlessly as he worked. 'Perhaps Poley is working for the Exchequer after all.' He pulled some of the contents loose, 'It is tobacco,' he told Ben, who had never seen the leaves withered, dried but complete before. 'It does not seem to have been here long,' he added, 'and that makes the packaging of interest too; for see, Ben, it is as clean as your own tobacco doublet. These passages have been well used over a long time – certainly since the winter gales died down. I dare say Martin Danforth could confirm how calm the weather has been this month and more, were we to ask him – calm enough to allow a ship to run up overnight from the Scillies; or from Spanish Flanders, whence these wares come. But still,' he added, rising, 'I doubt all these smuggled goods are as important to our affairs as is this.' He gestured to the lantern. 'It has such a peculiar odour, does it not? Let us take it and proceed.'

Ben did as he was ordered, but thoughtlessly, his mind wrestling with the relevance of what Tom had shown them – and what he had said to them. Because he was paying scant attention to what he was doing, Ben caught up the handle of the lantern and straightened – which was a mistake. For, even with the shutters wide, the heat of the lantern still came rushing up the metal chimney of the thing and all but consumed his fingers there and then. All the little hairs on the back of his hand caught fire and before he could put the thing down and nurse his hurts with a curse or two, he had added his own particular savour to the tell-tale stench of the thing.

Five minutes later, Tom led them through a narrow doorway into Agnes Danforth's temporary resting-place. They did not linger here, but went upwards into the lower chambers of the keep's more public areas. Here they had some distant sight of servants hurrying about their business, but Tom kept them clear of the bustle as he guided them past the working areas and into the maze of passages immediately beneath King Henry's new additions of curtain-wall and gun-placements. The closest they came to being swept into the preparations was when they passed the kitchens where a whole ox was being turned slowly on a spit above the blazing fire, and giving off – to Ben's sharp senses at least – a tastier version of the odour his hand and the dark-lantern seemed to be emitting.

'Leave that here,' ordered Tom as he led them up into King Henry's workings. If Ugo was surprised by the ease and speed with which they could rise from one balcony to the next, passing the long-barrelled culverins as they glowered out across the calm of the Channel, then he said nothing. Soon the repetition of the design fell into a predictable pattern and Ugo was content to take the lead until Tom's hand fell upon his shoulder and the three of them stopped. They were halfway up the outer wall now, and their view south was clear and uninterrupted in the calm of approaching evening. Away on the horizon, several sets of sails gleamed pale gold with tobacco shadows in the sunshine.

Ben glanced at them as the other two turned inwards. 'We'd need Agnes Danforth and her sharp eyes to make anything more of those,' he said.

'Indeed,' said Tom dismissively. As he spoke, he opened a trap-door at the back, beside the inner door that led into whatever room of the original keep stood behind and below them. Ugo looked down the trap and Ben peeked over his shoulder, down into the throat of a long, dark corridor with a dead end at its head, except for the trap. Then Tom let the wood drop and it slammed shut noisily. 'A long drop there,' he said. 'Or a short flight of steps here.' He knelt by the door, picked the lock with his dagger, opened the way and led them down. As Tom waited, Ben glanced through the inner window as he followed and was surprised to see not Lady Margaret's quarters but the armoury.

The three of them came out into the warlike room one by one, Tom last, because he lingered to relock the door. As the other two hesitated at the edge of the fencing *piste*, Tom crossed to the wall and pulled down the falchion that Ben had used in practice yesterday. It came in a black leather scabbard with a considerable swash figured in gold.

'Give your Toledo to Ugo. Just for tonight,'

said Tom quietly. 'You will cut an altogether more impressive figure in this – especially if you have to use it. There is much of the swashbuckler about you, Ben, and there will be hearts lost to you this night!'

Ben opened his mouth to reply – perhaps even to demur; but even as he did so, the most unexpected sound rang out. It was the brassy blare of hunting horns.

'We are summoned to Lady Margaret's feast,' said Tom. 'She would have preferred the bell in St Michael's Church, I expect, but she cannot ring it without a bell-rope.'

'Such a sound!' said Ben, quite awed. "Tis almost as thrilling as the hunting horns in Shakespeare's play of *A Midsummer Night's Dream*!'

'Better than Plautus, perhaps?' teased Tom.

The drama of the moment won through to the truth in Ben's jealous heart. '*Much* better than Plautus,' he said.

CHAPTER 27

Feast

What struck Ben most forcefully about the feast was the importance of the guests. It was not the pomp or ceremony with which the occasion was conducted – though that was enough to rival Queen Elizabeth's court at its most formal. It was not the food – though he was hungry and it was the best that he had ever tasted, offering a range and quality of removes that he had hitherto never even dreamed of. It was not even the entertainment – though this was varied and amusing, and he had never in all his life heard a baron reciting Homer in Greek or seen one fighting with a quarterstaff, and these were amongst the least of the attractions.

What really struck him was the way in which every local lord, knight, gentleman and justice had been invited here; and they had all come, with their ladies at the very least. As he arrived at the entrance to the great hall hard on Tom's heels, Danforth was just announcing to the Baron Cotehel and the Lady Margaret his mother and Countess Cotehel, the arrival of Justice Pinnock and his wife, followed by Lord and Lady Keane and Lord and Lady Trematon.

'When Hal comes into his majority,' said Tom, *sotto voce*, as they joined the queue to be announced, 'he will not only be Lord Outremer and Castelan of Cotehel, he will be the Senior Justice at the local assize and Lord Lieutenant of the County. It is the price he pays, as his forbears paid, to the memory of King Henry for the work done here and at Elfinstone. It is no wonder that everyone at this end of Cornwall and the latter end of Devon wants to know him. In due course he will be their lord and leader in peace and war.'

'It is no wonder, then,' said Ben in reply, 'that the Lady Margaret wishes to have him master of every social, legal and military art.'

Then the social arts claimed the three of them, and discussion had to wait. They were announced by Danforth and then guided past the reception line, where the Baron and Lady Margaret greeted them with the same formality they used on the greatest of their neighbours. Ben was not a man to be easily impressed, and yet the simple magnificence of Lady Margaret's gold and silver dress, suiting so perfectly, as it did, with the newly furbished decorations of the great hall, simply took his breath away; and when he stole a glance across at his master, he saw that Tom, too, had been simply stunned by the Lady's impact.

Their placing at table was clearly a compromise between the Lady's wishes for the master, the apprentice's obvious lack of polish and the Dutchman's unexpected arrival. They were the last three above the salt, but on the favoured right hand and, if not at the top table itself – raised on a dais so the great and the good could see and be seen in careful precedence – then immediately beside. Indeed, though Ben was suspiciously proximate to the great medieval ewer of white crystals that marked the line between the honoured guests and all the others, he was so well pleased that he hardly noticed.

The courses came and went. Each one was introduced first to the Baron, as master here, and then the Lady Margaret. Then each was brought down the tables as each guest, in strict social order, carved himself a chunk to lay upon his trencher; or, if he preferred, Danforth in all his glory would perform the office for him. Those courses that survived the entire table – like ceremonial baron of beef, presented first in honour of their host, the ox, the great pie of larks and blackbirds and the porpoise baked in golden foil – were placed on the remove tables at the side of the hall.

And so the evening began to pass, the whole of it as well rehearsed, prepared and presented as any of Will Shakespeare's plays. At first, the food and the conversation were enough to claim the full attention of the guests as they all began to fill their bellies and broaden their acquaintance. Then, as they continued to eat, they were entertained. The tables were set in a horse-shoe shape so that diversions could be presented in the midst. After the first ten courses, when the edge was taken from appetite for food and conversation alike, a little choir of servants schooled by the Reverend Wainscott sang some modern catches by the likes of Thomas Tallis. This they followed with the short but unseasonal 'Audivi Vocem' from his Christmas Mass. These were succeeded by a consort of viols, and the viols by a boy with a lute, who sang like an angel. Ben recognized him as Kit the butcher's boy, and wondered – with a vagueness for which the *boutellier*'s excellent vintages were entirely responsible – that he should play his instrument as handily as he could steer a skiff.

Kit was succeeded by the Baron himself, who recited the opening of *The Iliad* in Greek to much applause. Then he suited the warlike theme of the poem with some action, falling to an exhibition bout with quarterstaves fought against Ulysses St Just.

Then, as the wine continued to flow, the manly theme of combat dominated. The blacksmith and the most massive of Quin's postillions gave a bout at wrestling, which was declared a drawn match after some half-hour of equal effort. This garnered the loudest applause of all, the clapping led by the soft-hearted Lady Margaret, who clearly did not like to see winners lording it over losers.

Then St Just appeared again. As Ben was looking vaguely around for the opponent chosen for his next bout, the sword-master crossed the open area with swift and purposeful stride. And stopped immediately opposite. For a chilling moment that sobered him more effectively than a bucket of water, Ben supposed St Just was going to challenge him – but no. With a kind of blessed inevitability, Ben heard the words: 'Before we clear the room for dancing, perhaps Master Musgrave...'

Tom put down the fork that he had brought from Italy for occasions such as this and stood. He turned slightly and bowed to the shimmering vision of Lady Margaret at the head of the table, then stepped back. As he walked round to the makeshift *piste*, he undid his belt and took off his rapier and his dagger. By the time he stood opposite his challenger, he was ready to lay them on the table and accept whatever weapons St Just had chosen. This was an exhibition bout, performed with courtesy, for the amusement of the guests – it was no formal challenge to a duel such as might have given Tom the selection of the weapons.

No sooner was Tom ready than Danforth himself appeared, hot-foot from the armoury, with two old-fashioned sword-and-buckler sets. Tom accepted the set that he was given and weighed the short-sword easily as he watched St Just prepare for battle. Tom was used to such bouts. He usually fought on his own terms and with his own swords, but tonight he was content to follow his opponent's lead. He did not remove his red-slashed doublet, therefore; but he did pull out the black gloves he carried, like the Italian fork, for special occasions, and pulled them on. Then, side by side with St Just, he went through a standard series of exercises to loosen his joints, and ensure his clothing would not restrict his movements at a crucial moment. At last satisfied and readied, the two of them straightened, and fell into the first position, face to face, some pair of yards apart.

Tom had studied George Silver's *Paradoxes of Defence* and, although he found it old-fashioned in the face of Capo Ferro's teachings, he was well able to employ its advice. With his buckler held low, he waited, therefore, adopting a square-on approach almost like that into which the wrestlers had fallen. His sword was a well-balanced falchion with a blade a little longer than his fore-arm, almost as wide as two fingers, sharpened on both edges and coming to a decent point. He placed it in the Fool's Guard and watched St Just's point, waiting. He did not have to wait long.

St Just was quick and confident, but he favoured the edge and made his strikes a little wide and showy so that, fast though he was, Tom had warning enough to block and turn either with his own blade or his buckler. He was content to fight defensively at first, but soon began to dictate the rhythm, so that the pace of the battle became relentlessly faster. There was little thrusting – it was all cut-and-parry work, beating out a ringing music as though a blacksmith was racing to fashion a horse-shoe in the least possible time. Blade against blade chimed like discordant bells while blade against buckler rang like gongs.

Tom had the advantage of having seen St Just at work against the footpads at Farnham and, as his defensive game relentlessly explored his opponent's technique, Tom soon began to define its limitations. No sooner had these been defined in the dazzling, pounding display of cut and parry that had characterized the bout so far, however, than Tom was presented with a problem: if he took the initiative now, he could win the bout. It would not be easy, but he was certain he could do it. As he thought – albeit at lightning speed – Tom eased the relentless rhythm of the bout. St Just sensed victory and had no scruples such as Tom harboured. He drove at once for total mastery, and Tom was forced to focus entirely on his technique, suddenly concerned that St Just was about to add some more red slashes to his crimson-puffed doublet. It was St Just's livelihood at risk here – and his standing before his household, his student and his mistress: he could not lose. But Tom suddenly found that, damage to his flesh and doublet aside, he did not want to lose in front of Lady Margaret either. The rhythm of the bout picked up again and Tom began to take the initiative. He stopped moving his feet and stood there, toe to toe – a benefit, given the guns wedged in his loose boot-tops. He pulled both blade and buckler in, controlling the size of the gestures he made in order to attack or defend; and as his strokes became tighter, so they became faster and less easy to read.

St Just's style was not so adaptable. He had clearly not been bested in a long while and never felt the need to explore his limitations as Tom sometimes did with Ugo and his other masters in the Corporation of London's Masters of Defence. And he was beginning to tire. Grimly, relentlessly, Tom pushed the rhythm of the bout on to another, faster level. Their arms were almost blurred now and the ringing of blade on blade and buckler was almost continuous. Tom's eyes flicked away from the firefly point of St Just's blade and up to the violet of his extraordinary eyes. There was desperation there, and not a little madness. Here, thought Tom, was a man that would take death before dishonour – who had, at the bottom of his wounded heart, little else to live for.

Tom froze. His blade and buckler were high, for St Just was attacking from The Falcon, high over their heads. The strike arrived and Tom turned his fore-arms, wedging both the blades in place, and holding them there. 'Master St Just,' he gasped, his voice filling the ringing silence, 'a moment's rest, I beg of you.' His level brown gaze held St Just's, and in the instant that followed he saw the madness drain away – saw something else replace it; but St Just glanced away before he could read exactly what it was. Then, once again, the Lady Margaret was pleased to lead the thunderous applause for honours so dazzlingly won – and so equally shared.

'That was kind,' observed Ugo quietly as Tom caught up his swords then stood back against the wall while the room was cleared for dancing.

Tom gave a bark of laughter. 'Charity's always painful,' he said. 'I might well have made another enemy there.'

'What are you talking about?' demanded Ben, all afire. 'Such a bout! I have never seen such swordplay. You were Castor and Pollux, two twins of equal brightness.'

Tom was content to leave it at that, hoping Ben's view was the general one. The consort of viols returned and the dancing began; but this, as everything else before midnight that evening, was dictated by the strictest order. Had Tom hoped for a moment or two that Lady Margaret might dance with him, he was disappointed; but he did not give up hope. As with the sword fighting, the dancing here was old-fashioned and country-style, but none the worse for that, and, as he could read George Silver, so he could dance a pavane, an allemande or a galliard with the best – or a bergomask or a dump, come to that. This ability remained untested for the moment,

307

however. He stood with Ben and Ugo, entertaining a passing array of other guests – mostly men – who were also not dancing for the moment and who wished to express their admiration of his swordplay.

Although the two side tables had been removed, the top table remained on its dais so that between dances Lady Margaret and her most influential guests could take their ease and continue to test the *boutellier*'s cellarage. Tom kept a careful eye on this, and on the Lady as she came and went, her cheeks aglow and her eyes a-sparkle.

She was seated here at midnight when the great doors behind her were suddenly thrown wide. A strange procession entered, headed by Percy Gawdy dressed in Danforth's costume, gold cross-garters and all. Behind him came Kit the butcher's boy dressed in Hal's gold brocade and, beside him, Gwynneth the servant girl in one of Lady Margaret's dresses. Behind them came a small army of servants rather nervously in fancy dress. The consort of viols fell silent and the guests fell back from the dance floor.

'Of course!' spat Tom. 'They have planned it early! Fool that I am not to have seen it! We must be quick or we shall be lost!'

Gawdy's moment was come, albeit two days early, and he claimed it with theatrical relish. 'My Lady, you must yield your seat,' he said, holding up his hand. Though preoccupied and already seeking to take action, Tom noticed at once that the bandages were off

308

now. The brand on his thumb burned red and painful still – indeed the whole fist seemed to have been scalded back and front.

At Gawdy's gesture, the strangely dressed servants gathered round the Lady Margaret and Hal beside her. As he continued to speak, they rose and were led quietly out of the hall. All eyes were on Lady Margaret as always, and none on Tom and his companions – for the time being.

'For I am your Lord of Misrule,' Gawdy called to all there assembled. 'And these are the King and Queen for a day. These are their servants and the feast and the day are theirs.

'It is *All Fools!*'

'Quick,' ordered Tom under his breath so that only Ugo and Ben could hear him. 'This is it. Let's go!'

CHAPTER 28

All Fools

It was only the speed and decision with which Tom moved them forward that allowed them to escape. Not that it felt much like an escape at first – certainly not to Ben, who was intrigued by the possibilities that the Feast of Fools traditionally offered. The guests were of Ben's mind: many of them had experienced the fun and games, and sport – of childish and more adult sort – that the temporary exchange of power often offered. Like the country celebrations of May Day and Midsummer, part of the enjoyment of the feast was the way in which social barriers were lowered and a great deal of licence allowed; and the fact that many of the motley band of servants – men and women alike – were masked only added to the deliciously mysterious possibilities.

The three of them pushed swiftly but not too obviously through the press towards the great door, therefore, the only eddy of movement in the sudden calm. Gawdy's wildly dressed followers had come right in through the door and none of them as yet had thought to step back and close it. Instead they were nonplussed for an instant – taken aback by the ease with which their plans were proceeding. Even Gawdy's ringing announcement faltered a little.

In that instant Tom had reached the door. He paused for a heartbeat on the threshold and looked back as the other two caught up with him. His cold brown gaze raked over the frozen tableau of the room, drawing up a swift catalogue of who was there and who was not, as far as the masks would allow an accurate tally. Then, side by side, they stepped out into the empty entrance hall. Lady Margaret, Hal and their costumed escort were gone. The great echoing cavern was empty – but, Tom calculated, it would only be so for a moment; and in that moment, if they were to sound the wicked bottom of this seemingly innocent charade, they must disappear themselves.

'Up or down?' asked Ugo, seeming to read Tom's mind.

'Out, for choice.'

'Best be about it then, or we shall be discovered.'

And so, like the most craven cowards on the face of God's creation, the three of them took to their heels. By the time the doors into the great hall swung closed, they were crouching in the shadows outside the main door; and by the time that door too swung shut, they were invisibly pressed against the wall of the powder store, where the shadow of St Michael's-within-Cotehel offered the best escape from the light of the rising moon.

'What's the plan?' asked Ugo. 'I take it we'll not run any more.'

'I will expound as we go,' said Tom in a tone that Ben had never yet heard him use; 'but we are not stood here merely for safety's sake. Our quest must begin with the sally-port.'

'Why?' asked Ben simply.

'Because, apprentice mine, if we have enemies and to spare within the castle keep, we have a goodly army more in Whitsand Bay – if I have read matters here aright.'

So saying, Tom turned and, with the other two at his shoulder he crossed to the little iron door and swung it wide – to reveal, under Ben's bulging gaze, a pair of galleys snug against the big stone jetty there, and the cliff-side dark with men. After allowing his companions a brief glance, Tom eased the door shut and slid the bolts hard home.

'Smugglers?' croaked Ben, his voice awash with utter disbelief.

'Spaniards,' answered Tom, grimly, 'and we must stay ahead of them until we can work out how to stop them and organize those that might help us do it. Meanwhile, we must keep out of the hands of the men that are helping them. We must find the Lady Margaret and young Hal, if we can; and we must warn Poley. I had not thought they would make Kit the King of Fools. That may make things more complicated.'

'That's your plan, is it?' said Ugo dryly: 'stay free, organize resistance, alert Poley and rescue the Lady.'

'Part of it,' Tom answered grimly.

'Can someone please explain to me,' croaked Ben, 'what in the name of God is going on here?'

'In a way it seems to have started with God,' said Tom, lifting the trap at the back of the powder store, 'though that fact was not made clear until we got to Winchester; and even there, some doubts remained.'

Down the ladder they went, one after the other into the strange silver-and-black maze of the moon-bright cellar. They moved on tip-toe and spoke in whispers – and even then only when they were close enough almost to touch lip to ear-lobe. 'For Gawdy was forced to claim benefit of clergy when he killed Lean Green. He did that, I would guess, because the footpads had failed in their commission to kill St Just as the footpads in London had been employed to kill Mann and Hammond – failed in their commission but refused to repay the money. Get the dark-lantern, Ben; I calculate it will have been returned to the foot of the ladder by now. And watch: it may still be hot. Gawdy burned his hand upon it most fragrantly when he was signalling the Spanish galleon on our first night here.'

'Well, I guess what you say might make sense,' said Ben, obeying without a second thought as Tom in turn crossed to the moon-bright door out to the cliff-face path and bolted that tight closed as well. 'But why would Gawdy wish to signal Spaniards or to employ footpads to attack St Just – and what of the benefit of clergy?'

'Gawdy was forced into declaring it to stay alive, for he would certainly have hanged otherwise; and so he revealed a secret he would rather have kept – the central secret of the whole, I think: that his father was burned at the stake.'

'Martyrs were ten-a-penny in those days,' said Ben. 'How many did Bloody Mary burn?'

'But he was burned while Gawdy was still in his mother's womb. Not under Mary, therefore – under Edward; and that made all the difference. He was not a Protestant martyr; he was a Catholic, or held some services that offended the Protestant sensibilities of the good men of Kent around him – and ultimately those of the Lord Protector. But whatever his fatal miscalculation in those dogmatically dangerous times, who was it lit the bonfire under him?'

'The local justices.'

'Indeed. At the local assize. And who is the leading justice of the Rochester assize? – when he is in residence at Elfinstone, at least, as he was then?'

'Lord Outremer,' breathed Ben.

'The Lady Margaret's grandfather,' said Tom. 'And so is the lovely lady brought to the vengeful attention of an already dangerous man; a man who, prompted by a confederate, was planning to let his madness run riot under the protection of the Spanish; a man who, therefore, needed anyone that might fight to the death to protect Lady Margaret out of the way – to wit, St Just.'

As they had this discussion they were feeling their way along the passage leading into the tobacco store. Only when they were in here did Tom pause to light the lantern, certain its brightness would be safely hidden from prying eyes for the moment at least.

He paused in the chamber and pointed the narrow beam of brightness down at the bundles on the floor. 'We discussed the contents of these packages when we last were here,' he whispered, 'but not the wrapping. Look closely, Ben. What do you see?'

'Markings and writing.'

'Ugo?'

'That great "V" there is the port marking of Vlissingen, I think.'

'And I agree. But the writing?'

'Spanish,' said Ben.

'As you would expect. The tobacco has been smuggled here from the Spanish Netherlands. And it does not stretch imagination too far, does it, to suppose that where Spanish tobacco can go, an enterprising Spanish force might follow? – given some promise of a warm welcome and a good haul of important prisoners: every important social and civil leader in the Plymouth area, in fact, assembled here for their feast of welcome tonight while we have been focused on the danger to the Lady threatened for two nights' time! Thank God Drake and Raleigh have not come.'

'Hence the importance,' whispered Ben, returning to the original thought, 'of the smuggler held in Plymouth Clink.'

'Indeed,' said Tom, 'of the smuggler held by Robert Poley; but also, I suspect, of some whisper from a spy in the Southwark Clink on the day he first sought us out at the blaze on Water Lane – a blaze designed to rid our conspirators of a canvas and a chapel alike. For he has had wind of this, or something unsettlingly like it, but not enough to take any action – until now.'

'Now that it is too late to warn him. 'Tis a long night's ride to Plymouth.'

'Perhaps,' said Tom. 'And that was the point

of the Fools' Feast: to make him think of April and catch him unprepared tonight. But he's less than an hour's sail away on the back of a rising tide and the wind coming out of the south and west – if I can get Kit to the little skiff he keeps down at the foot of the cliff.'

'But Whitsand Bay is full of Spaniards,' quavered Ben.

'Not there,' said Tom. 'Round the point on the Penlee side – a straight sail across the Sound and he's there.'

'Is there no other way of raising the alarm? Has the castle no alarm bell?'

'Indeed it has,' said Tom, 'and no great distance from here, in the bell-tower of St Michael's; but the bell cannot be rung because I cut the rope – as I was bound to do – when I took down the body of Agnes Danforth. You see the cunning of the mind at work in this? Or should I say minds? For there are two, as I hinted earlier.'

On that he turned away from the tobacco and crossed to the little inner door that led to Agnes's resting-place. He eased them into the silent chamber and paused for an instant, shining the light down upon her. 'As I mentioned in the garden of our burning house, it took two to carry Master Mann; and, as I demonstrated when I slammed the trap leading down from the gun platform into the end of the passageway beside the armoury,' he said, 'only two men working together could have surprised Agnes. One held the

316

trap up while the other jumped silently down behind her and ran forward to take her by the neck – one-handed, as you see.'

'Gawdy again,' said Ben, his voice awed by Tom's ruthless logic.

'And, therefore, Rowley holding the trap behind him, and helping him up again when they were precipitated down the stair and it no longer mattered who heard the trap-door shutting. When was it done? While we were all at dinner, I would judge – and Lady Margaret's robe taken while she was with us. Why was it done? Originally because if the cut-up portrait was Gawdy's, the chapel that housed it was Rowley's. A Doctor, no less, of Poley's College for Spies at Cambridge. He was in correspondence with someone called Lane – Poley himself, I assume – who was known as Hogg to his other spy. Hogg Lane is where he lives, you see. A good spy on his own spy and on Lord Robert's spy – Lord Robert Devereux, the Earl of Essex, who employed close eyes upon the woman he hates and the boy whose person and fortune he covets. But in the end, Agnes simply saw too much – saw, I am certain, something to make her suspect that they were here when they were not supposed to be here; and so they moved. With Agnes out of the way, a little of the sin-worm's madness took hold, and the cunning we have noted. For, with the portrait, have they not beheaded her? Aye and burned her too, in effigy at least – so they planned in the house in Water Lane. Now, in her golden robe, they hanged her; using an empty barrel from their hiding-place to do the deed; keeping us all riveted upon the Lady Margaret, who was at once their eventual target and immediate distraction, to be attacked, as I have said, on the day we have all been led toward like chickens following a line drawn in the dirt: Saturday, April the first.'

'Of course!' said Ben. 'But I said myself it could not be them because they had not yet returned from Winchester.'

'Ah, but they had. They arrived quite soon after the rest of us and were hidden in the cellar beneath the powder store while they completed their plans for tonight.'

'And how was this achieved?' asked Ugo, frowning down at the dead woman. 'They must have had help.'

'We live in an age where our names mean something,' said Tom, apparently irrelevantly. 'In the future I would guess all places will be like London now and a mixture where names and lines and families are all too easily lost; but that's not true of most of the country yet. Find the most common man called Smith and you know that within a generation or two his forebears were shoeing horses. Ben, I'd guess that, were we to climb into the lower branches of your father's family tree, we'd find some clan along the Scottish Borders that would own him, for Jonson is a border name, like Musgrave.'

'Aye,' allowed Ben. 'And so?'

'If not of trade or clan, then of birthplace,' Tom said, snapping the lantern shut as he crossed to the next inward door. 'Where was that village, hard by Elfinstone, where the smith re-shod your horse?'

'Wainscott,' said Ben. Then he repeated in a much more thoughtful tone, 'Wainscott.'

'I told you Kent was all-important,' said Tom, and swung the door an inch ajar. 'Now this is our most dangerous path so far,' he added after a moment's silent look-out. 'We must get through the area controlled by Rowley, Gawdy and their revellers, and our absence will have been noted by now so there'll be look-outs posted. We must get to the tunnels under the gun emplacements and work our way up. If the Lady Margaret is in the public rooms, or her private chambers, we'll be able to reach her from there. But that will only happen if we avoid the Spanish soldiers who'll be coming in through the ancient tunnels we've just come out of. Rowley's opened those for them while Gawdy was preparing his Feast of Fools. The gun placements will also lead to the roof. Anyone else trying to get out of this will likely head up there, for the great gate will be well secured by now, so we've a chance of picking up some help if we're lucky; and if not, then we'll use the culverins to raise the alarm one way or another. In the meantime,' he added grimly, 'we keep an eye out for the main chance. For I've not given up all hope of enlisting young Kit on to our side.'

Before they found anyone to help them, however, they first found someone else who needed their help. For, as Tom swung the door wide, ready to make a run for it again, he glanced back at Agnes; and there, in the brightness from the open doorway, lay Martin, trussed up like a Christmas goose and laid out cold on the floor beneath her. So they hesitated in the place a little longer, using the dark-lantern once again and continuing their whispered conversation until Martin was unfettered and strong enough to walk with them.

'It was at Elfinstone I first became certain there were two,' said Tom as they worked. 'For while I could just about imagine one man able to hollow out that extra passage within the wall, how much easier it was to see how two working together could do it – and one at each end of the tunnel itself: the master and the secretary. How well it must have fallen out for them – for Gawdy particularly, forced by his employment to share in so many of his mistress's private thoughts and transactions, but never allowed to see her in her truly private moments. It must have been a kind of hell for him to be so utterly consumed by the person of the victim he was preparing to destroy. What an unutterable release to be able to play peeping Tom to her Godiva; but what torture to know that he was bound to destroy what he coveted so dearly. No wonder the Earl of Essex's secret gift came to such a mysterious end – especially if, by the most delicious irony, Essex was using Gawdy as Poley was using Mann, to watch her in any case. For the picture also says, does it not? that *I have eyes so closely set upon you that I can have your likeness made without my artist even seeing you.* A chilling prospect indeed; and,' he added, as Martin began to stir, opening his eyes and frowning in the lantern's glare, 'were Gawdy to mention my name to the Earl of Essex as someone the Lady Margaret was wishing to involve, the Earl's reply would likely be enough to get the letters to me stopped, no matter what the price. For was it not at Elfinstone we first crossed swords and I cost both Essex and Southampton the fortune Lady Margaret now possesses.'

'So,' said Ugo slowly, 'you think the Earl of Essex is involved in this? – that these Spaniards are somehow working to his orders?'

'No,' said Tom. 'I think the Earl lost control of his creature long since. I think this is nothing to do with the Earl's plans for revenge. It is all to do with Poley's creature Rowley beginning to doubt his faith and think of Spain – of a spy spying on another spy and seeing thereby a way to use his man. Only a man such as Rowley could have sent a message such as Master Mann to the "Master Lane" he knew would be always watching him, unknown from the shadows. It is all to do with Gawdy's revenge against the Lady for what her grandfather did to Gawdy's father; and I think he and Rowley have transmuted

321

two strange desires into one great scheme, so that they share the madness now. They have nothing to hope for but that the Spaniards will allow them licence now and afford them protection later in gratitude for the service they are rendering tonight. You are welcome back amongst us, Master Martin,' he added. 'I hope you are able to walk, for we must run. The Spanish will be here at any moment.'

With Tom in the lead and the chamberlain staggering between Ugo and Ben, the four of them raced across the store-room behind the kitchen to the door that led into the tunnels beneath the new works. Tom tore this open and froze: there in the mouth of the first tunnel a wild figure stood facing him. It was dressed in a mad assortment of rags and shreds, and where its face should have been there was an almost featureless vizard mask. Tom charged forward at once, even as the monstrosity grappled under its robes for a weapon. As he ran, Tom stooped and slid one of the dags from his boot-top. As he did so, however, he saw another unconscious body sprawling on the floor. This he recognized at once as one of Quin's ostlers, dressed only in shirt and breeches.

Tom straightened as his shoulder took his opponent in the ribs. A familiar hissing sound completed the train of thought and he pulled back, minimizing the damage of his impact, but bringing him face to face with the falch- ion that he had fought to a standstill earlier that evening. He froze. As he did so, the other three staggered through the door behind him. 'Master St Just,' gasped Tom. 'We are here to help.'

It was the sight of Martin Danforth that stayed St Just's hand. As Tom explained what they were about, St Just sheathed his sword again. 'You stand a detter chance of finding her than I do,' he allowed at last.

'Can you get back into the great hall and take King Kit to one side?' asked Tom. 'He's our best chance of getting help in that little skiff of his, if we can get him to it before the Spanish close every loophole in the place and Gawdy has leisure to think what he wants to do to Lady Margaret. We'll retreat upwards if we get the chance. A last stand on the roof, if nothing else. You'll be welcome to join us there if the fates allow. We'll be all fools together!'

CHAPTER 29

Desperate Measures

'The best we can hope for is three hours,' said Tom as they ran for the tunnels leading to the lowest gun emplacement. 'That will see us through the darkest hours and into the hope of dawn.'

'If we can survive that long,' gasped Ben, 'with such fearful odds ranged against us; and such desperate plans for rescue and relief.'

"Tis not so bad,' said Tom. 'Consider, Ben: if Gawdy and Rowley are in league with the Spanish, the worst of the rest will be in league with nothing worse than smugglers; and most of the celebrants at the Feast of Fools – in mask and costume or not – are good honest yeomen like the postillion whose costume St Just has taken. If the Spanish have the castle, then, they will find it full of enemies themselves – and all of them led by the redoubtable Captain Quin, as like as not.'

Tom had no sooner delivered himself of this observation than the first of the shots rang out and a great outpouring of shouting and screaming swept all around them like the roaring of a nearby waterfall – only to be stilled by the next brutal volley.

Martin Danforth stopped, brought suddenly to full wakefulness. 'Those are my people,' he said. 'I must go to them.'

'You'll be more good to them out here with us,' said Tom, 'and a sight more use to Lady Margaret and the Baron – not to mention the chance you'll have to revenge your sister's murder.'

That steadied him. A steely look crept into his baggy, watery eyes and the set of his jaw firmed under his jowls.

'But if Gawdy and Rowley are working with the Spanish, how have they managed to make all these complicated arrangements?' asked

Ugo. 'I can see how Gawdy would want to, in the strange, fantastic world of lust and revenge he seems to be sliding into; but how in heaven's name would he manage it?'

'With the Lady Margaret's letters,' answered Martin suddenly. 'That's it. I'll swear that's it.'

'Explain,' invited Tom, leading the way through to the first of the well-armed balconies.

'I had thought nothing of it, for I have never met the Lady Margaret until now ... but ... Since time immemorial it has been the right of the Outrams to take a little easement from the smugglers hereabout – for use of the cellarage and such; and Quin has been sending letters to his contacts here and in Flanders on his own behalf and that of the Outrams for thirty years and more. So when he started sending letters from Lady Margaret, he thought no more about it. He told me so. It was secret amusement between the pair of us that she had fallen so swiftly in with family ways. But nothing has ever come for her – a note or two of reply, perhaps, now I think of it, but never any lavender or lace or silk or such as might be expected. And now I know a little of her face to face, I cannot believe she would do such a thing as trade with smugglers. And...'

'And the letters were never in her writing, were they?' asked Tom thoughtfully. 'They were in her secretary's hand – and no one thought anything strange about that. You are

325

right, Master Danforth, this has been easy enough for an evil, secret and cunning man. You have all made it so easy for the pair of them. Let us not make it quite so easy for their confederates, shall we? These doors are solid and the steps up to them narrow on the inside. Do they lock as well as bolt from both sides?'

'They do, master. The keys are kept on the insides and the locks were put in at the old King's direction, so each level needs a new key.'

'Well, let us open the first here and remove the key. So. Now let us lock the door and close the bolts. They'll be lucky to come through that. Now this trap-door. I see it also bolts. Now this level is isolated. And up we go to the next. Do these ladders lift off? I see they do as well. This is very good indeed. With luck and care we can isolate all the guns from the castle keep until the Spaniards find a way to break down every door, level after level from the inside, one after another. That should slow them – and, indeed, should allow an intrepid band such as we to face them off upon the roof to some effect, in the hope of Poley's arrival with the dawn.'

'With the dawn and a regiment of horse,' added Ben feelingly.

'Only until they get their hands on Lady Margaret,' warned Ugo. 'We'd have to come down for her.'

'Then it is doubly in our interest to get to her first, is it not?' answered Tom with absolute command.

Level by level they worked their way up-wards, opening the doors to retrieve the keys, then locking and bolting them from the outside; locking down the trap-doors that opened into the dead ends of the passage-ways; lifting the ladders out of their brackets behind them and tossing them over the cliff. 'We need only keep the topmost,' said Tom; 'then with a little cunning we can get down again if we need to. But tell me, Master Martin – and truly, for it is of no little moment – does Master St Just have any truck with smugglers?'

'No, sir. For a sailor he is most law-abiding and proper. I think even Drake would have traded with the men from Flanders before Master Ulysses would. Or the woman from Scilly.'

'Is she an important smuggler, this Scillon-ian woman, then? For she is in the hands of a fearful man.'

'In our local waters she is something of a pirate queen – like that Irish woman that lately won her freedom from the Queen for running a pirate fleet across the Western Approaches. But what information she could give I cannot tell.'

'Of the movements of Spanish galleys out of the ports of Spanish Flanders and Catholic France, no doubt; and able to tell of this night's comings and goings – did he not have her securely under lock and key!'

They actually saw their first Spanish guards

when they looked down into the armoury. Tom had warned them of the likelihood of this, though any of the others could have calculated the probability with but a moment's thought. It was a squad of four grim-looking *tercio* men, well trained and professional – professional but clearly desperate for money, for their uniforms were as patched and shredded as their armour was bright and burnished in the candle-light. They had already rearmed themselves from the best of the weaponry around them and were standing on easy guard, looking every bit as lean, hard, hungry and deadly-dangerous as they actually were.

As quietly as mice, Tom and his men went grimly on about their business, balancing the danger of alerting these men to their presence against the equal danger of leaving them an easy route to follow in their rear. On the next balcony up, with the ladder sticking out over the low wall beside the culverins, they gave the greatest heave that they could manage to send it far away from the cliff-edge to tumble silently into the night. Tom lingered for a moment, watching the ladder fall end over end into the Channel. Away to his left suddenly, out towards Penlee Point, he saw the flash of a white skiff's sail catching the moonlight as it swelled under the gentle sou'westerly wind. Then, with his heart in his mouth on the sudden, he turned to look into the Lady Margaret's private chamber.

The four of them were in there, but at first

it was difficult to recognize Lady Margaret. In the inverted tradition of the Feast of Fools, she was dressed as a kitchen maid in little more than a slattern's shift, the golden glory of her hair bound up beneath a dirty kerchief; and yet she still stood straight and tall, her hand firmly on Hal's shoulder as he stood protectively in front of her. Gawdy and Rowley stood shoulder to shoulder filling the doorway, looking in at the pair of them with frowning concentration, their eyes catching the light of fire and candles to glint and shimmer with the same silvery chill as the Spanish soldiers' armour.

'My only regret,' said Gawdy suddenly, his voice unexpectedly loud in the breathless hush that the four secret watchers had brought with them, 'is that I won't be able to hear you scream as you burn. I heard my father scream as he died. My mother was there, with me within her, and she says how I kicked at the sound; and I can hear it still, you know – whenever I sleep. That's why I sleep so little. That's why I could spend my nights in watching you, more closely and more closely still, and readying my plans for to-night.'

'You are mad, Percy,' said Hal with quiet dignity. 'But still I shall see you quartered for this treason – hanged and drawn and quartered.'

'Oh I think not, Hal. For you see I shall be in Cadiz, living a life of rich and unimaginable indulgence with the good doctor here, and you will be in Essex House – if you are allowed to live.'

'Raise your voice, brat, and it'll be the worse for you,' hissed Dr Rowley in a bitter, sneering tone Tom had never heard him use before. 'There's none to hear you but Spanish soldiers and they'd likely as not enjoy the use of both of you before handing you back to us. They owe us a debt it'll be hard to pay with all their promised wealth and ease, no matter how bright our futures will be at King Philip's court; a fine repayment for the indulgence shown by My Lord of Essex and others to the renegades of Spain.'

Tom crossed to the trap-door that opened on to the corridor where Agnes Danforth had died and Ugo lifted the trap as Rowley must have done to let the murderous Gawdy fall on her. Tom hesitated for an instant, then reached out his hand to Ugo. 'The Toledo,' he whispered, sliding out the deadly steel reach of his Solingen blade as he spoke. An instant later, a rapier in each hand, he was gone to save the Lady and her lad.

Ben strode across to follow him but Ugo stayed him silently. 'He'll be better alone,' the Dutchman breathed. 'Get out your dag and watch his back through the grille as earlier. The Lady may not call for help, but these two will, and the door down into this chamber here is the only one we cannot get through – unless someone has the speed and wit to unbolt it for us.'

Tom landed like a cat, lightly and silently.

The solidity of walls and floor aided him as surely as it had helped Agnes Danforth's murderer. Still, he crouched on landing, mouth wide, gasping in air in great soundless gulps. Then he straightened and began to creep forward. He was as well aware as any of them that stealth and surprise were his best weapons for, although he was confident of taking Gawdy and Rowley hand to hand, they were as likely to be carrying guns as swords and, in the face of his reputation, as likely to raise the alarm as to fight like the men they were patently not. The four *tercio* guards downstairs would finish him off in an instant – for they all had guns as well, and were not likely to stand on form or deal with him honourably.

For this, for them, was war.

One door opened inwards to the right at the very head of the stairs. It stood ajar now, showing the width of Lady Margaret's private changing-room – made up still as a bedroom for young Hal. At the far end of it the inner door opened into her bedchamber, and the doorway was empty now. Tom gritted his teeth and stepped in over the threshold.

Such was Tom's concentration on his silent movements that he hardly registered the sneering, one-sided conversation from the next room at all. The words themselves were of little moment to him – and indeed, might well be a dangerous distraction; but the simple sound the men were making allowed him to locate them in the chamber although he was not yet able to see them. Like a favourite stage set from one of Will Shakespeare's plays, he brought the scene he had watched from the high grille back into his mind – and immediately saw another possible problem. He could still creep up behind the men if their backs were to the door, but the moment he came close to it, Lady Margaret or Hal would see him, and their faces would betray him. All hope of surprise would be lost unless he could rely on their quick thinking in this most terrible of extremities. He really began to hope that Lady Margaret had been so badly frightened she would unhesitatingly abet the two deaths that were her only hope of life. It would be a close call for a woman such as she was.

Then Hal gave a chilling sort of sobbing cry and Tom was spurred into action at once. He ran in through the inner doorway, throwing all his thoughts and calculations to the wind. He kicked the door itself wide as he entered, hoping to hit one of his enemies at least, but no such luck. The four of them were over by the bed. Each of the men held one slight figure, wrestling with silent fury in his arms.

'*Hold!*' spat Tom in a vicious undertone, and both men swung towards him, stricken by their discovery. With a strangled cry Dr Rowley threw Hal on to the bed and ripped his sword out of its sheath. The action was automatic and unexpected; but, never one to look gift-horses in the mouth, Tom threw himself forward. Rowley was on his left, between Tom and the low-banked fire, and so he engaged at once with Ben's Toledo blade. The Doctor had an unexpectedly firm wrist and a confident, showy style. Tom remembered what James Hammond down at Elfinstone had said about the time the Doctor and St Just spent together in the evenings: clearly there had been more than abstruse calculation and obscure speculation going on; but the pupil had all of his master's faults and few of his strengths other than overconfidence. As he would have done with St Just, had he not been so blessedly charitable, Tom slid the falchion's blade away with a flick of his own, hurling himself unstoppably along the line of his attack into the most absolute lunge of his life so far. Rowley had an instant to try and pull his edge back in against the steely strength of Tom's left wrist, but he never stood a chance and he would have died there and then had not Gawdy shot Tom in the shoulder.

The ball from Gawdy's dag took Tom at the very point of the left shoulder, tearing through the muscles right at the top of his arm, which was tensed for the killing stroke. It simply hurled him back across the room, so that the point of Ben's rapier ripped open Rowley's belly instead of running him cleanly through the spine. Stunned by the shock of the massive wound, Rowley fell backwards, clutching at himself and folding over, as though winded by his dreadful wound. One tottering step further, and he fell backwards

333

into the blazing fire.

Tom hit the wall and bounced. His shoulder was numb and Ben's dripping blade hung uselessly in his insensible fingers; but Tom was used to shock and pain. He remained on his feet and swung back instantly with his own Solingen blade held high, pointing exactly where his steely gaze was directed – at Percy Gawdy and Lady Margaret. So it was he stepped safely past the hearth just before Rowley, clothes ablaze, rolled out on to the floor behind him and began to throw himself about the floor, trying to put himself out. Feeling a little as though he were flying, Tom stepped forward once again. Gawdy was standing before him, tall and straight and confident. He held Lady Margaret tightly against him with his burned and branded hand clutching her silent throat and the second barrel of a vicious little double-barrelled dag hard against her head.

Because of his years of association with Ugo, Tom recognized the weapon for what it was. The weapon itself, of course, he recognized from Water Lane and Winchester. For, unlike most such weapons, the barrels were over and under instead of side by side. It had two firing mechanisms and two triggers, and instead of side by side, they were placed one behind the other. Gawdy's finger was resting on the second trigger, right at the rear, only a quarter of an inch in front of the weapon's solid grip. Logic and a wisp of smoke dictated that it was the ball from the first barrel that had just gone through Tom's shoulder, and that suggested that the weapon was well primed and would fire again the instant that finger moved the trigger far enough back. Tom tried not to look at Lady Margaret or the madman who was holding her. He tried to look only at that finger. Almost on another plane of concentration, he was trying to look *through* the finger to the gap between the trigger and the grip.

But Margaret forestalled him. She simply willed his eyes to hers. Almost distracted, he glanced at her. And she was speaking; her lips were moving. In utter silence, but with all the force of the loudest screams she mouthed: *KILL HIM!*

Tom's instant of distraction, the movement of the jaw against his forearm, made Gawdy glance down as well, away from Tom and the tip of his deadly blade.

'*HA!*' Tom shouted in pain as he threw himself forward. Such was the shocking, unexpected velocity of the action that not even this guttural sound gave Gawdy the extra speed he needed to thwart the impossible blow. With the accuracy only total mastery allied with constant practice can bring, Tom sent the point of his rapier past the unflinching orb of the Lady's right eye; past the soft white hollow of her temple, and through the ringlets of her golden tresses as they escaped from the kerchief; along the uppermost, delicate curl of her ear; in through Gawdy's tensing trigger-finger; through the fat little muscle beneath the bone, severing it before it could tense any further; in behind the trigger itself, wedging it immovably into place; on through the pit of the gasping throat behind it; on through the choking larynx and out through the vertebrae behind, severing his spinal cord as it went as cleanly as a headsman's axe. The gun wedged on the thickness of the blade then and smashed back into Gawdy's throat with the full weight of Tom's powerful frame behind it. Dead already, Gawdy flew backwards almost as powerfully as Tom had done when the dag-ball hit him. Lady Margaret spun sideways out of his grasp and staggered backwards, only her iron will keeping her erect.

'My Lady!' called a voice from on high with a reassuringly Dutch accent, 'unlock the door and come up before the Spaniards come.'

Gawdy landed on the bed where Tom's jutting blade wedged, and Tom managed to control his wild lunge just before the bending blade snapped.

Lady Margaret, quick-thinking even in these extremes, paused only to pull him erect and see his sword safely reclaimed before she ran to unlock the door. Hal ran to the door by her side. Tom jerked his sword-blade free and turned. Rowley was lying still now, clearly as dead as his mad associate, and still ablaze. Tom hardly had time to draw a shuddering breath before the bedding caught fire too. There were no hangings, but the fire still spread with disorientating speed. Tom swung

336

back, yelling again with the pain as his torn shoulder moved. The door was open and Hal had gone up. Lady Margaret stood silently waiting for him.

He took a step towards her. 'Go on!' he called, but his words were lost in a great explosion of sound. More smoke came billowing into the room from the high grille and Tom turned back, utterly disorientated, to see the bodies of four Spanish guards lying strewn across the changing-room.

From behind them, a wild figure stepped out, body all shreds and patches and head an almost formless, faceless mask. 'Good,' hissed St Just. 'That's saved ne sone work.'

CHAPTER 30

I Love You

It was fortunate that St Just joined them then, for they needed all his wiry strength to help them with Tom. Tom could walk swiftly enough, though his legs were weakening at the knees with shock. He could manage stairs, given a little time; but, especially with his wounded shoulder, ladders were more of a problem. And they did not have time to linger: the noise and mayhem they had caused were guaranteed to bring all the

Spanish soldiers not immediately involved in holding the hostages. St Just emphasized this with his answer to Tom's first question: 'How did you find us?'

'Like the *tercio* men, I followed my ears – and my nose. You were fortunate with your gun battery up in that grille.'

'Every dag and pistol we have in one blast and they all fired true,' said Ugo, quite awed himself. 'Eight of them, for mine were both double-barrelled. Amazing.'

'Effective, at least. Four down. A couple of hundred to go.'

'That many!' said Tom, surprised. 'Out of two galleys!'

'These are hard men,' answered St Just. 'No galley slaves for them. They rowed themselves in. And they'll row themselves out again, with half the gentry hereabouts as hostages and the castle that fired first on the Armada a blazing ruin, like as not.'

'That'll be a good trick,' said Tom. 'Most of it's built of stone.'

'Not the central section of the keep,' said St Just. 'Except for the roof, there are wooden beams and floorboards there. It's lucky you set fire to Lady Margaret's bed. Even Hal's would have set the roof and the floor ablaze.'

'That'll be an interesting experience,' said Tom explosively as they heaved him up into the next gallery and pulled the ladder up behind him. 'Up on the roof with the whole place ablaze beneath us, we'll be like a set of griddle-cakes cooking.'

'Let's hope not,' said St Just, heaving his seemingly drunken charge up on to the last ladder.

St Just was not the only one to notice Tom's state. As he came through on to the vertiginously open roofing there was a group of concerned friends there working to make sure that he fell inwards not outwards – if he fell at all; but in fact he did not fall. He staggered a little but remained erect until Lady Margaret, firmly taking charge, led him into the safe and secluded area made by the rear of the nearest gun carriage and sat him there as though upon a throne.

They still had the dark-lantern with them, and by its light she tore the shoulder off his doublet and shirt, exposing the thick red welt of his wound. Then, oblivious to petty propriety, concerned only about cleanliness and the risk of infection, she pulled up her slattern's skirts and ripped makeshift bandages off her petticoats. As she bound up his shoulder, Tom looked over at the setting moon.

'Still a while to go,' he said. 'Check all the trap-doors and bolt them shut. We want no more surprises here.' He turned to St Just as the others went off, obeying his orders. 'I saw young Kit take sail, but he'll not be back for a brace of hours – always assuming Robert Poley's awake and ready to go.'

'Is that likely, do you think?' asked Ben, calling over from the nearest trap-door.

'I cannot be certain sure,' admitted Tom. 'It

all rests upon the second letter. That Mann had a secret message in the heel of his shoe is possible, for, as Poley said, it was one of the ways Babbington and the others used in their treason with Mary of Scots; but the message was so simple and its transliteration so obvious that I wondered whether Poley showed it to us for some secret reason of his own.'

'Such as?' enquired Ben, piqued that his hard work be so lightly dismissed.

'To point us in the Spanish direction. To show us how Gawdy might have talked to Spain. To warn us that we should look beyond mere smuggling. It certainly did all of these things; but then again, perhaps it is just that Poley wanted to make assurance double sure. He had seen almost all that was in the thing, but thought perhaps we could tell him more – uncover something he had overlooked. 'Tis entirely possible either way, given the man. Are all the traps bolted fast? Good. Now, Master St Just, can these culverins be made to fire inwards as well as outwards?'

'Indeed they can. That is why they are on carriages with wheels and trunnions. That is why the top of the keep has been made the way it has.'

'And were we to move the culverins, could you guide us in the loading and the laying?'

'Of course I could. I laid the guns aboard *Revenge* for Drake. Why do you ask?'

'Were Poley to come to our rescue and ride up Rame Head with the troop of horse we hope for, what would he be faced with?'

'The great gate, portcullis down and full of well-armed *tercio* men. The great approach would be a killing field.'

'And they would have good reason to slow him down and hold him back because...'

'Because the rest of the raiding party would be taking their hostages down to the galleys,' answered Ben, used to the Socratic method.

'But if the galleys were no longer available, what then?'

There was a short silence as they all considered their answer.

Then Ben, the apprentice bricklayer, whispered, almost breathlessly, 'Why, master! You have looked with a bricklayer's eye!'

'I have, apprentice mine. But yours is the craft, so you must explain.'

'The back wall is built upon an overhang. The rear of the powder store – aye and of the church itself – sit out upon a ledge above the bay. If the guns were laid so as to make them fall outwards...'

St Just, the sailor, took up the theme. 'If the walls fell on the galleys, then the galleys would no longer be there. Then they would be like the men from the Armada galleys wrecked along the Irish coast: lost and with no retreat.'

'And what did those men do?' whispered Tom, ever more faintly.

'They gave up. Gave in.'

'Precisely. Then, with Lady Margaret's permission, and under the Baron's direction, let us lay the guns.'

The demi-culverins were heavy even though their barrels were shorter than the full culverins below. The wheels and trunnions on the carriages were by no means free and easy. In the end, everyone except Tom was needed to wedge the gun-pikes into the cracks between the flags and lever the things around. All of them except Tom were needed to shoulder the ropes attached to the fronts of the carriages and pull them across the level plain of the roof. Protesting, creaking and screaming, they went. Fortunately they only needed two in place, but each took the better part of an hour to position – especially as they both needed complex and specialist treatment. The Baron and Lady Margaret joined in with all the others under St Just's grim tutelage as they learned how to load and lay a demi-culverin. The barrels needed especially careful loading because Tom insisted on overcharging each. Double loads of powder and double loads of cannon-balls were needed, then extra wadding to keep it all in place – and extra wadding rammed in hard on top of that, for the barrels were to be angled sharply downwards. Wedges were hammered under their rear wheels to tilt the great guns downwards at Tom's suggestion and under St Just's expert direction.

Perhaps because they were so few in number, perhaps because there was no way of knowing who they were or where they had gone after the inferno in Lady Margaret's room, the Spaniards left them alone. Bereft of their English turncoat allies, the invaders had enough to occupy them, and clearly no one amongst them even dreamed of the mayhem the determined little band could cause.

'Gawdy was never down here,' said St Just grimly as they worked. 'And even if he had been, there was no way he could have understood these fortifications. If the Spaniards are relying on his information, then they will find themselves sadly misinformed.'

'Will they take the hostages straight down to the galleys, do you think?' asked Hal, ramming the wadding in with all his strength.

'They'll do that last of all,' Tom assured him. 'They are easier to control where they are in the great hall. And besides, they will do as surety should anything go amiss. They are needed on hand until the last possible moment.'

Lady Margaret took her son's shoulder and mouthed to him.

'Galley slaves?' he asked on her behalf.

'The Spanish soldiers rowed themselves,' Tom assured them both.

The culverins were laid by moonset, and the last of the light spurred them on. 'Poley is due with the dawning,' whispered Tom.

'And that's not far away,' whispered St Just. 'Do we wait for sunrise or attack at once?'

'Attack,' ordered Tom. 'As soon as the darkness comes.'

They didn't have long to wait. The last of

the moon sank down behind Plymouth and the pre-dawn darkness closed down. Even the stars seemed pallid, so that the brightness of the fuse was like a flambard when St Just lit it at the blazing chimney of their dark-lantern. The moment that he did so, a shot rang out and he was thrown backwards just as Tom had been. In the darkness it was impossible to see how badly he was wounded – and clearly, opening the dark-lantern would simply invite further attacks. So Tom grabbed the burning fuse and crawled to the culverin. He had been the one who had suggested the target, though St Just had done the final aiming. He was best placed to fire, therefore. He jammed the fuse into the culverin's open pan. The powder of the charge caught at once.

'Get dack!' called St Just weakly but clearly.

Tom took him at his word and threw himself back at once – and just in time. The gun exploded with the most colossal sound, hurling itself back wildly, like an unbroken stallion. The whole carriage came apart and the barrel reared and fell on its side, smoking and burning.

What happened on the roof was nothing compared with what happened below. For the culverin had been aimed at the powder store. Two cannon-balls, of cast iron, heated alike by the explosion of the powder behind them and by the friction of their flight because of it, smashed through the walls and into the piles of barrels there. They all exploded at once, hurling the roof upwards and the lighter walls inwards. But there was enough power to hurl the heavier walls outwards as well – not just the walls outside the powder store but the sally-port beside it and even the tower of St Michael's-within-Cotehel. All of the outer walls tumbled off the cliff and fell three hundred feet straight down on to the galleys at the jetty below; and the great bell in the church tower at last got to ring the alarm as it fell, like the wrath of God himself, upon the heads of their enemies.

'Shall we fire the second culverin?' asked Ben into the great cave of silence that followed this.

'Why not?' croaked St Just. 'I doubt there'll de any other guns tointed our way after that. And we want to welcome Naster Toley when he arrives, do we not?'

Tom passed the still-burning fuse to his apprentice. 'Open the gate, Ben,' he commanded.

So it was that, when Robert Poley reported his arrival with a troop of horse in the grey light of dawn next morning to the Council, he wrote that he had found the great gate of Cotehel Castle not only open but blasted wide with shards and splinters littered all down the great approach.

There were Spaniards still within the castle itself, he wrote, but they were quiescent and willing to negotiate, for their ships had been destroyed and their defences thoroughly demolished – indeed, they were seemingly under the command of the young Baron himself. Certainly, with the exception of his mother, all those who might have been expected to guide and advise him were in a dire state. His tutor was dead, apparently killed in the attack together with his mother's secretary. The household's master of horse had been killed in the first Spanish attack. The boy's tutor in the science of defence and the visiting Master of Defence were both sorely wounded. Various other persons too unimportant to name had lent their help; but it was the young Baron, by all accounts, who had organized the defences and seen the invaders off, except for those his troop of horse had taken into captivity to answer questions at the Council's leisure; and all this information went off with the swiftest horseman in the first clear light of morning.

The only other news he had to report was that he was bringing the wounded heroes back to London at once himself, for they were both feverish and in need of the finest treatment.

So it was that Lady Margaret stood in the morning looking out through the ruins of the great gate at the pair of litters rolling northward surrounded by familiar riders. In the wreckage of the great hall, which – like the gate and the sally-port wall – she would have to repair at once, her portrait stood, repaired by Tom and returned to her. No longer did it make her think of the Earl of Essex, whom she hated, but of her protector, on whom she could always rely – no matter what the danger.

As she watched the litters wind away out of her sight, she looked down at a piece of paper on which she had written earlier, hoping to pass it to one of the wounded heroes.

I love you, Thomas Musgrave, it said.

Clear-eyed and accepting the dictates of fortune for the moment, she folded it and slipped it into her sleeve.

There would be time enough to give it to him in due course, God willing, she thought.

Acknowledgements

On the morning of 23 July 1595, 110 days or so after the story of *The Silent Woman* closes, four Spanish galleys from the Spanish Netherlands landed in excess of 200 men westward of Mousehole, in Cornwall, and burned the town. Then they came ashore at Newlyn and attacked and burned sections of Penzance. This was the first – and last – invasion of the south since 1066 and it caused a great deal of shock in Elizabethan England. It also gave Essex his excuse for attacking Cadiz, which he did as co-commander with Lord Howard, the Lord Admiral, in 1596. I am indebted for this information to the West Penwith Resources website. I am indebted to more traditional sources – to wit, G. M. Trevelyan's *English Social History* – for the information that the smuggling of tobacco between the Spanish Netherlands and the south of England was big business by 1597.

To be fair, there is a slightly shorter list of authorities required than usual this time, for the two major settings – the two castles, of Elfinstone and Cotehel – are purely fictional. Cothele House exists well up the River

Tamar, and is one of the best-preserved Tudor country houses in existence. Its interiors inspired those of Castle Cotehel; but there is no castle on Rame Head – only St Michael's Church, which is much as described.

The landscapes both in Kent and Cornwall were based on the Ordnance Survey's relevant Landranger series of maps. The travelling between them was based upon Gamini Salgado's *The Elizabethan Underworld*. The households of these two establishments are based upon Juliet Gardiner's *The Edwardian Country House* and *The Elizabethan Household*. The way in which Lady Margaret runs both is based upon Bess of Hardwick, a powerful historical character who moves through various chapters and references in both Antonia Fraser's *The Weaker Vessel* and Alison Sim's *The Tudor Housewife*. I am also indebted to Elizabeth Burton's *The Elizabethans at Home* and John Dover Wilson's *Life in Elizabethan England*; to texts as ancient as Cunnington and Cunnington's *Handbook of English Costume in the Seventeenth Century* (1955) and as modern as Hart-Davis's *What the Tudors and Stuarts Did For Us* (2003). I am happy to thank the librarians at Tunbridge Wells Library and my own librarians at the Wildernesse School who have helped me – yet again – with these authorities, some of which are long out of print and very difficult to get hold of. I must also thank Mike Gray, Head of History at the Wildernesse, who has always been unfailing in his knowledge and advice.

Ben Jonson is also 'real', and as close to 'historical reality' as I can manage. He was the son of a clergyman, who died before his birth, leaving his mother to fall back upon the hated brick-maker as stepfather to her brilliant, but bellicose and self-opinionated, son. Ben won a scholarship to Westminster School. He went to the Spanish Netherlands as a gentleman-adventurer, killed his man, a Spaniard, in hand-to-hand combat and stripped him of his armour and sword. Soon after the 'events' in our story he may have gone to Cambridge; he certainly married 'a shrew, but honest' and settled to a theatrical, literary life, which saw him in and out of jail on a fairly regular basis. Even so, his reputation eventually rivalled that of Shakespeare, whom he was to survive by twenty years or so. He was lucky to do so. In 1598 he killed Gabriel Spencer, the actor, in a brawl and was sentenced to hang. He pleaded benefit of clergy and instead he was branded on the thumb with a letter 'T'.

Amongst Ben Jonson's most successful plays of later years, first produced in 1609, was *Epicoene, or The Silent Woman*.

Peter Tonkin,
Tunbridge Wells